THE NEXT PAGE BOOK PROJECT:
The Masks We Wear

To those who have yet shed their masks, may you find the courage in these pages warmly welcomed, door open, from us, writers all over the world.

Contributors

Samantha Pearlman • Nicole Landwehr • Vianney Gonzalez • Anita Brown • Sheila Diaz • Seema Bhatnagar • Susan Jachymiak • Sophie Brookes • Linda Amici • Bonnie Servos • Nicolas Correa • Will Malone • Stacy Parish • Judy Seitz • Chris Fancher • Veronica Valles • Jesse Wren • Carly Spina • Alexandra Crawford • Melanie Luebbert • Rachal Gustafson • Cheryl Mallicoat • Lizzie McLaren • Gina Pepin • Mary Hui • Corina Oana • Nyesha James • Chandra Battles • Jyotismita Das • Heather Nizzio • R Jason Wallace • Larry Laraby • Aadila Tilly • Julie Ramirez • Nancy Buonaccorsi • Amorina Carlton • Katja Philipp • Gina S • Naomi Harm • Beth Romines • Laura Anna • Dr. Paul Blair • Melissa Jane Knight • Jennifer Fuller • Angela Tee • Tesa Standish • Megan Ladwig • Jerry Toups • Rajaa Abu Haya • Joanna Gillespie • Mark Saenz • Katie • Maren Kelly • Andrea Aguirre • Melissa Rathmann • Jennifer Barrett • Tracy Kelly • Dr. Joanne Fullerton • Kelly Hantak • Megan Cannella • Paula Rawson • Christel Norwood • Caroline Chase • Alexandra Knight • Michael Kidd • Charlotte Rodricks • Ashley Auspelmyer • AL Berggren • Folasade Olayemi • Gina Antonia • Smriti Iyer • Tri Nguyen • Sam Campbell • Noelle Chandler • Jo-Anne Oakley • Lisa Whitten • Amaziah Shalu • Elyse Hahne • Cassie Soliday • Paula Januzzi-Godfrey • Kelly Esparza • Susan Lowe • Kanwar Sonali Jolly-Wadhwa • Paul LaTorre • Maggie McHugh • Matthew Gilbert • Patricia

Darien Cope • Kaitlin Kilby • Mark Nechanicky • Gene Glotzer • Attiya Batool • Lucie Frosl • Melissa Dean • Allison Dunajski • Bret Williams • Jennifer Haston-Maciejewski • Akshaya Kishor • Jane Shore • Natalee Tangen • Teresa Lien • Erik Youngman • Jeff Dase • Kathy Andrew • Robin Green • Jessica Delfino • Alexandria Hulslander • Antonio Romayor Jr. • Barbara Sapienza • Tu Vuong • Sheila Atuona • Walid Abu Haya • Jonathan Taylor • Annabelle Perston • Mary Dawood Catlin • Dr. Rob Martinez • Melissa Pritchard • Julia Knight • Aubrey Lynn • Veronica Jarboe • Mike Breza • Anna Lindwasser • Kimiko Shibata • Lynn Sawyer • Neha Vashist • John Lawson • Ezikiel Holm • Olivia Lauritzen • Marie Sinadjan • Breanna Struss • S. Kensington • Molly Miller • Kim Elder • Dr. Angela Thompson • Brad Darnall • Phoebe Miles • Soma Kar • Ana Sofía Castellanos • Breanna Tsingine • Benji Reese Carter • Dominique Margolis • Sydney Barcus • Jessica D. Frazier • Kimi Hardesty • Anne Maguire • Nidhi Srivastava • Dr. Deepika Kohli • Jill Devin • Troy Knowlton • Melody Serra • Julisa Basak • Bonnie Lynn Nguyen • Joshua Gray • Dubravka Rebic • Keira Lane • Jo Smith • Chris Keilman • Rachel K Jones • Kathy Whynot • Gina Marie Elia • Christine Alice Coc • Megan Gabellieri • Vira Bunoan • Jody Matey • Victoria Noe • Steven Kolber • Christine Salek • Kyle Ross • Miriam Walsh • Tega Brakz • Maria Kornacki • David Betancur • Lindsay Avery • Sarah Wallace • Jonathan Squirrell • Emily Français

☺

About Us

The Next Page Book Project started in March 2021 during the Covid-19 pandemic. As most of us are aware, the pandemic flipped our day to day lives upside down. Personally, I felt isolated and had a difficult time finding the connections I had prior to the pandemic. This project came to me in a dream – One story written by 100+ people around the globe. In times of isolation, we can connect and come together to build a story.

The next morning I started on bringing this project to life. The next few weeks, I posted the book project idea and connected with people around the globe. The 150+ people in this project came together to create this story. Regardless of race, ethnicity, age, gender, religion, sexual orientation, gender identity, gender expression, disability, economic status and other diverse backgrounds – everyone was welcome to be a part of this project. I am extremely grateful that in times of isolation, we were able to connect and make this story.

It was quite an undertaking & I had no idea if it would work or be of interest to others. Two years later, we ended up having 175 people in total join this project. I am extremely grateful to have connected with each and every individual who has contributed to this project.

This story discusses topics that are important to so many; mental health, identity, growth & acceptance. This project is all about collaboration, inclusivity, creativity, and diversity.

I am so honored to have so many individuals participating & creating an amazing story. The world could use a lot more togetherness and in disconnected times, I believe this project has made it less isolating.

Thank you for going on this journey with me.

Acknowledgements

I would like to take a moment and recognize each and every individual who has joined this project. Thank you for trusting me with your words and thank you for going on this journey.

Special thanks to Paula Rawson, Phyllis Pearlman, Jo Baker-Smith, Linda Amici, and Brittany Lane for assisting with editing and making sure our story flows. Without their input and help, this story would not be what it is presently.

Shoutout to the following artists for their creativity & amazing design work.

Book Cover: Michel (@michelmrr)

Map Illustration: Ana (@goldenflower.arte)

Chapter Illustrations: Rachel Zolotov (my amazing aunt)

Huge gratitude to my family. Thank you for always supporting me in this journey and giving me the encouragement to pursue this daunting project. Thank you Bryan Pearlman, Lena Pearlman, and Matthew Pearlman for believing in me and actively supporting me throughout the past two years. A special thanks to my grandparents, Phyllis Pearlman and Jeffery Pearlman for always cheering me on.

If you are reading this, I am so glad you exist.

You're not alone.

One: The People We Meet

The People We Meet

For me, like many others, every day is like Halloween; we dress up and show others exactly what we want them to see. Wearing a mask allows me to disguise how I feel. A false smile, hiding behind headphones, and now in the time of Covid-19, wearing an actual mask. I'm not alone in this performance. We all wear masks on a daily basis, depending on where we are, who we are with, and what we are doing. For some, makeup can be a mask of sorts, a barrier, a protective shield. For others, humor or being the class clown is a performative mask used for deflection and protection. Our masks hide our true feelings.

I sometimes wish I had a superpower to see how people are really feeling under their masks. How freeing would it be to just be ourselves? Isn't it heavy, day after day, wearing a mask? We are constantly hiding in fear and being inauthentic – is it because we feel unworthy? The hats we juggle and the performances we put on are exhausting. We are not born with these masks – we learn to put them on as a defense.

The truth is that most people are anxious, lonely, and overwhelmed. I would say I'm fairly perceptive of how people are feeling. As I walk around, I wear my headphones and completely dark clothing, trying to not stand out. All I see are people glued to their phones, like it means anything. I'm one of a few individuals at this school who doesn't have a social media presence. Not because I can't, but because I don't need yet another mask.

Junior year didn't exactly end as I had planned, and so far, this year hasn't been the dream I thought my final year of high school would be. After months of isolation, we are back at school and there has been a drastic shift in priorities. I realized that the

The People We Meet

person who left in March is radically different from the one who came back in February. I think I'm ready to begin my next chapter.

I make my way through the narrow, desolate, school hallways, listening to "Ghost Town" by the Specials. This song has been an essential addition to my morning playlist since we returned to school. It's surreal, really. We've only been back for a couple of days now, but I haven't adjusted well to this new reality. Hallways that were previously lined with students – many finishing last-minute homework assignments; scarfing down their breakfast; or being corralled by homeroom teachers, anxious for the morning announcements – are now bleak and lifeless. No colorful, handmade posters for school events, or sign-ups for the theater department's next production. I often question why we returned in the first place. We're more alone and isolated than ever. I get lost in thoughts of what could have been – this year, my senior year. I'm startled back to reality when I hear the sound of the morning bell ring, hardly muffled by my headphones, and realize it must be 8 a.m. I head off to first period.

I take a seat in the back of the room, keeping to myself, though Advanced English Literature and Composition is my favorite course this semester. I've always enjoyed reading; I can get lost in a book just as easily as I can get lost in a good song or movie soundtrack. Our reading list this semester centers on BIPOC, Latinx, Asian and Native American authors who have historically been underrepresented in the literary canon. This has been a welcome and much-needed change, in my opinion. I just wish my classmates took this course seriously. They seem more interested in the latest social media trends than having any deep or meaningful conversations, inside or outside of the classroom.

The People We Meet

I've always felt a little different, different from my peers anyway, but this past year has highlighted that discrepancy.

Some people can mask their anxiety and depression, but I can tell that they are not like everyone else. Even though I never get too close to people, I know that they have battles they are fighting internally. Why is it that they still try to hide that part of themselves? If only people knew that they weren't alone, maybe we would all be able to get the help we need. My peers continue to hide behind the façade that "everything is okay" and that they are totally fine, but deep down, I know they aren't. We are not okay. Even our teachers seem out of sync. Everything feels so lifeless at this school; we're just routinely going about our days without actually living them. It's as if we are all having an out-of-body experience, but we don't even know it's happening.

We're so eager to get back to our "normal" that we aren't taking the time to really mourn the loss we've experienced this past year. Brushing it off as if everything is fine and we need to act like our normal selves. I'm tired of pretending, tired of seeing everyone around me not being authentic because they're scared about what others will say.

I'm determined to be unapologetically myself. I'm tired of hiding behind this metaphorical mask we are forced to wear. When did we even learn to hide our true selves from the world? I'm jealous of those comfortable enough in their own skin not to care about the opinions of others. I want to start living, truly living. I'm not sure what that will look like, but I know it will be better than whatever this current "life" is, that's for sure.

The People We Meet

New day, same headphones. The playlist has changed. P!nk – she is empowering. Is she pop, rock, or somewhere in-between? Am I somewhere in-between?

Walking down the science wing, as it is not so aptly named, to my English class, I collide with a person I have never seen before. I see an apologetic smile in her eyes as she says "I'm so sorry. I guess I have some pep in my step today seeing all of you back in the building. We have waited for this for a long time. I hope you have a fantastic day!"

I exchange a return glance, more of an acknowledgment of sorts. Truth be told, my head was down and I'm not walking on the appropriate arrow on the appropriate side of the hallway. Who is this "Ms. Pep in Your Step"? I wonder if I have a pep in my step.

I sit down in my assigned, socially distanced, seat. "Open your Chromebooks and click on today's link in Google classroom." How many times have I heard this very sentence in the last year?

The link takes me to a Native American author's poem, "Peace Path." Wow, all my classes are coordinating now! The last stanza of the poem says, "…history the tall grass opens for us. Breathe the incense of sun on prairie. Offer peace to the sky…" I glance out the window. I raise my hand ever so slightly, "can we leave our Chromebooks, go outside and discuss the lesson today? We just want to talk, unmasked." I see my peers turn and face me, wondering who had the courage to say that. There is a brief pause. Others join in the plea. We head out the door.

I will find out later who the "pep in your step" lady is.

As the class rushes to the grassy area of the main quad, the most populous area on campus, my classmates bombard me with praise and enthusiasm. While the fresh air brings about a sense of freedom, an overwhelming sensation of guilt and remorse immediately floods my mind. Did I seriously just say my thoughts aloud and lead my entire class out here without the approval of our instructor? I don't know whether to be joyful or completely terrified of where my actions will land me. All of a sudden, my heartbeat starts to race, and I can feel that familiar flushing sensation take over my face - the kind where I can easily be mistaken for an overripe tomato. It becomes hard to breathe, and I begin to gasp for air. Before I know it, I'm hunched over, dizzy, feeling like I'm outside of my own body, with no control.

From a distance, a distinct, somewhat familiar voice shouts, "Go along now, get back to class boys and girls. Everything is under control, she will be alright, and PLEASE PUT THOSE MASKS BACK ON!" When I open my eyes, there are three individuals hovering over me. I hadn't realized I'd fallen, but clearly, I'm looking up at these faces from the ground. I recognize the nurse and the assistant principal gazing into my eyes, checking my pupils, asking what just happened.

In my sophomore year, I was sent to the nurse's office when one of my teachers was concerned about my well-being after an accident. That's where I was introduced to both the nurse and the assistant principal as well as their familiar questioning techniques. As I maneuver myself into an upright position that allows me to get back on my feet, the third person, whose familiar voice is strangely familiar, turns around.

It is at this very moment I learn "Ms. Pep in Your Step" is the new senior class school counselor.

The People We Meet

She has a very soothing effect on my thoughts. Her voice is soft and she seems to have a calming presence. Is it possible that she knows what is going on in my mind? No, I don't think so! My mask is strong, stronger than "Ms. Pep in Your Step." It occurs to me that maybe "Ms. Pep in Your Step" has the ability to read others through their eyes? My eyes speak volumes and so do hers. What about nonverbal communication like hand gestures and body language? I realize that even with masks on, I have a strong language of communication that allows me to be myself, at times. I have been waiting to hear this soothing voice for quite some time now. Suddenly the feeling of being free settles in me.

I love being close to nature and what I really want is to discuss the poem "Peace Path" in the fresh air and open ground with classmates. But her eyes ask me "can you walk?" and through my eyes, I reply yes. Her hand points toward the nurse's office and I follow her. After routine questioning, "Ms. Pep in Your Step" asks me to rest for an hour in the nurse's office so the nurse can observe me. I relax, but my thoughts are racing.

> Oh, the beautiful mask on my face
> You hide or not
> I shall be out of you with my peers
> With my loved ones
> It would be me, unmasked,
> It would be me, myself
> I would then fly high
> Like a bird, to my own destinations
> Oh, beautiful mask on my face
> You will not be able to bind my spirits.

The People We Meet

Yes, I always have pep in my head and now in my step, too. Thanks "Ms. Pep in Your Step." I move toward my designated classroom in the hallway with authenticity on my face and freedom in my thoughts, breaking the barrier of the mask.

As I enter my classroom, I feel renewed and full of life. I remember a time before all this, before all these tensions and anxious thoughts, when I felt like myself.

I recall a vacation I took to the beach, remembering the feeling of warm sand between my toes and the sound of ocean waves moving in and out. At this moment, in this present time, the memory makes me feel the comfort and peacefulness that trip brought.

We are always told to be ourselves because we are all unique in our own way, and I desperately want to be myself in this sea of sameness. The truth is, we all care about what others think to an extent, and I feel like young people are glued to their phones and social media. Why is it that we are connected now more than ever yet remain out of touch with those around us? How many times do I walk behind someone in the hallway, silently judging without knowing their story? It would take a few seconds to spark up a conversation and get to know the individual behind the mask, behind the sea of people all trying to belong. But, knowing that, why don't I do it?

Suddenly, I'm brought back to reality. While looking around, I notice that my classmates have the same puzzled expression on their faces. How can we create a positive change in our classroom, our school, our community, and our world if we don't connect in other ways?

The People We Meet

I know they say my generation is the future, the generation that will speak up for those who don't have a voice but it's the same generation that doesn't have the ability to ask a waitress for extra ranch dressing. We cannot keep living the way we do; we will break this cycle with our passion for justice and equality. As this thought runs through my mind, the bell rings, and I head to my next class now craving pizza and ranch.

Walking down the corridor, I manage to answer my own question. I join the meandering line of evenly-spaced students; akin to lifeless objects on a factory belt, waiting to be manipulated into shape by soulless workers, their hands working on auto-pilot. I shake my head, grinning to myself. Isolation has turned me cynical.

Anyway, the answer to my question. Yes, it sounds so simple, just to talk to someone. I've seen it with the more extroverted of my peers, engaging in breezy, flowing conversation, like birds in the wind. But the reason we don't do it is simply that we can't.

Social anxiety usually starts as a child. Left unchecked, it gets worse. "Oh, you're just shy, you'll grow out of it." Isn't that what the adults say? Except we don't grow out of it. Instead, we build up walls around ourselves, a fortress of solitude, and now, it's hard to find the right things to say.

Then there's social media, with its illusion of contact. Yet another mask for us to wear, allowing us to be anyone we desire to be behind our screens. Something about being a faceless insertion point in a text box brings forth confidence from even the most timid of people. The student who struggles to answer questions in class is also a vocal and unfiltered social justice warrior on Twitter.

False contact, false confidence. A substitute, perhaps, but is it sincere? Take off the masks and tear down the walls. Say hello instead of typing it. Before I can contemplate it further, the factory belt halts. I walk into the classroom, ready to be molded by the next pair of hands.

Sociology has been my least favorite class during the remote time of quarantine. Mrs. Williams' hair perpetually in a tight bun, blouses always buttoned to the top. The kids have been placing bets on her daily shirt color; black, brown, and navy seem to be the extent of her wardrobe options. I take a deep breath and brace myself for a long 40 minutes of boredom.

What I encounter when turning the corner into room 213 couldn't be further from my expectations. My initial clue that Mrs. Williams is missing is the stark difference between this space and the lackluster, monochromatic beige of the rest of the school walls. It is hard to believe this is the same classroom.

There is a distinctly different vibe here: walls the color of the ocean, squares of student artwork, and hand-lettered quotes spanning from floor to ceiling. The large windows are as wide open as the eyes of every student walking through the door.

The next surprise is the teacher sitting casually on a desk next to the doorway. His brown eyes connect with each student, enthusiastically greeting each one as they enter. Elbow bump, air high-five, thumbs up. The way his eyes sparkle makes it obvious, despite his bright mask, that he is smiling.

The People We Meet

This clearly isn't the teacher we have grown accustomed to seeing in the two-inch box on screen the first part of the year. I glance around and everyone else seems just as enamored, caught up in reading the walls. It's as if we have entered another planet.

"Welcome back to REAL life school. I'm Mr. Alexander, but most people call me Joe. I will be your sociology facilitator for the rest of this year. Let's begin by getting to know each other."

All at once, I know that in room 213, I'll have nothing to hide behind.

I take my seat and sling my headphones around my neck. So far, my return to in-class school experience has sucked, but something about Mr. Alexander's classroom makes me feel reluctantly optimistic. Maybe it's the open windows across the room, but I begin to see myself and my classmates a bit more vividly. As we settle into our socially distanced desks, Mr. Alexander faces us, clasps his re-sanitized hands, and begins again. "Welcome, Seniors, to your final sociology class. I hope you don't mind the windows being open. It is just such an unseasonably warm day that I thought we should take advantage of it, face masks or not."

With that, a fresh breeze ruffles our hair and despite the slight chill, I catch myself taking a deep breath. I feel some of my earlier anxiety fade, and the tension in my shoulders relax.

The rigidity of both Mrs. Williams' backbone and her lesson plans had always seemed counterintuitive in a sociology classroom, virtual or not. Now, the memory of all that is being washed away by Mr. Alexander's casual, open, nature. He's the exact opposite of Mrs. Williams, and with every passing minute, I'm becoming more interested in what he's saying.

The People We Meet

"Thanks to the current pandemic, we have in this classroom an unprecedented opportunity," Mr. Alexander says. "We have a chance to look at our entire world in a new light and discuss how our society has changed; how it IS changing. Much of what we have taken for granted as a society has changed dramatically and will continue to change for many years ahead. What values have we commonly held, and how will these be forced to change? How will we choose to interact and live in a post-pandemic society?"

I sit up a bit straighter and feel the tiniest spark of enthusiasm deep within my core. Maybe this will be the place to find my answers, or at least to begin searching for them. I glance around at my classmates and see that they are listening as well, and in that moment, I feel my own emotional mask begin to fall away.

As Mr. Alexander (or Joe as he regularly insists in a playful way) continues, I feel the atmosphere of the room change. Each student is engaged in a way that isn't possible on a laptop or tablet screen.

There's a level playing field with no one person dominating the discussion. Introverts become involved and those of us who are usually shy feel empowered to speak. Each of us is on even ground and suddenly these discussions around the study of structure, interaction, and collective behavior become the most fascinating topics because of what is happening around the world.

The science of society, social relationships and behavior of humans is dictated in so many ways by our facial expressions. Without sharing the facial expressions we normally have on display, we must adapt in other ways to make our point understood.

The People We Meet

The tiny spark of enthusiasm I've been feeling is growing. Even with masks on, I can sense the rest of my classmates feel the same. Mr. Alexander engages us as we dissect the traditional forms of social interaction and collective behavior. He jokes that these classes have never needed an update more than now.

We walk again out to the grassy area of the main quad. This time I don't feel dizzy. As if choreographed, my classmates remove their masks for a deep breath of fresh air and smile in perfect harmony.

One teacher has single-handedly turned my day around. After Mr. Alexander's class, I have a new sense of self-confidence that only a short while ago would have felt like an eternity away.

We each put our masks back on as we head back into the building before the inevitable instruction is shouted and I even walk to my next class with a bit more pep in my step!

I will admit, I'm slightly afraid that Mr. Alexander is setting a standard other teachers won't be able to reach. Still, I remain hopeful. While on my way to history, I reach in my pocket for gum only to find out my pen has busted. Honestly, I'm not even mad. I'm still running on the high from sociology. I go to the nearest bathroom, hoping no one is inside.

When I open the door, there's a girl washing her hands. She is wearing all black, from her Vans up to her Joy Division hoodie. She even has a pair of black headphones around her neck. I feel like I've just walked in on myself.

She glances up quickly with a startled look and shouts, "Hey! Do you mind rolling out a paper towel for me, please?" The tone of her voice echoes through the bathroom with urgency.

"Um, sure," I reply. After she thanks me, I wonder why she can't possibly do it herself.

As I wash my hands two sinks away, I hear whispers of pain under her breath. I don't want to openly stare at her, so I guide my eyes as best I can in her direction, keeping my head down at my own sink. I first notice soap everywhere, then the blood on her hands. They're red and inflamed.

I'm instantly reminded of an article I read about an individual who struggled between the lines of Covid precaution and mysophobia. Though I know I'm in no place to make assumptions about her situation. That is, until she looks over to me and cries, "I'm sorry, I'm having a really hard time right now with my eczema and OCD in all of this mess."

"I'm Ruby," she adds, then averts her eyes from mine. "Probably not the best way to make a first impression."

"No," I say. "It's cool." This is the most real anyone's been with me for over a year. I appreciate the intensity, actually. "I'm Sid." I hand her some paper towels and suddenly realize that all barriers of social distance have slipped our minds as we both tend to her sore arms.

At this point, getting to history on time isn't high on my list of priorities – if it ever had been – but getting better acquainted with Ruby is. Besides, I already know that my new ally in the guidance office will write us both passes if we need them.

"Nice shoes," I say, as I brandish my own checkered pair for her to see. Mine are old and worn and I've taken to writing letters inside of the white boxes to spell out words. Hers look brand new.

The People We Meet

"Thanks," she says, as she pulls away from me slightly and blows a lock of her hair out of her eyes. Her messy hair isn't exactly curly but it's made up of wavy "s" curls that just sort of do whatever they please. I appreciate her I'm-not-here-to-impress-you aesthetic.

My assumption about Ruby is that she is new. By senior year, I pretty much know everybody in my class. But the Covid-world has screwed up my perspective enough that I can't be sure there aren't people who might've slipped under the radar for the last three years.

So I go ahead and ask her, "Are you new here? I can't believe we've never met before."

She props herself up on one of the sinks in a familiar way and says, "Yep. Just moved here. My Dad's the new sociology teacher."

"Oh, I just got out of his class and was headed to history when I came in here to wash some pen ink off my hands. Your Dad is different from every other teacher I have had."

"Oh, is that bad or good?" she says with a worried tone in her voice.

"Good. He has given the class more energy and actually got the whole class to participate. It has really made my day. Is your Dad like this all the time?"

"I don't know, to me he is just my Dad. I guess we need to get to class. Thanks for your help."

As we head out the door, I turn to head toward history class and Ruby turns the other way. I yell, "Hey, what class are you going to?"

"History!" Ruby yells back.

"Follow me, it is this way," I say. "So I see from your hoodie and headphones, you like music. What do you listen to?"

"I like the older bands like Fleetwood Mac, The Cranberries, and The Cure," she says.

"Wow! Those are some great choices, I'm impressed. This is it." I exclaim.

We enter the classroom and I go toward the back where I normally sit. I notice Ruby walks in slowly and seems undecided as to where to sit. As she looks around the room, I catch her eye and motion for her to come and sit down back where I'm sitting. As she walks over, I can tell she appreciates the gesture. As she settles at her desk, she whispers, "Thank you," which makes me feel good.

Last class of the day. At home, I would probably already be watching Grey's Anatomy or listening to music. Today seems like the longest day of the entire year. Will I ever get used to being back at school and the tedium of the school day?

Honors World History covers historical events from 1000 BC to the present. Mr. Salvatore is good but the readings he gives us are better. I actually enjoy learning how connected current events in the world are to those that happened hundreds of years ago. I lean over to Ruby and ask her if she likes history. Ruby whispers, "It's usually boring." I tell her she will enjoy this class. "It's a great way to end the day," I say.

Mr. Salvatore starts by telling us we have finished all the history he intends to teach us for the day. I actually hear myself cheering along with my classmates. "But," he says, "we have an end of the year project we need to start looking at." Groans fill the room. Jenny, sitting in front of me, says, "Can we do it alone? I don't like anyone else in this room." Several students laugh and a similar number say, "Yes, no groups please."

He lets us know that we have to work in groups, but says we can pick one person to pair up with in the group. Like a roller coaster ride of highs and lows he follows with, "but I'll be putting two pairs together to make groups of four students." I quickly look at Ruby and say, "want to work with me?" She almost shouts "Yes!" in reply.

It takes forever before Mr. Salvatore gets back to Ruby and me to talk about our group. "I hoped you two would pair up," he says. My mask doesn't hide my reaction. He quickly follows that up with, "Sid, you may not realize this, but you have one of the highest grades in my class and no one in this class writes like you do. Ruby, I promised your Dad that I would put you into a group with someone good and the two of you took care of that for me."

"Best in class," teases Ruby. "Lucky me to meet you on my first day."

I feel my face flushing the shade of a Roma tomato underneath my mask and my right eye begins to twitch in embarrassment. I did declare that I was going to be unabashedly ME senior year, so now I take a few deep breaths and settle into my core. I'm done hiding and I'm dismantling any façade of less than that's propping up my insecurity.

"Yeah, I'm a nerd that way. Binged on the History Channel as a kid but something always stirred deep down inside with every documentary. An uneasy feeling lingered that the truth was being covered in the veneer of the victors in their grandiose ways of proclaiming superiority. That's why I'm loving Honors World History. Give me the voices of the ancestors buried beneath the ashes of defeat. Let them rise. What really happened? Tell me the stories of those who survived the massacres but assimilated, hiding their stories in indigenous patterns on blankets and art that only their descendants could decipher. I want to know the truth."

A twinkle in Ruby's eyes punctuates our kindred spirit ways. Was it random or a supernatural force that guided me into the bathroom as she cleaned up the crimson stains on the sink? Maybe the answer is in the project.

I'm startled when my ears begin to tingle at the sound of the bell. I don't know if it is the random encounter with Ruby or the buildup of exhaustion from the long day, but the rest of class went by in the blink of an eye.

My eyes follow Ruby closely as she gathers her things. The rays of the afternoon sun smash through the classroom windows onto her face. She has profound, luminous, eyes that feel so obtrusive. When she looks at me, I feel as if she can see right through my mask and into the deepest pits of my heart and soul. Part of me wants to stand on my desk and shout my life story to Ruby as I embrace myself wholly. And the other part wants to cease to exist, scared that she will discover my most treasured secrets.

In the midst of this daydream, she slips through the classroom door and is gone in an instant. I'm so desperate to know more about this mystery girl. Who exactly is Ruby Alexander and what is her story?

The People We Meet

Daydreaming has almost caused me to miss my bus. I'm not exactly pleased to still be riding the school bus as a senior in high school. My parents are convinced that I have no need for a car quite yet and that riding the bus builds character. My Dad could repeat this sentiment in his sleep. "Riding the school bus allows you to build character, form friendships, and stand up for yourself when faced with unkind people." It's not convincing, especially on a day like today.

Our high school is hosting its first spring football game since the start of the pandemic against our crosstown rivals. It's my senior year, and I'm determined to be involved. Sweat begins dripping down my neck as I step into the spring sun that drifts slowly toward the horizon. I need to rush home if I want to eat dinner and get ready before the big game. A sudden thought comes to me: will I see Ruby Alexander there?

"What's up, Sid?" a familiar voice calls out. It's Charles, the only other senior on this bus. We've never talked about it, but I assume his parents also believe in "character building." I throw my bookbag on the ground as I sit down in the seat across from him, suddenly feeling exhausted. I return his eager wave.

"Hey, Charles. I'm wiped. How are you adjusting back into this in-person weirdness?"

"It was… well weird," he replies. "It felt strange walking around. I always thought I'd feel so confident inside this place when I was finally a senior. Now, I'm a senior, walking around back here in the hallways. I honestly feel like a stranger to everyone. I don't know… I just feel off."

The People We Meet

I can't believe how well Charles has captured my thinking. I know lots of people at school, but today has brought its fair share of "new," including some new faces. There's this feeling of being a stranger that brings me a sense of comfort now that Charles has called it out.

"I felt a little off today, too. I almost passed out earlier," I admit.

"Yeah," says Charles. "I'm not used to wearing these masks all day, either. They make me feel hot. I just want to be unmasked for a bit."

I shrug, but a shiver goes down my spine. I let him assume that I almost fainted because of my mask, but I'm quite sure that's not what it was. However, the fact that he also called out the desire to be unmasked, even if he was being literal, stops me in my tracks. I freeze. I have no words left to say to him without revealing too much. I just need to not think for a bit. Today has felt heavy.

The day continues to weigh on me as I enter my house, the door creaking to a close behind my tired body and shutting out each ray of light. As I peer around the empty rooms, I desperately want not to be alone. It would be reassuring to keep the mask on for my family. Pretend that I'm all right, that I'm not ready to peel it away for the day and see who I really am. My parents are still out, acting in the roles they are assigned each morning. For a brief moment, I let myself wonder what it would be like to be around my parents, unfiltered and undisguised by the forced rudiments of society. Instead, I shed the person I'm forced to be at school and let myself fall into the fluffy ravines of my bed.

The People We Meet

One recurring name runs through my mind as I sink further and further down into the mattress. Ruby. Why do I care about seeing you again? Why did I feel no fear when you took my mask from me? Why do I want to become something to you, Ruby?

A surge of energy pours over me, flinging me from my bed and throwing me toward the closet. If Ruby shows her face at the game tonight, I feel a lurking desire to impress her. It is unnatural how quickly I waver through my emotions, but I cling to this feeling: the feeling of value. I feel an entirely new weight upon me, one that is not heavy and does not drag me down. I decide to literally strip myself of the all-black clothing I started the day with. Even though I'm not looking for attention, I want to dress more like myself. I dig through my closet to find my vintage corduroy teal overalls that I have not had the confidence to wear. I pair it with a yellow scrunchie and a white shirt, and white Converse, and I'm ready for the game. As I peer into my mirror, I notice that I actually like what I see. I just hope Ruby does too.

I take a deep breath as I get out of the car at the game. It seems strange to be going to a football game this time of year, but the pandemic has changed a lot of things, including the school's varsity sports schedule.

"Bye, Sid! Text when the game is almost over and we will pick you up!" my Dad says as I walk away. My mood and my clothes did not go unnoticed by my parents at dinner. I could see the questions in their eyes, and their general excitement to see me happy. Thankfully, they did not press me for details. That's good because I'm not ready to divulge anything about meeting Ruby. I'm not even sure how to explain it, or exactly how I'm feeling. I just know that it feels exhilarating to have met her, and that I want to know more about her and to spend more time with her. Instead, I told them about Mr. Alexander and how sociology seemed like it was going to be fun, and about Mr. Salvatore and the group project we were assigned for history. I think they knew something other than my classes was contributing to my good humor.

I scan the crowd as I walk toward the stands. It's hard to identify people, as masks are still required to attend the game. As I get closer to the student section, I notice a few familiar faces looking over my outfit. It definitely isn't my typical attire, but I feel more like myself than I have in a long time, and I don't mind the stares.

Then I see her. Ruby is standing near the concession stand, looking around, but seemingly not finding what she's looking for. I notice she has also changed her clothes, and I feel a flutter in my stomach – was that because of me? I casually change course and make my way toward her.

I sidestep some middle schoolers decked out in blue and gold hoodies emblazoned with the school mascot – The Mighty Falcons. The boys are howling hysterically over some TikTok nonsense. I cringe at their antics. Ruby turns and notices me as I walk toward her, causing my pulse to quicken. I suddenly feel incredibly nervous.

"Hi, Ruby!" I say a little too loudly, too enthusiastically. I feel my face flush under my mask.

"Oh, hey," Ruby replies, still distractedly looking around. "I'm waiting for my Dad. I drove myself here because he said he had to wait for something at our house. All he told me was it's a surprise he's bringing to the game. I'm nervous about what it might be. You know my Dad isn't exactly what some would consider conventional." My curiosity is piqued. My parents' idea of a surprise is to allow me to skip doing the dishes or folding my own laundry. I've never met someone whose parent would bring a surprise to a public event. In reality, I would be mortified if my parents, or anyone, surprised me at a school function. I feel mildly anxious for her and my hands become clammy.

We stand there awkwardly for a moment when suddenly her eyes widen, and I can see the part of her face visible above her mask go white. In a barely audible whisper, she says, "I can't believe it," and takes off in a sprint as though I don't exist. I quickly spin around and see Mr. Alexander, eyes grinning, standing next to a woman I don't recognize. Ruby jumps in the stranger's arms and holds on for dear life. I can see her body convulsing into sobs.

My stomach drops and my mouth goes completely dry. I can't believe what I'm seeing.

Two:
The Bonds We Form

The Bonds We Form

I see Ramon Hernandez, my ex. He attends our biggest rival in high school, Middletown High. We went to elementary and middle school together, and we agreed when we broke up over the summer, to remain friends but give each other space. What is he doing here?

I broke up with him because I was tired. I was tired of trying to be something I wasn't. Being his girlfriend didn't feel right; in my opinion, I enjoyed his company more when we were just friends. I had dated him, if that's what you call it, from eighth grade up to my junior year in high school. I really did try, because that is what I thought I should be doing at that age.

I have never "liked-liked" Ramon. I care about him, but my heart has never been in it. He's cute and fun to hang with, but I know I like girls. Before now, I have not been ready to be my authentic self. So even though seeing Ramon brings back some old feelings of insecurity, looking at Ruby holding onto the lady she obviously knows and cares about evokes more from me in three minutes than three years with Ramon ever did.

Looking back, I have always had a feeling I was "different" from those around me. Ever since I can remember, society has expected me to dress and act like a lady. When I was a little girl, reading stories about princesses, I would mention how pretty the princesses were over the handsomeness of the princes. My parents would tell me it was normal to think the princesses were pretty. "But aren't the princes cute, too? Look at how handsome they are."

I would nod my head, but I knew how I felt. Growing up, I would notice when other kids were cute or if they gave me butterflies. It was always girls I noticed, never the boys. Now that

I have met Ruby, I know this heavy mask is starting to fracture and come off for good.

Ruby gets a hold of herself and stands up straight, one hand still holding onto the lady, whom I see now has a military uniform. It doesn't take a genius to realize something big is going on. Ruby has family drama that is clearly a whole lot more important than me, or the game, or anything else, I guess.

Ramon joins the TikTok guys and a noise like barking hyenas erupts. I run-walk away from it, putting some distance between me, them and Ruby's family. No way is she going to want to watch the game with me now, and why the hell else am I even here? Waves of heat engulf me as I see myself, like a scoreboard lit up in my team colors, here to make some public statement about – what? No one knows but me. No one else knows that I'm anything on the inside other than the girl who's always listening to music and dresses in dark clothing.

All the weird stuff I have done today, the out-of-character, no-mask, stupid, stuff I've done is like fixing a target to my chest. The back of my skull is buzzing. There are so many people here. I suddenly really need to know what all the laughter is about, and at the same time, I don't. I wish I could drown everything out with ABBA or Queen.

I push through the pastel "unicorn" girls, whose heads turn like a Hydra's to follow me. I stagger out from the crowd with no idea where to go or what I can do to get back inside myself again. Can I even find a safe place, my hidden place? What if I have no way to put the mask back on – just stuck with my own frightened face, naked, for everyone to see? In one day, somehow, I've left myself no choices at all.

All of a sudden, I hear Ruby call my name. She runs toward me through the chaotic crowd and invites me to sit with her and her parents to watch the game. I'm not interested in watching the game, but I happily accept her invitation. We go up to the press box and watch the blue and red jerseys intertwine and dance across the field. It turns out that her mother surprised her this evening as she had been deployed overseas as a psychologist prior to their move.

The game ends with a total loss for our team, but this night has been one of my favorite nights of my high school career. All because of Ruby and a new perspective.

On the bus ride to school, I spend a good amount of time thinking about the past few months. I realize Covid has been remarkable for many changes – good and bad. I continue to be amazed by everyone's different perception of things. The people that I thought would be following the guidelines and policies are not the ones doing so. Some people are adapting to the new "normal" really well. Others are making up the rules as they go. Some people are spending a great deal of their time fighting expectations and voicing their "rights." I know it is a touchy topic and I'm not quite prepared to have this conversation with anyone else.

As I walk to class, I know today's topic of discussion is going to be about the effects of Covid in regard to social norms. I walk into the classroom with my physical mask on, ready to debate my perspective. I don't think I'm ready, but Ruby proves me wrong. Over the past few weeks, my time has been consumed with Ruby, when we are not spending time together in person, we are constantly texting each other. Ruby has constantly surprised me with her ability to defy my expectations.

Mr. Alexander gives the usual elbow bumps and air high-fives as we filter into class. Ruby isn't here yet. I slide into my seat, catching fragments of chatter about the soccer game last night. The TikTok guys are hooting about the 3-1 win while a few of the "unicorn" girls are giggling while liking the posts of the goalie. They ignore me as I go by. "All right class, let's start," says Mr. Alexander. "We've been talking about changes in values brought on by Covid-19. We may be doing 'this' for a long time." He gestures to his mask and our distanced desks.

As he takes a breath to continue, Ruby sidles in the doorway past him, hugging the wall. His eyes crinkle in a smile as she ducks her head and quickly takes an empty seat close to me. She darts a glance at me through her tangle of brown curls. The sleeves of her black top are damp. She turns away as her father begins speaking again. "We can all get sick and die from this: rich, poor, young, old, white, black, or of color. Doesn't matter. All the talk is confusing, scary, and sometimes outright wrong. Tell me, how does it change how you behave and how you live your life?"

A few hands shoot up. Charles says he was skeptical about there being a disease at first, but then his grandmother caught it. She is still in the hospital. One of the TikTok guys, Logan, says he doesn't watch or read the news anymore. He gets what he needs from social media. He added that he has not started to apply to colleges since the in-person touring stopped, not to mention, how can college be on anyone's mind considering the state of the world…

My heart starts to beat faster and I feel a familiar warm tingle on my face. To my surprise, I see Ruby's red, cracked, hand edge up out of the corner of my eye. Mr. Alexander nods at her and she takes a deep breath before starting to speak.

I can see her hands curl into fists in her lap from where I sit. And above her mask, pink color is blooming on her high cheekbone and the tip of her ear.

"I'm sad for everyone whose health has been affected. Charles, I hope your grandma recovers soon. I relate to you too, Logan, turning away from the TV news to social media, in an attempt to control what information we take in. I have deleted my accounts because the uncertainty makes me anxious. My grandma, who visits all the time, asked if I could help her in our garden. So I have turned to spending time outside with her. I'm learning from her about growing food, identifying edible weeds and how to forage for food in the woods behind our house. She has taught me about perennial vegetables like asparagus and Turkish rocket, and fruit vines that bear harvest twice a year like some raspberries do. We have started seedlings and planted heirloom tomatoes, peppers, and winter squashes and we tend to the garden each day. Between the beds she points to edible weeds like dandelion, chickweed, and plantains whose young leaves we harvest early in the spring to make salads or sauté. In the woods, she shows me where wild edible foods grow. We've found wild leeks called ramps, stinging nettles that can be cooked as spinach, and elderberries. She is full of knowledge about plants, and I'm learning how to grow and harvest sustainably without disturbing any of the wild roots. I wonder if others would be interested in gardening or a food growing club this year?"

Ruby's idea and passion lands squarely in my heart. To know about wild, edible, plants is so cool. My parents garden too, and I have always loved interacting with nature. I see others waiting to raise their hands along with me. Does Ruby have more to say? I see her take a glance my way. Does she catch or maybe sense that behind my mask, I'm smiling encouragingly?

Ruby's glance nudges me to raise my hand and show her that I'm willing to join her in a food-growing club this year. Her tense and furrowed brow relaxes when I raise my hand. I can sense her relief that she isn't out on a limb by herself. A familiar sensation rushes over me and before I know it, I'm suggesting that we use the community garden and the food we grow there could be donated to families in need. I ramble on about many families being affected by the pandemic by financial hardship, physical illness, and even death. When I finally come to my senses, not only is Ruby smiling at me with her eyes, but half of the other students in the class have their hands raised to join this cause.

Mr. Alexander starts a round of applause in the classroom, before introducing Ruby and me as the leaders of this new gardening program. He tasks us with coming up with a cool name and getting even more students on board. I'm absolutely positive he is giving more feedback, but I can't hear him over the screaming voice in my head. Yes, I love nature, but do I have what it takes to help lead such a large project? I hope so, but I don't know. I'm not sure.

The Bonds We Form

I feel my anxiety ramping up. My palms are getting clammy. I feel a cold sweat coming on. My stomach is getting queasy. My heartbeat is racing. I tell myself, "don't faint! don't faint!" in between the racing thoughts of who, what, when, why, and how all this is going to get done?

I can hear Ruby asking if I'm okay, but I don't see her. I feel a hand grasping for my own, but the room is moving like a roundabout.

As my eyes slowly open, I see the most beautiful face staring back at me. Oh, she is so beautiful. Her eyes are the color of the ocean on a clear day. As she leans in, the sweetest smell fills my nostrils. I can feel my heart beating out of my chest. Suddenly, I hear a familiar voice saying my name. I try to speak, but nothing comes out. A throbbing sensation is filling my head like someone is beating on it like a drum. I begin to shake, and everything goes black. What is happening to me?

Suddenly, I take the deepest breath I have ever taken and open my eyes once again. I see Ruby's face; she is sobbing uncontrollably.

"Hey Sid, Sid, can you hear me? Are you okay?" says Mr. Alexander. Why is he screaming at me?

"What happened?" I ask. As I try to sit up, my head feels like it is going to split open. I reach around to stop it from coming open. As I touch my head, I feel a knot the size of a golf ball and my hand becomes damp. Why is my head wet? Did I land in water? What is going on? Mr. Alexander takes my hand. "Sid, take it easy. Let's wait for the nurse to come."

The Bonds We Form

"What happened?" I ask again. Mr. Alexander slowly says, "You fainted, you fell and hit your head on the edge of the table." He is pressing paper towels onto my forehead and tells me to stay calm. He slowly helps me to a sitting position. It feels as though a thousand bricks have landed on my head. I start to get up, but I feel dizzy and fall back. "Oh!" I moan. "Take it easy, Sid," responds Mr. Alexander.

Ruby sits down next to me. Tears are steadily running down her face. However, she is no longer sobbing uncontrollably. "Are you okay? You really scared me when you fainted!" she exclaims.

I hear the door open, and a woman's voice say, "Well, what do we have here?"

The nurse, Ms. Wilson, comes in. She stands there with an expression that speaks louder than words. Her eyes are talking to me. They say, "Again?!" To this I reply with my eyes and say, "Errmm....yeah. Sorry!" with pressed lips, enlarged eyes, and raised eyebrows, slowly rubbing my throbbing temple. Ms. Wilson rolls her eyes while shaking her head sideways.

She takes me to the infirmary and dresses my head wound, feeds me with glucose and gives me an aspirin to make me feel better. She is speaking, but no words reach me. I'm listening to her with my eyes and not my ears, and I eventually drift into deep thought. I find myself collecting my thoughts about Ruby.

Certain recent incidents point toward the forming shape of the foundation of my dream castle. In my thoughts, I zoom into the future, in flashes, just like movie scenes. I physically freeze in the moment and hop from one scene to another. Me confessing to Ruby, hop, Ruby asking me for a date, hop, watching countless sunsets together, hop, at the wedding altar, hop, buying an apartment, hop, a puppy named Lily, hop, our baby.

Ah! The thoughts are mesmerizing. I don't realize that I'm sitting here on the infirmary bed with a silly smile stuck on my face, staring at the distant clouds outside the window. Suddenly, a whisper pops my dream bubble with a question. I know it's not the nurse, because it's a male voice.

The voice asks again, "How are you? Ruby is worried about you…" And it's none other than Ruby's father, Mr. Alexander.

I'm rendered speechless for what seems like an eternity, but is likely less than a few seconds. Despite that short blip in time, a million thoughts have time to race through my mind. One on top of each other, all at lightning speed: Ruby is worried about me? Does he know my initial pull toward Ruby feels like something beyond mere friendship? Should I be worried about what this means for Ruby? For myself?

Surprisingly, though a bit disoriented to be awoken in such a fashion, I feel a sense of calm rush over me. Looking into the eyes of Mr. Alexander – he doesn't seem angry or unsettled – he seems genuinely curious, and honestly, a bit amused. I begin to open my mouth, still unsure what response is going to pass through my lips. But my voice catches and my thoughts are halted by the most intense shock of pain coming from the back of my head. I have experienced many headaches in my short lifetime, but those have been nothing compared to what I'm feeling at this moment.

Mr. Alexander steps away from my direct line of sight, and I realize that my vision is foggy. Up close, the outline of his face and his expressions were clear as day; however, now at a distance, the rest of the room becomes a blur. I hear what sounds like a faraway door opening, and concerned, muffled, voices drift my way, discussing what seems to be growing concerns over my condition.

A panicked thought strikes me – perhaps my fainting spells are a result of more than just amped up adrenaline. I hope that my mother can step away from work and come to my aid shortly. I drift back out of consciousness.

My thoughts begin to clear, though my vision doesn't. I keep thinking how growing up I've heard so many adults say that kids today "have it made." They clearly haven't met any modern teenagers. So many thoughts running through my head about relationships, school, the pandemic, and my health, along with emotions that make me question who or what I am isn't easy at any age, but especially for me.

Needless to say, my school day is over and I wait for my Mom to come to get me. I hope I can rest at home and maybe catch some Grey's episodes. While waiting for my mom, a familiar face comes into the room to check on me. It's Ruby. Is she here as a friend or something more? At this point, I don't care because what I need is a familiar, caring face that won't put any pressure on me.

Ruby begins asking me lots of questions about what happened and I'm not sure what to say. I don't want to scare her away, but I also don't really know what the hell is going on with me. So I give her short, nondescript, answers. I know she's just concerned but I don't really want to talk about what happened and I'm just glad she's here. Although my answers seem to bother her, she also appears to sense my hesitation to talk about it.

She seems to really get me, which is ironic because I'm still trying to figure out who I want to be. After a few more minutes hanging out with Ruby, my Mom shows up. Is she mad? Sad? Scared? I can never be sure with her because sometimes I feel like I'm the parent in the relationship. I know my Mom loves me, but her needs are just one more challenge for my teenage mind to deal with.

Mom isn't mad, and I'm certainly glad about that. It's clear, however, that she is concerned. I think I know what's coming before she says a word. When she does start talking there are tears in her eyes. I can see that she is frightened for me. The fainting spells are possibly symptomatic of a more serious problem. "I'm not taking you home, Sid. We're going to the hospital. These fainting spells are not something we can just ignore."

"Mom, I really am okay."

"You may be, and I certainly hope it's nothing serious, but we are going to find out."

With that on the table, I really have no choice but to go along with her. My binge-watching hopes for this afternoon are gone.

As we get my things together to leave school, I start thinking of what things could possibly be wrong. I have watched enough Grey's that my imagination starts running wild. Brain tumor...cancer...brain cancer...diabetes. One perk of brainstorming all these crazy possible maladies is I'm not obsessively thinking about Ruby. Then it occurs to me, if I'm really sick, maybe even with something incurable, how could she possibly want to be with me?

We get into my Mom's Prius and head west across town to St. Michael's Hospital. I'm afraid for the first time and really glad my Mom is with me. Even though we don't always get along, I love her and I know she loves me.

"Mom, should I be scared?"

"Of course not! We are going to figure this out together."

As the Prius cruises quietly across town, I drift into a kind of trance as the possibilities run like a silent movie across my mind. I even make up things I imagine could be wrong with me. Gone for now, at least, are romantic thoughts of Ruby and what our lives might be like. Now it's just my mom and me, heading quietly to St. Michael's.

As we approach the hospital, a peculiar and uncomfortable feeling of trepidation sweeps over me. My body shakes involuntarily, almost as though it's trying to rid me of the strange sensation. This triggers the now familiar signs of an inevitable fainting spell. The last thing I remember before I succumb is strong arms preventing me from possible further injury.

Voices. Whispers. Before my eyes open as I regain consciousness, I hear them.

It's easy to fathom my whereabouts, despite my disorientation and the throbbing in my head, by the pervasive smell of disinfectant. There is something in the quality of the voices I'm hearing that averts my thoughts from my status quo. My brain is nagging me to focus attention on the discussion taking place around me. Precisely who's talking is currently beyond my comprehension. Mom's familiar voice is unmistakable. But there are at least two others in the conversation.

It's the tone of Mom's voice that piques my curiosity. At first, I can't identify why it grabbed my attention so forcibly. Then it dawns on me. Fear. Mom is scared.

I deduce instantly that my initial presumption is accurate – indeed, I'm dying from an incurable, fatal, disease. I begin contriving what I will say to Ruby, whether I will disclose how obviously attracted I am to her.

But then, the words of one of the strangers chills me to my core. I think my hearing is deceiving me due to my head injury. Mom's reaction to the stranger's shocking revelation confirms that I, in fact, have heard correctly. An animal-like sound, in stark contrast to the muffled conversation thus far, comes out of her. I wouldn't know it was Mom if my eyes weren't open and resting on her at that precise moment.

One phrase from the words of the stranger spins around in my head. "……undoubtedly, she is not your daughter."

What? Did I hear that right? I'm not my Mom's daughter? That just cannot be, can it? How can I not be her daughter? I've seen pictures of her pregnant with me, haven't I?

Mom moves at a slow pace as she enters my room. Her eyes, puffy and red, surgical mask damp from her tears, are trying to meet my eyes but just cannot. She sits beside me and it is at this point, I again jump out of my comfort zone, and blatantly ask, "That's not true, Mom… is it?" Mom seems just as astounded by the news as I was.

The Bonds We Form

"Darling, you are my daughter. We will get to the bottom of this and…" she is saying as I rudely cut her off.

"I just don't understand. What is going on? Did they mess up my test results? I just came in for a CT scan to figure out why I'm fainting. How did they determine I'm not your daughter?" I cry.

"Sid, it is a long and convoluted story that I just don't think you're ready to hear yet" Mom states.

"Excuse me?" I scream.

A moment of silence and then she says, "It was your sophomore year, right after your car accident that the doctors discovered you and I are not blood related. That does not change a thing. I'm your mother and I'm responsible for you until death parts us." She states this as a matter of fact.

My head is spinning more than it did before my two last fainting spells. Am I truly hearing this woman correctly? Is she truly not my Mom and has known this for two years? This is appalling. Now not only do I not have answers to my fainting spells, I don't even know who I am. I have the indescribable urge to seek out Ruby.

I need to see Ruby like I need to breathe. The one person with whom I feel like me, who gets me, who sees me. Who has deftly removed my mask. With Ruby, I'm more myself than I've ever felt before. A Sid I can fit into, totally, absolutely. The mirror that Ruby has held up to me reflects a person I can finally embrace, reveal, accept.

Words and questions scream in my head, ricocheting off the fragile walls of my skull. *"She is not your daughter."* Who am I? I have lost the end of my kite string. It has slipped out of my fingers

The Bonds We Form

and I'm floating in a space with no floor, no edges, no handholds. An abyss. Will I be reconstructing myself again? I need Ruby.

"Mom," I whisper. My mom urgently approaches my bed. I hear her frantic footsteps, sense her near, but her form is vague. Gray. Foggy. I rub my eyes. The void inside me is now consuming the hospital room. The room *darkens*, losing light. Shadows reach from all corners and engulf the bed, the hospital tray, the monitors. What is happening to me? In my brain?

My body tightens. It's hard to take a deep breath. Am I drowning in the depths of the bottomless abyss? Have the stars blinked out when I've finally learned how to look up?

"Mom"

"Yes, Sid. I'm here."

"Mom, everything is dark. I can't see you!"

"I'm here. Feel my hand."

"Mom," I say haltingly. "My friend. Ruby." My head throbs. I struggle for words.

"I have to see her. Mr. Alexander's daughter."

"There you are!" My Mom caresses my face. Her hand is familiar, but I still can't see it.

Someone else rustles around in the room.

"You've had us worried," a sweet, unfamiliar voice says. "You fainted again and you've been out for almost an hour."

I turn toward my mom's hand. "Did you call Ruby?" She's all I care about.

"Sid, I don't know who that is…"

"Is school still open? You can call and tell Mr. Alexander that I want to see Ruby."

"Sweetie, I'm sorry, but you can't see her. They're keeping you overnight for observation. Only your Dad and I can be here because of Covid protocols. He's on his way."

Another way the pandemic has changed our society, I guess. It used to be that anyone could come into hospital rooms during visiting hours. At the worst of the pandemic, patients couldn't have any visitors. Many died alone. The stories online are heartbreaking.

Mom squeezes my hand. "They have to run more tests, though. They've scheduled you for an MRI in the morning."

"The morning?" I don't want to be here in the morning. I want to be in class. With Ruby.

"How is your vision?" the nurse asks. I didn't realize she was still in the room.

My vision is briefly bright instead of gray. "I can tell you're shining a light, but that's it." The nurse sighs as I hear her press buttons on the machine.

"That's not good, is it?"

"I'm not really qualified to say anything." She puts her icy fingers on my wrist, checking my pulse.

"But, off the record?" I ask. "Considering I could see this morning."

She pats my shoulder. "You seem like a pretty smart girl. What do you think?"

I fall into a heavily loaded silence as I can't think of a reply to such a rhetorical question. My mind goes through whirlwinds and bouts of unconsciousness. I'm ravenous for answers but can't fathom shooting another guess at this uncannily calm nurse. As her hand leaves my pulse, a cold fingermark lingers where she had pressed for it. I still have no clear vision. I close my eyes and feel the throbbing inside my skull, like a dull finger beating on a faraway table. The hollow sounds resonate deeply within, bringing chills down to my core.

"Get some rest, sweetie," my mother's voice cuts faintly through the darkness. Her hand touches my cheek, and meets a rolling, liquid substance trickling down. Only now do I realize that I'm crying. The exhaustion of this day full of excitement and pain has come to a head. Tears stream down like a never-ending river. I taste their salt on the inside of my mouth. It's a silent cry that shatters bones to porcelain. Yet, a lingering sense of stillness comes with the release.

My mother shifts to the side of my hospital bed, her body weight pressing down my right side, a tucking feeling with a sense of overall presence on the blanket. Her arms sling over my legs, taking great care to not disturb all the lines. I can hear her sobbing now too. Another presence comes into the room or perhaps had been there all along. It's hard to make out time and space within the continual fading in and out of consciousness. Memory pieces overlap. Did I just hear Ruby's voice? Images of edible urban guerilla gardens swoosh by; Ruby and I next to each other, hands digging in the dirt, smiling contently. Then, suddenly, I hear more clearly, the baritone voice of my father. Something inside me clicks. I feel safe now.

Sounds fade in and out: the rustling of clothes, a chair scraping its metal legs over the vinyl floor, the clacking of the blinds against the window that was left open for air circulation. Then, there is a faint beeping sound.

Three: The Actions We Take

The Actions We Take

Back at the Alexander household, Ruby is trying to work on her homework. Between adjusting to a new school, her mother finally arriving home, and now worrying about her new friend, focusing on homework is difficult. Teachers have been supportive, and the other kids are mostly welcoming, but Ruby still feels out of sorts.

It doesn't help that her junior year ended so dramatically and abruptly. One moment, she was getting ready for junior prom, set to go with her best friend, Ian. The next moment, everything was canceled, and she was looking at her teachers and classmates on a computer screen in Brady Bunch-style class meets. Before long, her father was offered a new teaching position across the state, and they were off to a new home. She had socially distanced goodbyes with friends, promises of "staying in touch" with Ian, and reassurances from her Mom and Dad that, "You'll make new friends!" It just felt so bleak.

Suddenly her door flies open. "Jack! How many times do I have to tell you to knock?"

"Sorry, Ruby. Can you get me a snack?"

"Ugh! Fine. Where's Mom anyway?"

"I don't know. I think she said she went to the store."

"You're seven years old. Don't you think you're old enough to get yourself a snack?"

"I can't reach the chips."

Ruby grabs the chips from the basket on top of the refrigerator and tosses them on the counter. Just then she hears the garage door opening. "There's Dad," she says.

The Actions We Take

As her Dad walks in the door, he looks tired and heavier than usual. Ruby knows that he went to the nurse's office to check on Sid earlier, but she hasn't seen him since. "Hey, Dad. Is everything okay?"

Ruby's father's appearance and outward disposition reveal that he is drained. Ruby rushes to him, hugging as tightly as she can. Too many worried thoughts are now racing through her mind as she tries to figure out what has happened to Sid. Was the fainting incident more extreme than anybody suspected? Did Sid's serious fall in school, which resulted in her hitting her head, cause a traumatic brain injury? Ruby yanks away from her father's comforting arms and asks, "Dad, what's wrong with Sid? Please tell me, I need to know!"

Ruby and her father sit down at the kitchen table. After a moment of silence, he proceeds to tell her that Sid is in the hospital with her parents.

"Apparently, Sid's fainting episodes have been going on for quite some time. I have been told that her fainting is caused by a temporary drop in blood pressure, which affects her brain because it does not get the adequate blood flow it needs. This can lead to her losing consciousness, just like you witnessed in the classroom today. They are holding her overnight to do further scans to determine the precise cause of her condition and to keep her safe."

A tear rolls down Ruby's cheek hearing her father's words and declares, "I have to go see her. She must be so scared."

Ruby's father appreciates her heartfelt words and the value of needing to care for and be by Sid's bedside. He clarifies that, according to Covid protocols, only one other person can be in the room with Sid, and only two immediate family members are allowed.

Ruby is heartbroken and feels powerless.

I must do something, she thinks.

But...what can she do?

She feels so helpless. Sid, I would help you feel better, if only I could, she thinks.

Ruby goes to her room to find solace, and to hopefully get a little perspective on the current complications of her life. As she flings herself down on her tie-dyed quilt, a poster on her wall catches her eye. It reads, "That which does not kill us, makes us stronger." Surprisingly, this crumpled piece of paper with bright green ink-jet printed words feels very powerful, and Ruby thinks about how fitting this is for Sid's situation.

She had found that quote in a Google search and printed it along with several other uplifting sayings during the "philosophical" phase of her freshman year. Once Ruby officially became a high schooler, she felt the need to purge all her childhood decorations and instead show off her newly formed "deep thoughts." Funny, Ruby thinks. At the time she felt they would be words of wisdom for her to share with others in her life. But that poster turned out to be the perfect advice to herself. Just a year later, Ruby's life was turned upside down. She found out she'd been adopted and her parents were not biologically her own.

At the time, Ruby felt like this news would kill her. In her psychology class at her old school, she learned about the stages of grief: denial, anger, bargaining, depression, acceptance. She definitely went through each of those stages, plus others that could not be described by clinical textbook labels. Ruby went to some dark places in her mind and soul.

But after months of passing time, weeks of therapy with an empathetic and gifted therapist, and hours upon hours of yelling, crying, accusing, discussing, and forgiving with her parents – Ruby did not die. And she did become stronger.

Now, as she mulls over her long, difficult, and nonlinear journey to acceptance and peace, Ruby thinks that if she can get through that, then Sid can get through anything. Though they have only just met this school year, Ruby already knows that Sid is strong, stronger than the average person. Stronger than even Sid herself knows. Ruby wishes more than anything that she could go and visit her and help her feel better. But she can't.

She thinks about how little she has really considered the effects of Covid in these circumstances. Sure, she knows already that it has been hard for people in the hospital, people suffering alone and dying alone. She is sad for all of them, but it's hitting a little closer to home for her this evening. She can't stop thinking about how terrified Sid must be, getting all sorts of tests done and not having any friends by her side to distract her and laugh with her.

She also begins to wonder if Covid might be one of the reasons she's been feeling so overwhelmed by her instant connection with Sid. Has she been so starved of normal human interaction that her body cannot process the feeling of making a new friend? Are her emotions heightened from moving away from all her friends and family during a global pandemic, and is this causing her to cling to the very first person who seems nice? Or is there something else, something special about Sid? The truth is, this connection Ruby feels is something she has never felt before.

She tries to convince herself that there must be something psychological going on underneath the surface. Despite the fact that she can't pinpoint exactly what that something might be, it makes much more sense to her than the alternative, which is that she is completely enamored with somebody she just met.

As night falls, Ruby becomes more and more anxious about how Sid is doing. The fact that she can't go and see her is consuming her every thought. Then, a cell phone rings, and she hears her father pick up in the other room. She goes to the door to listen. She hears only her father's side of the conversation.

"This is Joe Alexander."

"Wow! Are they sure?"

"That is going to be hard for her."

"Is there anything we can do for her?"

"Okay, I will let Ruby know. She is a great kid, and we would like to help."

"Please take care of yourself and your family."

Ruby prepares for the worst as she hears her father's steps slowly coming toward her room. Her mind is full of the worst possible things. Is Sid dying? Is she going to be able to come back to school? Will she ever see her again? What would life be like without her?

Suddenly, the steps outside her door fade away. Her father is not coming in here at all. In fact, she hears the door to her parents' room open and then shut. The last thing she hears her father say before the door closes and she can't make anything out is, "I just got off the phone and there is some news."

Ruby runs to her bed. Flinging herself on it, she yells, "Why did this happen to Sid right when I found her?" She has been in "love" with other people, but this feels different. This feels like more. Not just some summer fling or lusty romance. Sid is the first person who makes her feel like herself. Sid is the first person who makes her want to love and be loved.

"IT'S JUST NOT FAIR!' she yells into the tattered and trusty stuffed elephant she's confided in for more than a decade.

Four: The Emotions We Feel

The next morning, I wake to the "beep beep beep" of the machine monitoring my heart. As I stir, the blue curtain is pulled back and someone wearing plastic scrubs comes in to check my blood pressure. The person is wearing a special medical mask and greenish gloves. If not for Covid, I would believe I'm dying of a terrible and rare contagious brain disease, and everyone has to dress like a nuclear attack is happening if they want to come anywhere near me.

"The doctor is coming to see you next," says the nurse. I watch as the machine tightens around my arm, tighter and tighter, until it jolts back and releases the pressure.

"Nurse Campbell says you like to be called Sid?" The woman in the white coat says, taking my chart from the bottom of the bed.

I nod. "Sid."

"Good morning, Sid,"

"Am I dying?" I blurt out. The doctor clicks her pen closed and clips it to her pocket.

"50 percent of people faint in their lifetime. Fainting itself isn't so worrying. It could be caused by dehydration or the sight of blood."

"Blood doesn't make me sick," I cut in, thinking of Ruby's sleeves.

"We do need to work out what's causing this," the doctor says gently. "Your body is reacting to something – stress, fear, some emotional trauma." She leans my way while still giving me my space. Her eyelashes thick with mascara, her eyes wide and sympathetic. "You can have complete confidentiality here,

Sid..." she stops. "If you want to tell us anything that's happening or maybe something from the past that's suddenly started to bubble up?"

I can feel myself panic again. I don't want to think about that. Not again. Not again.

I need to ease my mind for a bit. Having so much to process over the last several days, I need to go somewhere healing. At least somewhere healing in my own mind. I can't think about the past again. My thoughts wander to my happy place, my garden where plants are thriving and growing with love.

During the initial days of the shutdown, I remember standing outside in the garden. I was barefoot and feeling a special sort of stillness I had not felt in my short lifetime. It was almost palpable, standing on the ground and feeling the air. Even though it seemed the world was spinning into chaos, the quiet I felt from the earth was something I will never forget. I felt finally at peace, I felt as though this was my chance to finally breathe and take in my surroundings. Even though it sounds terrible, the pandemic was a gift, the pause I did not know I needed.

I remember reading an article about a group of international seismologists who measured a drop of up to 50 percent in noise generated by humans as we isolated in our homes. I think I remember them calling it the "wave of quiet." If I take anything with me from the Covid pandemic, I hope it is this stillness.

Some people believe the earth began a healing process as smog lifted from the skies, dolphins swam in the once murky canals of Venice, wild animals explored once busy streets, and whales could hear the songs of their ocean. I think of what needs

The Emotions We Feel

to breathe, swim, explore and sing inside of me. I think of my fainting spells, Ruby's hands, the revelation about my mother, and the eyes behind all the masks.

I think of things taken for granted and new chances. I think of the potentially bad news that will soon be revealed about me. Or it could be bad news disguised as good news?

Good or bad? Bad disguised as good or good thought of as bad? Is there any way of truly knowing or telling? My mind is racing but I try to quiet my thoughts.

These are unprecedented times…unimagined times.

The world…my world, as previously known, has changed forever.

Assurance, certainty, control has disappeared – seemingly overnight.

Did those things ever truly exist?

Everything has changed: classrooms, teachers, lessons, my health, my identity, my future…everything.

I remember a time in the garden digging up weeds.

Some weeds came out easily with roots fully attached. Some weeds were so embedded in the soil that when I pulled, the roots would often snap off! This type required further digging out or zapping with some eco-friendly weed killer.

I recall a third kind of weed I discovered: hidden ones. The ones whose roots I'd accidentally uncover, but at first glance did not appear to be attached to any visible plant. Were the fainting spells my body's reactions to some carefully guarded, hidden thing? Feeling calmer, I allow myself the chance to inhale and exhale fully.

I realize that my body, in an unconscious, protective response to Covid, has only been taking shallow breaths.

"Shallow breathing" seems to sum up my life so far.

Exhaling fully once more, I know it is time to dig deeper. Time to uncover what lies below the surface.

Is this what fully "taking off the mask" looks like?

"I'm not ready to talk about things at this moment. I would like to rest some more." I'm trying to avoid the painful memories and thoughts that I haven't shared with anyone since it happened.

My Mom clears away the remnants of the hospital cafeteria lunch that my Dad had fetched for me a bit ago. I only ate about half of it. My physical ailments and emotional thoughts are causing my appetite to tank. After a few more hours of rest, nurses and doctors are now reviewing my vision and blood results. I ask if my vision is going to get back to completely normal. They assure me that I'm not going blind and that it should resolve itself since I'm already starting to see more clearly.

The nurse informs us that the on-call psychologist will be in shortly. Basically, I just feel exhausted and weak from the upheaval of fainting again and hitting my head as a result. I'm relieved to have my vision almost back to normal. But my lingering thoughts about why I continue to have these "spells" and if they will happen again are causing me even more anxiety. On top of all of that, the most recent revelation that my Mom and Dad are not my biological parents is a shock to my system. I need to get out of this hospital and have some important conversations with my family. Am I strong enough to have these conversations?

It would be so nice to be able to see Ruby again and talk to her about these things on my mind. My thoughts are interrupted by the on-call psychologist coming in to chat with us again. He still feels that since my blood work is not showing any abnormalities, that some kind of built-up emotional stress or trauma may be the cause of the fainting spells. Yes, indeed I have the "weight of my world" on my shoulders. Not letting myself, my family or the world know who I really am. And with what happened the summer right before freshman year, it is excruciating to think about, much less discuss aloud and openly.

As the psychologist continues on, I feel myself beginning to lose interest in his doctor jargon. I try to follow along but keep getting lost in the vibrations of his vocals. I can smell the scent of spearmint permeating from beneath his mask. I'm aware of his expertise, and I know I should be listening intently, but I can't stop myself from being drawn to the pattern on his necktie. Am I imagining it, or do the crimson specks resemble red rose petals? I know that what I'm seeing may be due to the head trauma or my impaired vision, but I can't avoid the overwhelming feeling that this could be much more than a coincidence.

My thoughts start spiraling wildly like a tornado on a deadly path of destruction. I don't want to go back to those memories, but with every slow blink, images start to appear. The beautiful, white snow tamped by deep red blood. The moon is illuminating shards of glass that are creating a spine-chilling yet beautiful mosaic. The emergency vehicle sirens getting closer by the second.

The Emotions We Feel

The red and blue lights from the police car, ambulance, and fire truck arrive. The images keep fading in and out as I hear the song still playing in the distance… "Every Rose Has Its Thorn" by Poison.

I must drift off because I awaken to my "mother's" voice. I'm still having difficulty wrapping my head around us not being biologically related, but my attention rapidly shifts. She's on the phone with someone and her tone sounds somber as she requests an appointment to refill a prescription. Surely she would not be scheduling an appointment for me while I'm still in the hospital. Why have I never heard of my mother taking prescription drugs? Has my turmoil over the past year been to her detriment? As she hangs up the phone and turns around, I squeeze my eyes shut and pray for clarity.

My eyes close and I go back in time. I remember being in Coach Taylor's room during freshman Algebra 1. He was always so positive. I need all the positivity that was in his room every day, right now, all at once. His first rule "Always Believe in Yourself" with an emphasis on "Be You" still comes to mind in times like this.

I remember the stories he would tell us about his childhood. How the stick thrown in his eye when he was five changed the course of his life. When he was in fifth and sixth grades, he was called names every day. But he persevered and now he shows up to work every day filled with joy. He is truly an inspiration in my everyday life.

I never will forget how he told us at the end of the year to keep being who we were and the dots in our lives would one day connect. What is meant to be will be. We would find out the reason for the why in our lives. This seems like an impossibility now, but I know deep inside that Coach Taylor still believes in my peers and me to this day. Somehow, someway, I will get through all of this, just like Coach Taylor did.

Coach Taylor is one of the few people I know that loves every kid just the way they are. His love and empathy for the students is evident every day. That year, he always made us leave his room with a new perspective and a feeling of hope. His class was one where my mask was rarely necessary

He taught us way more than algebra. He taught us that we are all capable of amazing things, how to be kinder to ourselves, and that it is okay to be different.

Now I lie in this hospital bed, looking for clarity on why all of this is happening.

I open my eyes. My Mom is standing right beside me.

She has good news. She tells me that Ruby has called to see how I'm feeling. Holding on to Coach Taylor's words of positivity, this news raises a warm smile to my face. It's a smile forgotten over these anguishing days, a smile from the bottom of my heart. At this moment of happiness, I realize that life may be full of surprises…for good and bad!

I'm happy to hear that Ruby is thinking of me and really cares about me. Maybe she has the same feelings toward me. My Mom looks at me with a heartfelt smile and says that Ruby wants to see me. "To see me? How?" I ask my Mom enthusiastically. We are at the hospital and no one except family is allowed to visit, due to Covid.

The Emotions We Feel

"Zoom call, darling," she says with a smile. "Ruby will contact you in two hours after she comes back from school. She will send a Zoom link to your email address very soon; be ready, sweetie."

Hearing this good news makes me forget about the real world and what I'm going through. For once I feel happy, thinking about Ruby. I will see her, and talk to her alone, where we can express more personal things. I'm excited and looking forward to talking to her, even though it's through the screen. Suddenly, I come back to my senses. The sunlight catches my eyes through the window; the wind gently brushes my face, and the birds sing a melody in my ears. I feel alive! I feel in love! I will finally see her beautiful face and her ocean eyes! For the first time since we met, I will see Ruby, the real Ruby without a mask covering her shine.

I will be better soon. I can go through this and get back to my normal life. As I'm thinking of Ruby, John Wooden's quote pops into my mind, "I believe one of my strengths is my ability to keep negative thoughts out, I'm an optimist."

It is five o'clock now, time to get ready for my Zoom date with Ruby. "Mom, where is my iPad?"

I honestly never thought I'd be so happy to hear the two-note doorbell chime of Ruby entering our Zoom. As my Mom helps me prop myself up with extra pillows in my hospital bed, there it is – a happy little sound. *Ding Dong!*

After months of endless school Zoom classes, that chime has created a Pavlovian response to a seemingly cheerful bell. *Ding Dong!* Ugh! Gripping anxiety and dry mouth consume me as I would adjust my hair, my posture, my facial expression, the strings of my hoodie, the best angle of my background. Is there too much clutter showing in my room? Should I sit in front of the bookshelves? I look pale. I should go outside more. A deluge of stressful thoughts always followed that happy little doorbell chime. I think if I must endure another school year in a global pandemic, I'd rather wear a paper bag over my head than have to confront my reflection on a screen five days a week.

Ding Dong! Suddenly, this Zoom chime feels like a lifeline. Finally, FINALLY! After all the stressful Zoom classes, after all the hospital equipment beeps and alarms, a joyful sound!

Ding Dong! "Hi, Ruby!" I blurt out before she can even turn on her mic.

"Mom, would you mind?" I don't have to finish my sentence. My Mom understands I want some privacy with Ruby.

"Sure, sweetie. I'll get you a snack. I'll be back in a little while."

Ruby starts right in as my mom gathers her purse and closes the door to my room. "Sid! I'm so happy to see you. Tell me everything that is going on!"

Where do I start? What should I say? Do I tell her how this has happened before? The fainting? Do I tell her what I learned about my mother? I try to find the words. I stumble. My voice dampens.

I look up at my iPad and realize that Ruby is staring at me, frozen in time.

She is wearing a solid black baseball cap and a black T-shirt that says "Rush 40th Anniversary Tour" and underneath that "Aug. 1st, 2015, The Forum Los Angeles CA."

My thoughts turn to my Uncle Joe telling me about that band. He had been listening to them since middle school, which coincided with the beginning of his (yet to be outgrown) Star Wars geekdom. Uncle Joe was a history teacher who often quoted Yoda in his class, telling his students "Do or don't. There is no try," or "Always pass on what you have learned." Uncle Joe was always comparing everyday life to different movie passages, to the point where it was predictable.

When I heard the news about his succumbing to Covid, as I was mourning the loss of a relative to this global pandemic, I felt even sadder for his students, who would never see their beloved history teacher again. At his virtual funeral, I remembered one of his favorite songs in my head… "Marathon" by Rush.

As I refocus on Ruby, she is still frozen, staring at me. I say to her, "Hey, are you okay?" No response. Am I on mute, as I too often find myself in class? No, my mic is on. Suddenly, I realize her screen is frozen. Then she disappears and to my dismay, I see the "Call is ended by host" message, and then nothing. Wait… What happened? Why did my screen go blank? We got disconnected!

Five:
The Decisions We Face

Lora steps out of the room quietly to give her daughter some privacy. Honestly, she needs a minute too. Shutting the door behind her, she hears Sid hiccup several times before dissolving into muffled sobs. It's something she's done since toddlerhood – anytime she's overcome with emotion, a series of hiccups, and then the tears come.

She can tell from the tone of her voice that Sid has a crush on her new friend. On any other day, this might've been her focus – even though Sid has never told her, Lora is well aware of her daughter's sexuality. Sid will have to face the kind of adversity Lora has never known. She'll be judged by society, possibly even targeted, and it terrifies Lora. But she pushes those fears to the recesses of her mind; she has more pressing things to worry about. She's been handed yet another devastating blow about her daughter, once again, in a hospital.

Two years earlier, Sid had gotten into a fairly serious car accident with Ramon. He'd been driving when he hit an ice patch and slammed into a tree, the collision left Sid with a broken arm, a slight concussion, and enough blood loss to warrant an emergency room transfusion. That's what spurred the revelation – the transfusion.

As the doctor explained everything to Lora that night, the words "type A positive" washed over her, stopping her in her tracks. That isn't possible, she insisted to him. Both she and Sid's father had negative blood types and it simply wasn't possible for Sid to have anything else. Multiple additional tests confirmed it though. Sid was A positive. She wasn't theirs.

In the weeks following the accident, Bill had DNA tests done by three different labs. He'd spoken to countless doctors and administrators. They didn't know how to break the news to Sid. So instead, they kept it to themselves and Lora started taking Xanax to cope, almost daily.

I stay on the Zoom call just in case Ruby comes back. I hear *Ding Dong* again and I see Ruby. I can hear her calling me, "Sid, Sid, can you hear me?"

"Ruby, oh my goodness, finally! Hi! How are you? I miss you so much. It has been so weird and confusing being here in the hospital." I find myself rambling on and Ruby just sits there on the other side of the screen smiling. It feels so good to see her.

I pull out of my rambling trance just in time to hear Ruby say, "I miss you too, Sid. What is going on with you? I have been so worried. Why did you faint like that? Are you going to be okay?"

I find myself thinking about everything at once – being in the hospital, and what I learned from my Mom. But part of me just wants to leave that in the dark for now and only focus on the good things.

"Ruby, is it okay if we just talk about something else? I don't want to be sad. I'm talking to you, and that makes me so happy. I just want to stay happy."

"Sure, Sid, whatever you want to do. It's just so good to see you. I was so scared when my Dad picked up the phone and I heard him tell my Mom that they got bad news. I freaked out. I don't think I could bear something bad happening to you. But seeing you, even though it's through the computer screen, makes my heart happy! Sid, tell me you're okay. Tell me that and then we can talk about something else."

"Ruby, I'm okay for now. They are still running tests. I am on the third floor and the room they put me in has a great view of the park. It makes my heart happy to see you too! How is school going?"

"Ugh, do you have any idea what it's like to go to school with your Dad as a teacher? As if I didn't already feel like I had a magnifying glass on my every move. But he isn't that bad I guess–"

"Ruby! Your Dad is the coolest, you should have seen how he–"

"Did you just call my Dad cool? You're so dumb. Are we just gonna keep interrupting each other or are we gonna–"

"Are we gonna, um? Oh, I know. Let's play a game?"

"Or, do we tell each other deep, dark, secrets like twisted family secrets that nobody knows about?"

I feel my heart in the pit of my stomach. How can this, almost perfect stranger, be able to see me, the real me? Does she know, just like "Ms. Pep in Your Step" counselor, or have I said something that I can no longer remember?

It's starting to make my head hurt. Wait, it is hurting a whole heck of a lot and my vision is getting blurry. My fingers are trembling and I feel a sudden wave of heat rising through the thick of my neck. It's so pronounced, and the pain is so heavy, that I have a sudden episode of puking.

This is not what Ruby needs to be seeing. Correction, I don't want her to see this... I don't want her to see me as ill. This is not the impression I want to make. I want desperately to just be me, the charismatic girl without the mask, without the drama, without the intense dread that comes with being a teenager, fainting and stuck in a bed, puking her brains out, losing her vision, with a lady for a mom that might not be her mom.

This day just needs to end.

I must have blacked out because suddenly all I see are bright lights hovering above me. I hear people talking, only I don't recognize their voices. I can't make out what they're saying because the conversation is drowned out by the rhythmic beeping sounds of a heart monitor. What is happening?

"Sid." I manage to lift my eyelids open in response to the familiar voice of my mother. Although blurry, I can make out the outline of her face leaning over me. I can feel her hand tightly grasping mine.

"What happened?" I whisper with all the energy that I can muster.

"Oh, Sid! You lost consciousness and gave us all quite the scare!"

Then suddenly I remember that I had been on a Zoom call with Ruby. Oh no! Ruby! Had she witnessed my medical episode? I scan the room for my iPad, but I don't see it. "Ruby... where is my iPad? I need my iPad!"

"No, Sid. You need to rest. Please don't worry about Ruby. We both have enough to worry about right now." I know instantly that my condition is worsening. I can hear it in my mother's voice, and I can see it on her face. Disappointment consumes her, no matter how hard she tries to mask it.

Before I can respond to my mother, my thoughts are interrupted by a loud knock on the door. A nurse comes in and speaks directly to my mother as though I'm not even here. "The doctor will be in to see Sidney soon."

Bill remains in the waiting room once again. Lora has always been a take-charge kind of person, especially since Sid was born. Even though they both work full-time jobs, Lora is the primary caregiver listed on all of Sid's emergency contact forms. Bill has never made a big deal about this. He figures that a daughter, especially as she grows older, will prefer to have her Mom by her side.

There is another reason why he has relegated himself to the waiting room. He is not a big fan of hospitals, even when Sid was born. He was on a business trip when Lora went into labor. By the time he got to the hospital, Lora had been wheeled into surgery for an emergency C-section. So, he sat by himself and struggled to stay awake by drinking bad cafeteria coffee and occasionally pacing back and forth like many expectant fathers before him. He had just begun to nod off when he felt a tap on his shoulder. A young nurse excitedly informed him that he was a new dad, and that mother and child were in recovery. As he waited to be reunited with Lora and meet his first-born child, he strolled past the nursery and saw rows of full bassinets. He noticed a man peering into the nursery holding a small, knitted blanket. In his rush to get to the maternity ward, he had been oblivious to all the other expectant parents coming into the hospital that night.

He thought it was a wonder that the nurses could keep a close eye on so many infants.

It was in the same hospital where Bill found himself after Ramon and Sid's car accident two years ago. Lora got there first and had a complete rundown of all Sid's injuries by the time Bill arrived. As Lora waited to speak to the doctor, she asked Bill to go get her a bottle of water from the vending machine. Being the ever-dutiful husband, he proceeded down the hallway to the elevator banks. He suddenly stopped in his tracks, though, when he overheard a doctor and lab technician discussing Sid's case. "That's right, Doctor. I checked the parents' and daughter's blood types multiple times and they are not a match."

Bill's gut told him they were talking about his Sid. He just knew that they must be talking about his daughter. Why didn't they talk about this in private? The elevator dinged and the door opened. He entered, not paying attention as he did. The door closed.

He leaned against the corner, unaware that he had not yet pushed a button. His thoughts focused on Sid and her blood type. How could something like this happen? How did we not know? Or at least notice something? Where do we go from here? His thoughts tumbled over and over, like a big red ball rolling down a jagged mountainside.

The door of the elevator opened, and he exited. As he crossed the threshold, he looked up and realized he never left the waiting room floor. He had forgotten all about Lora's water and was struck by the idea of coffee. He wanted strong coffee!

He re-entered the elevator and saw that the floor of the cafeteria was already lit up. He looked up and saw another person in the elevator. The door closed and the two strangers traveled down in silence. His thoughts went back to Sid and Lora. He wondered how much of his life had been real.

He exited the elevator and headed toward the coffee bar; his mind focused now on how his wife would handle the news. Lora had always been a strong woman, but would this be her breaking point? How do we have this discussion? How do we tell Sid? Is our relationship strong enough to overcome this? So many questions. Bill was on autopilot as he reached the coffee bar and poured a cup, adding cream and sugar. As he took the first wonderful sip, he let his mind take him to a happier time. He saw his mom and dad, waving goodbye on his first day of school. Wow! That was a lifetime ago.

That happy feeling fades as he is shocked back into the present. Lora is calling his name just like she did that night. Same hospital, different year and for a moment it is like déjà vu.

"Sid's asleep. She knows, Bill, she knows," Lora says quietly. Tears prick her eyes and a lump gathers in her throat. "What are we going to do? What are we going to tell her?" She crumbles into his chest and cries. His familiar smell always makes her feel calmer. They haven't hugged in what feels like an eternity. The news of Sid not being their biological child has made them grow distant. Lora has been taking medication to quiet her thoughts and Bill is more engrossed in work. Both trying to distract from the devastating and confusing news that somehow, Sid isn't theirs. They haven't dared utter a word about what may have happened to their baby, for fear it might somehow mean they love Sid less. But they have each privately wondered and suffered pain over the loss of the baby they never knew. What is she like? Whom does she look like? Where is she now? The questions are endless.

"We need to find out what happened, and what is happening now," Bill replies matter-of-factly.

Lora stops sobbing and looks up at Bill. His body is stiff, his words seem cold. She wonders to herself why he isn't sad or angry or feeling something. Anything. She feels the anger begin to rise in her.

Just then Lora's phone rings.

"Who's calling—" she half-whispers to herself as she takes the phone from her back pocket, wiping the tears from her cheeks. She doesn't recognize the number. She answers, "Yes? I'm sorry but this isn't a good time—"

The voice on the other end of the line interrupts. "Hello?" The young female voice says, hesitantly. The hair on Lora's arms raises and she feels a sudden chill race from her toes up to her head. The voice sounds vaguely familiar but at the same time, Lora doesn't recognize the girl's voice or number.

Lora greets the voice on the other side of the line with a trepidatious, "Hello?"

The caller pauses for a moment. "Umm. Hello, Mrs. Simpson. This is Autumn Jones."

Lora inhales and holds her breath for a few seconds. Autumn lives next door to them and was best friends with Sid through their years in preschool, elementary, and middle school. Sid and Autumn were once inseparable and seemed to do everything together. They rode bikes together, went to the movies together, and played video games together. It was like they were sisters. But in middle school, it seemed like they were more than sisters. Autumn often would stay at the Simpson's house, eat dinner with the family, and attend weekly movie nights. Lora and Bill would hear the girls' laughter late into the night. They often wondered how the girls could function the next day on just a few hours of sleep several nights a week.

The summer before Sid and Autumn started high school, the girls suddenly stopped spending time together. Lora originally thought that Autumn's daily cheerleading practice was the cause. Each time Lora asked Sid about Autumn, she would say, "She's busy." Lora and Bill noticed that Sid began to withdraw into herself and had little to say. On some mornings, Autumn would give a slight wave to Lora and Bill as she left her home in her cheerleading uniform. They often noticed Autumn glancing in Sid's direction as Sid waited at the bus stop and Autumn jumped into a car with her older brother and his friends. They also noticed Sid typically stared at the ground when she heard Autumn yelling at her brother.

Lora's memory quickly comes to a halt as she hears Autumn's voice again.

"Umm, I was in class with Sid when she fainted. I heard she's been in the hospital, and I wanted to check on her. Umm, even though our relationship has been distant, and we don't hang out anymore, I still care about her. Since I didn't see anyone at your house, I wanted to call and see how Sid is doing. Umm, do you have any news?"

The Decisions We Face

"Oh, Autumn," Lora exhales exhaustedly. "It's sweet of you to call and check on her." She puts on her best mom voice – saccharine and noncommittal, anonymous in the most productive way.

"Oh…um…yeah! Of course. Of course, I would check on Sid. We've been friends… We've known each other since we were itty bitty, right? I couldn't just not know, you know?" Autumn chatters nervously. Autumn doesn't know what Sid has or hasn't told her parents.

"You sure have known each other a long time. That's something isn't it…" Lora trails off. The silence grows just enough to make them both feel uncomfortable. "But we don't know anything yet, Autumn. The doctors are running tests, and we're waiting."

This isn't true in the strictest sense, but Lora is too tired to discuss what's going on – the depth and worry of it. She has quit checking her Facebook because all she gets are messages from well-meaning people that she hasn't seen in years and likely has little in common with anymore. Would these people recognize her on the street if they ran into her today? No. Would she want these people to be in her life again like they used to be? High school friends, former coworkers, parents of kids Sid went to school with like Autumn's parents? Not especially. None of these people know Lora or her life. They only know the Lora that shows up at work or bake sales or school plays. She isn't telling Autumn the truth about Sid. She didn't tell Sid the truth about that blood work. She's sure there's something she's keeping from Bill, but even if she remembers what it is, she isn't going to tell him.

She should have Bill go by the house though, to bring in the mail and put the lights on a timer. When she realizes she's still on the phone, and that Autumn is still chattering, she interrupts. "Mmm. Hmm. Thanks again for calling. Tell your Mom I say hi." She hangs up before Autumn responds. She stands in the hall, phone to ear for another ten minutes.

When I open my eyes, I see two doctors gazing down at me. "Did my heart stop?" I ask.

"Nope." It's the psychologist I talked to earlier. His eyes are kind, and he says the words I've been waiting to hear. "We think we may have some answers for you, Sid." He gestures toward the doctor standing next to him. "This is Dr. Miller. She's a neurologist."

She sits down next to me and pats my hand. "Hi, Sid. Your parents are on their way in, and we'll talk about what's going on with you."

"What is it? What's wrong with me?" I can't stand another minute not knowing.

Just then, my parents appear and stand by my bedside. My Mom grabs my hand.

"Well, first of all, your scans show you have a serious concussion," Dr. Miller says.

I can't help but interrupt. "I had a concussion after my car accident, and it didn't feel anything like this!"

She nods. "This is certainly a more severe injury. When you fell at school, it looks like your head took the brunt of the trauma." She gives my parents an encouraging glance. "But the good news is, we have every reason to believe you'll make a full recovery."

"But her fainting spells," my Mom says. "What about those?"

This time the psychologist answers. "Well, that may be a bit more complicated." I read his name tag for the first time. Dr. Branson.

"What do you mean?" I ask.

"Sid," he says. "A lot of people have struggled with anxiety during this pandemic. And it's especially hard for you kids. So much of your world has changed, and most of it is out of your control." He pats my shoulder. "It's very normal to feel anxious about that. But sometimes that anxiety can affect us physically as well. I would like for you to try meditation, as it can be helpful for those with anxiety."

I know what he's saying and what he's trying to allude to. But really, is my fainting just another thing that's going to be blamed on the pandemic? He may be right that my body is physically reacting to my psychological state, but he's far from having the full picture. Can't this doctor tell from our conversations that I have my walls up? My walls have been up way before last March. There is all this stuff bottled up inside of me from the last couple years that is trying to ooze its way out. There are some cracks slowly forming but these walls are not going to fail me any time soon. Aren't psychologists trained in seeing the cracks? Isn't that their job?

I start to wonder how good of a doctor this guy really could be. After all, "Ms. Pep in Your Step" and Ruby could both see through my walls. I have had a complete conversation with this guy and even though I didn't tell him much, I did tell him I wasn't ready to talk. Doesn't saying "not ready" imply that there is something I'm not ready to say?

I must deliberately stop my mind from continuing down this path because I know it isn't going to help anyone. I remind myself that he did recognize there was more to my story and that there was no way for him to know it all started way before anyone ever heard of Covid-19. But where do I begin? Am I ready to let this stranger know my deepest secrets? Am I ready to remove all the masks?

If I want to figure out how to stop these fainting spells from continuing, I don't have a choice anymore. It's time to peel back the layers and I'm going to have to pull them off like a Band-aid. Fast and in one big swipe. I look the doctor right in the eye, open my mouth, and then – more blackness.

I guess I'm not ready to talk...

As I come back to consciousness, yet again, my Mom and Dr. Branson are both hovering over me with anxious expressions. Yet again. I suddenly realize that the common denominator for these fainting spells is my trying to verbalize the chaotic thoughts inside my head. At this moment, I recall some things my two favorite teachers have said.

Mr. Alexander has repeatedly encouraged each of us to "speak our truth" and creates an environment of trust and belonging that enables us to do that. Can it be that even though I know I need to share my story about what happened because I don't have a relationship of trust with Dr. Branson, I'm paralyzed with fear and am overcome physically as a result?

I'm frustrated by the fact that my body is rebelling against me. Just as it did after the car accident in terms of my physical being, now it is rebelling mentally – shutting me down when I try to talk about that day.

The Decisions We Face

I consider a couple of things Mr. Salvatore said. He has pointed out that history is written by the victors, yet it is seeking out the stories of everyone impacted that can give us the full picture. He has told us that each of our stories contributes to the human narrative and that our stories are vital to understanding where we are now.

I need to find a way to share so that I can start to heal.

Mr. Salvatore also remarked that day in class when I was with Ruby that "no one in this class writes as you do." It occurs to me that I can write it all down. I can share it with someone I trust. So, I ask Mom to hand me my iPad and open the notes app.

Dear Ruby,

I don't know if I will ever send this to you, but I wanted to express myself. Since I met you, I've unintentionally shown you a side that I didn't realize I had, someone who is not as strong as she looks. I may have been able to help you that day in the bathroom when you were at a low point, but now I'm ashamed to say that I can't help myself. I want to be stronger than this. I hate to think that my mess of a condition caused you worry or stress. I desperately wanted to tell you this before, but now I realize that I couldn't have. I need to tell you about how I've been feeling. When I'm around you, I feel happy. When I'm around you, I feel myself. You make me feel less alone. For as long as I've known you, I've felt connected to your beautiful blue eyes, the way you speak with passion & intention, and how I feel seen when I am around you. I can't tell if you've noticed how I feel about you. If you have and can only see me as a friend, I'm willing to accept that, but at the same time, I'm not ashamed to say that I would find it hard. As Cecelia Ahern once said, "If you love something let it go. If it was meant to be, it will come back to you."

The Decisions We Face

Something inside me tells me to stop typing. My mind is awhirl with possibilities and made-up scenarios that could result if I choose to send this to Ruby. Feeling as if I'm miles away, I sit there, half-staring at what I've written, and wonder what to do with it.

While staring at these words, I decide to delete everything.

My face flushes with horror as I realize that I almost sent this to Ruby.

This is the thing that finally breaks me. Years' worth of carefully controlled emotions come pouring into my mind all at once. I have used the phrase "my mind is flooded" before, but it isn't until this moment that I realize what that truly means. I feel like I'm being swept away. Looking at the world through water-filled eyes, all my hidden secrets and cherished memories float off and crumble apart.

Here I am, sitting in a hospital during a global pandemic. My doctor is trying to tell me that collapsing every few hours is a symptom of anxiety. Quarantining for a year. Losing friendships. Seeing my ex-boyfriend. Meeting Ruby. Knowing that my sexuality is frowned upon by a lot of individuals. Moreover, learning that my parents aren't my actual parents.

Is there a name for the sound made when laughing, sobbing, and screaming in rage simultaneously? I suppose not. I can't imagine enough people experiencing this emotion to bother naming it. I feel the familiar onset of another blackout coming. I almost brace for it, but my mind is too flooded. Too chaotic. I rise to my feet and yell defiantly, refusing to fall. I don't think this will work. And I don't expect what happens next.

Six:
The Choices We Make

The Choices We Make

Ruby Alexander spent a fair amount of time pondering her options before finally deciding she needed to see her friend in person before she could come to a decision, or for that matter, any conclusion. Although she'd dated in the past, she hadn't been able to form any lasting connections. Looking back, what she had with anyone else was barely a fraction of what she feels with Sid. She looks around her room at the messy assortment of books lying on the floor. Bending down to put them away, a page from her book of Japanese fables catches her eye.

It details how every person has an invisible red thread attached to their pinky with the other end tied to that of their destined soulmate. This person is their perfect complement in every conceivable way. With a heavy sigh, Ruby shuts the book and bolts off to find her Dad, musing in her head whether Sid is indeed the one. Her Dad is all dressed and ready by the door.

"Took you long enough," he says and smiles warmly at his daughter.

"You do know I could have just driven by myself to the hospital, right?" she questions.

"I thought you might want the support, so I'll drive you to the hospital," he replies as they walk out.

They drive along the road in comfortable silence while the car radio blasts hits from the '80s. It's a short drive and they reach the hospital quickly. Ruby waves goodbye to her Dad and proceeds to pass the busy reception area undetected. From there she quickly heads to the third floor to find Sid's room. Ruby opens the door just in time to witness her friend swaying precariously to the floor. Ruby rushes in, cushioning her fall.

The Choices We Make

When I open my eyes again, the room is quiet and dark and I'm alone. A cup of water is positioned on a rolling table to the left of my bed. I reach for it slowly, bringing the rim to my lips with trembling hands. Water. Ramon always hated water; tasteless, and boring, he said. But water is practically all I ever drink. A guest speaker our freshman year told us that the human brain is made up of 73 percent water, and Ramon joked that if I drank much more my brain would explode. I feel like my brain has exploded, with all the newness and chaos this week.

Two nurses come in, whispering, but leave just as quickly when they notice I'm awake. I wonder how long I've been sleeping.

"Going on nine hours." Dr. Miller stands in the open doorway. "I assume you're wondering how long you've been asleep."

Do neurologists also study mind reading? "Where is everyone?"

"Your Dad is at work, your Mom went to get groceries, and your friend is waiting outside the hospital."

Friend? "Excuse me, Dr. Miller. What?"

"Ah, yes, you were out cold when your friend burst in. She somewhat caught you, actually, as you fell, but security caught up with her and immediately escorted her outside."

Am I hearing this? Ruby, my Ruby, was here, in my room, and I missed it? And now waiting outside the hospital! Was it possible she missed me as much as I missed her?

Dr. Miller smiles. "You must be an important friend," she says. "All the more reason we're going to send you home today. You'll begin weekly counseling sessions with Dr. Branson and daily check-ins with your school social worker, Mrs. Busbee.

Accommodations will be in place until your concussion heals. I will be back to check on you shortly."

Dr. Miller leaves, but all I think about is "counseling."

"I don't need counseling anymore; I need to see Ruby." I think. It's time to let out the truth and rise above the fear of being judged. I, Sid, am no longer bound, believing in unrealistic perfect perceptions, or dated ideologies. I can rip off this suppressing mask. When the doctor leaves I suddenly feel the urge to get up from the hospital bed to find Ruby.

As I step off the elevator and find my way to the front doors of the hospital. I take one step out of the building and I see her sitting alone on a metal bench. Breathless, I run to her. "Ruby, you're here?" Ruby stands up and her face is red, but her arms are open. When I come near, she closes them around me in a warm and gentle embrace.

"So, I heard you broke into the hospital, found my room, and caught me as I was falling. Does that mean we are in this together?" I say with a sigh.

She replies with a nervous smile and soft voice, "Yes, of course, we are."

I'm bursting with the urge to come clean and reveal everything about myself. "I have so much to tell you."

But she replies, "Not now, save it until we're alone." Her father stares at us from the car for a moment before he respectfully rolls up the windows. Does he know? Ruby looks at me and says, "Do you want to walk?" I say yes without hesitation. We walk through the parking lot on light feet, holding hands. It feels good to have human contact. We walk in silence, full of anticipation, all the way to a little pond in a nearby park. At one point, I bend down and give Ruby's scarred hand a peckish kiss. This beautiful hand that brought us together. I feel weightless and proud of my truth and am instantly released from my prison of emotional hell.

Ruby needs to hear what caused me to bottle up a poisonous cocktail of guilt and fear in my soul. No more secrets. I open my mouth to spill the truth when I hear Dr. Miller's voice saying my name.

Yes, Dr. Miller. I'm stunned to see her walking toward us. How did she know where to find me? Us? Doesn't she have other more important things to do and patients to check on?

"You must be Ruby," she says, taking a good look at her before turning to me and holding my gaze, "Sid, can we talk?"

"I want Ruby to hear whatever you have to say. Is it okay if she stays? " I say not wanting to leave her side.

"Sure, I was telling you about counseling with Dr. Branson before you took off. I would also like you to try meditation. It's important that you try to do it. I want you to know you're not alone, and counseling with meditation is the first step toward getting better and living a healthy life. You are exceptionally and uniquely made. Never forget that." She finishes off in a motherly and soothing tone before she turns and leaves.

As I watch her go, I can't help but note that Dr. Miller just said so much to me without saying *too* much. I feel a heaviness lift off me. I breathe deeply, inhaling all the air and exhaling it in equal succession. I close my eyes for a second and open them again, making sure I'm not dreaming. Did Dr. Miller just recognize that I'm having difficulty expressing and letting out what I have been masking?

I feel peace overflow my entire body and I close my eyes for just a second, welcoming the feeling. Ruby whispers, "Sid, I think we should...I should...I mean. Dr. Miller is right about going to counseling and trying meditation. Maybe we could...I mean, I could do the same." I look at her and understand immediately. Our faces, inches apart, eyes locked and searching, seeking certainty. Ruby's hand touches mine as she fills the little space between us, kissing me first lightly on my forehead and then on my lips.

At this moment, everything from my past that has been keeping me trapped, keeping me restless, keeping me feeling so different from everyone else, seems to slip away. I have found my person. My person has found me.

For the first time in a long while, since maybe even before the start of the pandemic, I feel hopeful. I feel that peace may be available to me. Sure, I've just found out my parents aren't who they've claimed to be for my entire life. Sure, my emotions have been taking over so ferociously that my body is no longer able to stay upright. But now, with Ruby in my life, I will put in the work to be happy. Will I finally get to take my mask off?

I know a lot of kids who've gone to counseling since the start of the pandemic. Many parents have been worried about how their kids will respond to the upending of their worlds. It's hard enough being a teenager, let alone being a teenager during a time when we're told to fear the world around us more than ever before.

The Choices We Make

Even though I know some kids like their counselors, I just never thought counseling would be for me. Am I broken? Is Dr. Miller telling me I need to be fixed? Maybe she's right. For a long time, I've felt deeply alone, but didn't understand why. Ramon was never right for me, Autumn stopped talking to me and the pandemic did not help my social life. It seems everyone has been able to move on much more quickly than I have... To have transitioned easier, which left me feeling alone.

Maybe seeing a counselor will help me finally tell Ruby, finally tell anyone, what I really feel. Maybe these sessions will be the first step in allowing myself to really and completely, finally, take my mask off and breathe.

Ruby's quiet breathing draws me out of my reverie. My head on her shoulder, watching the sunset together, is so magical. My breath hitches in my throat as Ruby looks down. She gives my shoulder a steadying squeeze, and with a hesitant yet reassuring smile, says, "You're so strong, Sidney. Stronger than you allow yourself to believe."

Hearing my name from her lips sends shivers down my spine, and I can't help but beam. "Ruby. There's so much I need to tell you. I..." I look down at our interlaced fingers and try to center myself.

Am I trying to confess my feelings to Ruby? Am I about to unmask my past?

Overwhelmed by the answers, I squeeze my eyes tight and lean on her for dear life. I'm also reminded that perhaps I should wait for my counseling sessions with Dr. Branson before saying anything to Ruby. What if he feels differently or tells me I'm simply a lonely soul trying to dump my burdens on the first person who's nice to me?

I'm reasonably sure that's not how counseling works, but operating from a defensive space just feels natural now. I peek up at Ruby, and our eyes meet, her gaze crinkling with a smile. My withering defenses immediately crumble, and I find myself smiling too. In this wordless moment, I feel entirely weightless. Fainting spells, my parents, the car accident with Ramon. Everything seems unimportant. Everything else is unimportant, as long as I have Ruby.

"Sid, I know that you've got a lot going on." Shushing what I believe to be protests about our closeness, I try not to tremble as my mind jumps to the worst outcomes. Ruby persists, "No, Sid. I'm... what I'm trying to say is, I'm here for you." Her solemn declaration fills me with a strange sense of ease, and right then, I trust that I have an ally.

Is that why I blurt this out? I don't know, but I'm glad that I do.

"Ruby, I just found out that my parents are not my biological parents."

I let go of my words and immediately after they're spoken, Ruby gives me a look. A look that's so comforting it almost brings peace to my soul. Her eyes are beautiful, and her soft smile can break through even the strongest of concrete walls. She gently wraps her arms around me and gives me the warmest embrace I've ever felt.

Then she softly whispers, "Sid, I can't tell you that I know remotely what you're feeling and what you're going through, but

I once had my world turned upside down too…when I learned that I'm an adopted child."

This is exactly what I need. Not a person who assumes to know everything I'm feeling, because no one does. No one can understand exactly what I'm going through. But I do want someone who will be there for me. Someone I know I can count on and be vulnerable with. I want someone who will do the same. Ruby just said and did the perfect things. I feel freedom in my heart. A breakthrough. Can this change the brick wall I've been building around myself for years?

Ruby, holding my hand gently says, "Sid, you're not alone. We're in this together. I promise."

The sun is slowly setting, and the light of day has faded. It's probably time for us to go home. Mom has finished signing the discharge papers and she's waiting for me by the car. We walk back, hand in hand. For the first time in forever, I breathe freely, without covering my true self. Before we say goodbye, I hold Ruby tightly in my arms. I thank her for all she has said and done. It's time for me to go home after all.

Seven: The Secrets We Keep

The Secrets We Keep

I stand outside my house long after Mom goes inside. Not wanting to go in, I shift my weight from foot to foot. I look over the house's strong frame. Its faded and peeling coat of white paint, the dusty windows with curtains drawn. The house looks like it's sleeping, like I shouldn't enter and disturb it. I know my parents are waiting inside. I take a deep breath and walk in.

"Can we talk about a few things?" my Mom asks, with a knowing smile. It stops me in my tracks. I study her face. She has an expression I haven't seen before. Does she…*know?*

"Mom, Dad," I start, taking a deep breath. "We need to talk."

They nod and I walk toward the armchair across from them.

Dad plucks at a hangnail nervously and directs his words to the floor. "Honey, I just want you to know your mom and I love—"

"Dad," I interrupt. "Let me go first. Please."

He glances up at me and his eyes meet mine. I can see how scared he is. I usually think of my Dad as larger than life, strong, and capable of facing anything. But at this moment, I know he is terrified of this conversation. There's so much to address – my adoption, my health, and how to move forward as a family during this pandemic. I start to question if now is the right time, if I'm just going to keep making things worse for everyone. I close my eyes and I feel Ruby's fingers interlocking with mine. I feel her lips pressing against mine, and I can hear her whisper in my ear, and I know that I can't wait any longer.

"Mom, Dad," I say with renewed resolve. "I want you both to know that Ruby and I are more than friends."

My Mom sighs, placing her fingers against her forehead to hide a slight smile.

"Sid," she says. "Sweet girl. Do you...do you want to sit down?"

My first impulse is anger, of course. White hot rage sends a warm wash over the skin of my face. How dare they act as if intentionally unmasking myself is something to giggle about? "Mom, I'm telling you Ruby and I are–"

"Girlfriends? Wait, no, in your generation it's just talking, right? You're talking." Dad's shoulders start to shake just a bit. She shoots him a prankster's glare and he tries to contain himself. "Well, I imagine it's more than just talking, though, or else you'd..."

"Mom!" I barely stop myself from acting like a petulant child. "Why is this funny?"

She stands up and moves toward me, catching on to my very real feelings of humiliation. "Oh, honey." Her arms wrap around me and it feels like coming home. I relax into a low, deep sob. "I'm sorry, I didn't mean to hurt your feelings. We know you. And we love you. And we love whomever you love. There's nothing you can say to make us not love you. We are so proud of you, more than you will ever know."

There are things you know but aren't conscious of until you hear them or see them or feel them. Ruby kissing me was one. I thought she was special, but I didn't know absolutely until that moment. I know my parents love me unconditionally, but I didn't know the true meaning of the word "unconditional" until my attempt to come out struck them as more of a joke than a surprise.

I feel my mother's palm against my face, wiping away my tears. "We shouldn't have laughed, baby. I'm sorry. It's just...a parent knows their kid, you know?"

"You hid from me that I was adopted. For years you kept from me that—"

"Adopted?" My Dad stands up slowly. His face is genuinely concerned, and confused. "Did you think you were adopted? You're not adopted."

"Wait. What?" I'm on my feet without even realizing I'm standing up.

"You're not adopted," he repeats softly, gently taking me by the shoulders. "I don't know where you got this idea, but you're not adopted. Oh, Sid," he says, letting his arms fall back to his side. "This is not how we wanted this to happen." My Dad looks truly frightened, even more so than before I blurted out my news. This is the conversation he's been dreading. Seeing this makes my heart pound. I'm becoming conscious of my breathing.

"Please, both of you, sit down. Please," my Mom begs as she returns to her spot. I stare from one parent to the other and fall into the chair with a heavy thump. Mom is no longer smiling. She looks as panicked as I suddenly feel. The entire vibe of the room has gone from loving to terrified in a single beat. "Sweetie," she starts, "I'm so, so sorry, but we need to tell you. We should have told you after the accident, but…"

My parents turn toward each other and the look that passes between them is something I've never witnessed before. I'm seeing them for the first time without their masks. It scares me to my core. I'm not sure I want to hear this, but I feel like I've been waiting for this moment.

"Told me what? What! What's going on?!" I scream. My head is now throbbing, but I refuse to pass out. Not now, please not now!

"Okay," my Dad relents, "we'll explain what we can." He takes a deep breath. "After the accident. You needed a blood transfusion. We thought we could donate our blood to you."

"But our blood didn't match!" My Mom can't hold onto the truth any longer. "It didn't match! That's when we learned…"

"What do you mean didn't match?" This is madness! Nothing is making sense. How could our blood not match?

"Somehow, Sid," my Dad continues, "we're not your biological parents. We think you were switched at birth."

My father's words twist and turn inside my brain as I try to make sense of them.

Wait. Can I still say he's my father?

Yes. No. I don't even know.

I look at the faces of the two people I've called Mom and Dad my whole life and try to find little pieces of me. She has a crescent moon dimple on her left cheek when she smiles – just like me. And he has the same hair color, mocha brown with caramel highlights. But these are just coincidences. We're not related. We're just connected by a lifetime of memories.

"My parents?"

Mom's sigh is audible.

"We are your parents," my Dad says as he reaches his hand across the table.

"I...I'm sorry. I know that." I bite back any further words and wonder about the two other people out there in the world who are obliviously living their lives with a child that isn't theirs. Do they know? Have they had their world turned upside down or are they still blissfully unaware?

And then a thought comes that has me spinning and struggling to breathe. If they did know, would they even want me?

"Sid, are you okay?" My Mom comes around the table and wraps her arm around my shoulders. The warmth and weight of her embrace grounds me, and my breathing slowly evens out. I look up at her and she smiles.

"Yes, Mom. I'm okay."

I'm not. I don't know if I ever will be, but for the moment, I'm a bit closer to fine. I close my eyes and hear Paramore singing in my head. When I was younger, I would sing along and pretend to be a member of the band. I was happy. Those times seem so far away – like a balloon drifting into oblivion.

Eight:
The Stories We Tell

No one was happier to be expecting a baby than Bill and Lora Simpson. They were matching outfit-wearing, high school sweethearts who dreamed of marrying and owning a house, with a dog and two children. After graduation, they drifted apart but found each other again after college and having their hearts broken a few times.

On their second wedding anniversary, they decided to start a family. On their third anniversary, it was still just the two of them. On their fourth anniversary, it was no different. By their fifth anniversary, Lora had grown weary. They were on the verge of giving up hope and considering other options when they learned that Baby Simpson was finally on the way.

The months seemed to fly by as Bill devoured books about caring for newborns and inspected every flutter inside Lora's growing belly. He wanted to be ready. In contrast, waiting for the baby made Lora feel exactly like she felt as a child when she fought away feelings of excitement. In her mind, she thought that if she allowed herself to get excited about going somewhere special or doing something fun, she would jinx herself and it wouldn't happen. So, she spent years trying to avoid getting excited about going to amusement parks, birthday parties, and sleepovers with friends. Now, she was spending her days trying to stay busy enough to keep her mind off the long-awaited gift that was growing inside her. Years of unsuccessfully trying to start a family had taught her to avoid disappointment by expecting nothing. However, once a day, at bedtime, she would allow herself to feel gratitude for Baby Simpson. Each night, she would close her eyes and wrap her hands around her belly and whisper "Thank you, God, for this baby. Held in hope. Wrapped in love. Unconditional. From above."

Bill and Lora Simpson had it all figured out. Their lives would be complete with the arrival of their child in just a few short months. Day by day, the anticipation built for Baby Simpson's birth. Little by little, they anticipated how their lives were going to change. However, one event would change the course of their child's life.

Had my Mom lost her mind when she told me "We should have told you after the accident" and Dad chimed in with "Switched at birth?" Waves of anger, frustration, and sadness swirled around my head along with countless questions.

"How exactly did you think I would feel about being switched at birth?" I ask. My parents start to say something and then are quiet for the longest time. Thoughts and questions race through my head. "Switched at birth?" I look down and say nothing else. This whole idea rages inside of me.

"Tell us how you're feeling, Sid." my Mom says.

My Dad continues, "This is not something we meant to hide from you. The time was never truly right for this to be brought up."

I sigh and stare off into space. I can tell by my parents' worried faces that they're concerned, but I just don't care. How can I explain this to Ruby? How can I explain this at all? Will people look at me differently with this news? I sigh loudly and shake my head. My Mom moves closer to me and takes my hand. "Sid, are you okay? What can I do to support you?" she asks and looks at me.

The Stories We Tell

"Tell me the story of what you know and how you found out," I tell my parents. "I want to know everything."

So, my Dad tells me. Twice. It doesn't change, but he tells me once more. He said that they believed I was their child until my accident two years ago and think I must've been switched at birth. How else do you have one child and then suddenly have another?

Dad reaches a comforting hand out to Mom. I haven't seen them hold hands in a while. "Nothing changes how much we love you, Sidney."

Then it dawns on me. I'm not the real Sidney Simpson.

"Your real daughter is out there."

I see their hands slowly break apart. Dad has tears in his eyes now, too. Mom reaches into the side table for her pills. I've blasted open the wound they so desperately wanted to keep covered.

"I still think about her. Nine months singing to the little bean as she grew in my belly. What happened? Where did she go? But, I have you now and I don't want to…I don't…" The words fail to come out of Mom's mouth, so Dad takes over.

"We were afraid that if we continued searching, we'd find what we were looking for, but lose you in the process."

My world will never be the same, but there's another person out there who has no idea that her world won't be either. "I have to find my biological parents." I feel confused, sad, angry, and a whole range of emotions I've never experienced before. Just as I'm beginning to feel like I can be who I am in the world, this happens. Oof, I really could use a Ruby hug right now.

The Stories We Tell

I'm ready for Mom and Dad to stop me, to calm me down, but they don't. Instead, they agree with me. "I think it's time we push through our fear and continue the search. With your medical condition, there's still so much we don't know. If we find your biological parents, maybe we'll find the answer to what's happening to you," my Dad says.

It seems like the logical place to begin our search. The hospital is, after all, where it all began. It all started here. In this hospital. My parents, or at least the people I call my Mom and Dad, had their dream come true right here when they held me in their arms for the first time.

Wait. Was I the first baby they held, or was it their real daughter? When did the switch happen? My head is spinning. My heart's racing again. I know this feeling, but I will not let it happen. Not now. I take some deep breaths and the feeling subsides. I try to stop thinking, but uninvited, the questions keep coming.

I can't help but wonder what will be revealed if I find my birth parents. Aside from the answers about my health condition, what else will I learn about my genetic makeup? Do I want to know? Did my parents choose to take home another baby? Did they know I would be a potential burden? There's a possibility that a hospital employee was responsible. If we find a person who knows what happened, will they be willing to admit it? I have too many questions filling my brain!

We find out that all the Covid protocols in place at the hospital right now will add to the frustration of trying to find answers. We're going to have to go back home and do most of our detective work online or by phone. How can we tell if people are telling us the truth if we can't meet with them in person and read their body language, look them in the eyes, and hear the tone in their voices? I want to say, "Maybe this isn't such a good idea after all. Let's just go on with our lives as they are." I don't say it though. Dad seems more determined than anyone to find his real daughter. There's no stopping him now.

Even though I'm back at home, I once again feel dizzy. Squeezing my eyes shut to make the room stop spinning, I take a moment and hope I don't faint. I take a few deep breaths, steadying myself before reopening my eyes.

Mom reaches over and places a hand over mine. "Hey," she says, her tone warm and soothing. I look at her, her eyes smiling at me with kindness and compassion. I wonder if she can tell that I'm overwhelmed because she suddenly seems gentler toward me. Maybe this is a motherly instinct? Moms seem to know everything. She squeezes my hand. "Everything is going to be okay. I know this is some jarring news. But, honey, you aren't ever going to be alone under any circumstances, okay?"

"That's right, Sid. We're here for you, always. You're our daughter. We'll figure this out together, I promise," Dad chimes in, walking over to me and giving my shoulder a soft squeeze.

Sucking in a breath through my teeth, I nod repeatedly. While allowing this new information to sink in, I find I can't speak right now. Yet my mind, as always, runs a mile a minute. I wish Mom and Dad's words would quiet my thoughts, too, but maybe this is how I'm processing the situation at hand. Once, I read in a book that it's better to allow oneself to feel one's own emotions, rather than shoving it all down. Usually, I keep my emotions hidden, but for some reason, right now I let myself think, process, and feel.

At this moment, I'm wondering silently what my biological parents are like. Do I look like them? Do we have similar interests, or are they completely different from me? Does my personality match theirs? Suddenly, guilt settles in the pit of my stomach. My non-biological parents are offering me support, but here I'm, wondering about my biological parents. Am I a horrible person?

I shake off that thought, knowing deep inside that wanting to explore my roots is a natural desire and doesn't change how dearly I love my Mom and Dad.

My mind wanders. I think back to Ruby's idea of planting a garden. She had learned from her grandma about harvesting sustainable food without disturbing any of the wild roots and identifying edible weeds. Maybe I can search, without guilt, to uncover my roots. They may have answers to my health and bring me closer to understanding my authentic self.

Needing a moment alone, and feeling exhausted, I head outdoors. I take my shoes off and stand in the dirt and allow my body to absorb the earth's energy. I have read that "earthing" grounds you and helps you recover from stress more quickly. It shifts the body to a restorative healing mode. My anxiety begins lifting as I let the gentle wind soothe my body and soul. I take deep, unabating breaths. The only thing that would make this moment better, is to have Ruby by my side.

Thoughts of Ruby run through my mind. My desire to see her again is growing stronger by the moment. I must share with her this new reality I've come to know. I just know she will go on this

The Stories We Tell

journey with me; our paths have crossed. I walk back inside and sink into the fuzzy, lavender, bean bag chair in my room. I see a photograph of some wildflowers on my wall with the quote, "May all your weeds be wildflowers." My eyes see new meaning in this. I'm so tired, but I want to pick up the phone and call my love. We can find our missing pieces together.

Nine: The Moments We Fear

The Moments We Fear

Ruby, please answer. Aah! Finally, after what seems an eternity, "Hey...Ruby!" Beep! Beep! Oh! Disconnected. Bell's ringing again. "Hello... Ru...!" Beep! Beep!

Why does the phone keep disconnecting?

Mom's texting me to come to dinner. I will try Ruby once more before I go. Ringing again. Ringing...ringing...no response. I look up to see my Dad at the threshold. "Dad?"

"Sid, dinner's on the table. Mom sent me to get you. Even if you're not very hungry, she wants you to try and eat a little, and get some healthy sustenance. Let's just sit together around the table as the family we are." He adds, "and always will be."

I pull my mask into place. Drawing the curtains on the turmoil wrought by the weird experience of calling Ruby's phone, I simply nod. Now Dad and I are both masked. We're masquerading, like actors circling the dark circumferential periphery of the spotlight, center stage. Neither of us are willing to reveal ourselves.

My thoughts whirlpooling, I plug in my dying phone and follow Dad to the dinner table. I can feel my pulse racing, my chest thudding, and my ears getting the familiar spacelessness that's a precursor to my fainting episodes. I reach the table and brace myself, holding on to the back of the chair, my knuckles white. My mom, the woman who raised me, is now so in sync with me. Or rather, always was. I took it for granted and never saw it then, back when I still believed she was the one who'd brought me into this world. She rushes over to me, even before the darkness sets in. She holds me and gently lowers me into the chair, resting my head softly on her chest. Slowly, the darkening buzz halts, the moment passes, and I start to breathe normally again.

The Moments We Fear

Feeling my breath pulse through my chest, I settle into the chair to attempt to have a "normal" meal with my (non-biological) family. Mom's cradling of my head brings me back to a fragment of a deeply buried memory — one I wasn't aware I had access to. I've heard before in audiobooks and podcasts about the theory of deep repressive memory digging. It's almost like lucid dreaming where you can tap into natal and infant memories. For a second, I confuse this with one of my fainting episodes, but it seems like something much more powerful. I'm nearly pulled out of my mask — from my chair at the dinner table — from this mortal coil. It's a surreal feeling, really, but at this point who am I to question reality?

I'm pulled back into what I know is a memory, where I can see someone looking down at me in surprise. With all my might, I'm trying to lift this gargantuan container of a cranium, but it's not happening. I can feel warmth surrounding me as I'm picked up and I feel safe in the arms of this stranger.

Honestly, I never thought I could pull out a memory THIS vivid from this long ago. I look down at two tiny, balled fists, and have the sudden urge to wail, to cry out - although I know I can't form words at this age or stage of existence. I mean, within these lucid memories — can I truly control and reshape my history?

Wait, am I still at the dinner table? Can Mom and Dad see me desperately struggling? Did I just scream out loud? I'm tempted to pull myself out of this hazy dreamlike memory and back to the dinner table. I clench my eyelids shut and try to thrust myself back with a kick, as hard as I can into reality.

When I look up, I see my Mom and Dad, their eyes brimming with concern. "Sid, honey, can you hear me?" my Mom's all-too-familiar voice squeaks out.

"Yeah, Mom. I just, I don't know." There's too much there. Too many words. Too many feelings. Too much confusion, and yet, it feels like the answers are just beyond my reach. "I'm just so confused…and angry. How could the hospital mess up like that? I mean, I need answers! WE need answers." My Dad slides the Kleenex box across the table before I realize the tears are falling down my face, identical to the tears in my Mom's eyes.

"Sid. Bill. For two years I've had an inkling of what happened, but it's only a feeling. It may not be what happened." Mom pauses, choked up. "I've just…I never told anyone about this." I'm not sure I want to hear what comes next, but I reach my hand across the table to encourage her, the woman I'll call Mom, no matter what blood runs through us.

"It was in the middle of the night after you were born, Sid, or after I gave birth. Bill, you went home for a bit because you didn't like the hospital room. Hospitals still aren't your thing." Mom ekes out a small smile at that. I can tell she is trying to stay strong. "I couldn't sleep, so I wandered over to the nursery. When I got there, the nurses were in a panic. A newborn baby had been left outside a fire station. This baby was alone and hungry and screaming. She wouldn't take a bottle. She just kept wailing her tiny little lungs out. I couldn't take it. I just asked for the baby girl, scooped her up, and nursed her. It was the first time she got quiet. I sat in the nursery with her until she had her fill. I guess I thought it was what any mother would do."

"Mom, what are you saying?"

"It's my fault. I had so many emotions flooding through my body. Sid, I wanted you so badly. Maybe it was because I nursed you. I was so tired. I don't remember. I don't know. I had an instant connection and felt complete with you. I thought I dreamt it until your accident"

The room is quiet for a moment, and my Mom continues.

"I really thought it was a dream… How could I do that? How can I not remember? Please understand… I love you." She looks directly into my eyes, and then down at the floor.

"Mom. I love you. Truth is, this is really confusing. I don't know what I am supposed to say. I will have to live with what you did and you will have to live with the decisions you made that night and face the repercussions." I know in my bones she had good intentions, but there are consequences to our actions.

I try to push my anger aside and speak my next words slowly – carefully.

"Mom, I am feeling really upset at the moment and I do not want to say something I will regret. Moving forward, I want transparency and I want us to figure this all out together. I want to know where I come from, who I come from. I want to figure out who I'm supposed to be."

As I run through the scenario in my head, just as my mother described, I make up stories. Maybe my real parents dropped me off because they were obsessed with partying or had me when they were too young to let their parents know about me.

These thoughts make my chest burn.

The Moments We Fear

I create another story. They left me because they knew I was sick and they wouldn't be able to give me the attention I needed. I imagine a woman, a young artist painting downtown on the corner of the street, red paint swept across the image of a brick building she'd just watched be demolished. She wanted to capture the essence of loss in the moment because she knew she'd never have the stability she needed to keep me. My father — whoever he may be — I can't imagine. Perhaps because I don't want to erase my Dad's face in my head.

We sit motionless for what seems like hours. We are together, yet the world has never seemed so lonely. My father sits motionless in shock.

This room has become a watery, drowning place. As my parents sit down, I get up, perfectly in rhythm as if circling in a carousel. Let's all just keep our distance. We seem to slouch, a half-time weariness, as though a football has been tossed hard into our midst. Nobody's catching. Nobody's reaching. I'm watching but I'm done listening. Once again I feel a slipping away overtaking the invisible arrows on this floor we're sharing in this ironically named "family" room.

The next couple of days are one big blur. I remember talking to Ruby and sleeping a lot.

I'm laying on my bed and I can hear my parents discussing family counseling, I hear them tiptoeing and talking quietly around me like I'm fragile. I feel like this house is becoming more and more unfamiliar as the days go by. My head starts to hurt. I need to breathe...

I don't need, want, or require family counseling, parents, or heritage moments right now. The stitching on all the multi-layered masks is unraveling. What I need, want, and require right now is to leave this house. I take, unnoticed, the keys which hang languidly like the burgundy-colored bougainvillea twining atop the garage door. Those flowers have been trained for years to look just so, grabbing onto each perennial growing season.

As I step outside the house to breathe in the wind and sky, I look to my left and see Autumn sitting on the porch with a blanket and a book. Enjoying the nice morning weather. She waves in my direction and smiles at me.

Of the two cars, I choose my Dad's ruby red car. Seatbelt secure, Fleetwood Mac's "Landslide" playing through the speakers. I tell myself I will carefully back out and not blackout.

The road is quiet for a Saturday morning. No one rushing around to go shopping or meet with friends for a brunch tradition. A world in isolation, and here I'm breaking free from it to feel something other than looming dread and debilitating guilt. The adrenaline from driving when I shouldn't be is enough to suppress the noise echoing in my brain. I allow myself to take everything in.

Ramon drove us everywhere. He was always so careful, calmly maneuvering us on our little trips. To the park on a warm sunny day or to our favorite cafe, where I would always get iced coffee and he would get a soda because coffee was never really his thing. I never felt unsafe with him behind the wheel, until that day. I saw no purpose in getting my license after the accident.

The Moments We Fear

Why would I want to be certified to do something that could get me killed? I avoided car rides for months after I recovered. I jumped at every horn and siren. Yet today, the road doesn't seem so hauntingly intimidating.

My recent trauma has replaced all of that, burying the rest.

As I pass my old elementary school, city hall, and the relic that is Wilson's Hardware Store. I forget about my parents. I forget about counseling. I even forget about Ruby. I also forget about turning around to go back home and find myself on a street I haven't faced in two years. More cars. More headlights. My heart is racing.

A horn sounds, blasting into my ears as if a speaker is sitting next to me. As my breathing quickens, my hands begin to shake uncontrollably, the steering wheel no longer in my possession. I don't know where I am, I feel overwhelmed, hopeless, and afraid. I knew this was a bad idea... I need my parents.

A scream escapes before I lose control of myself.

Ten:
The Paths We Travel

The Paths We Travel

I open my eyes with a faint sensation that I'm already sitting up. My mind races as it grasps at the flood of dream fragments. But then, relief washes over me. It's just a dream, I tell myself. Nothing bad happened. With the help of the dim moonlight shining through my bedroom window, I grab the journal I keep on my nightstand and try to jot down as much as I can before it all slips away.

My dreams almost always start with a strong sensation of fainting. Often, they end with me facing an unknown. Unfortunately for my parents, it isn't that uncommon for me to cry out before I realize I'm awake. My dreams are always convoluted, vivid, and emotional.

I'm not sure of the meaning of the mystery of my parents in this one, so I draw a large bubble question mark after that. I pause and stop trying to catch all the other details. What was the dream about? I jot down the words "Autumn, Ruby, past, & future." So much of the past feels like a lie and the future feels hopelessly unknown.

I turn the page and write "Landslide" in large letters and underline it twice. This is a song about the challenges and changes life throws at us. Being a senior is a challenge – so often I'm asked about my plans. College? The future? How? Why does everyone ask me about unknowns?

I stretch my arms, shifting my attention to the waking world. It's hard to believe that spring break is next week. Where has the time gone? I know I want something to happen this year but I'm not sure what. The only "known" I hold dear is that meeting Ruby has been important. We have grown close these past two weeks. First as friends, then finally as a couple. We've been working on the food growing project since I've been released from the hospital. But I wish I knew how to fit the pieces of my life together. I put the notebook away. I can already hear Ruby's sigh and can picture her smile as I tell her about my crazy dream.

Of course, Ruby knows about my dreams. She always makes sense of them. What is disjointed and fragmented to me becomes coherent when I tell her. I'll tell her about this one when I see her, and it will make sense. I only keep the journal so I can hold onto the dreams long enough to tell Ruby.

I know I should be doing homework, but it just doesn't seem that important right now. What's school when I have so many real-life issues I'm learning about? I've been seeing Dr. Branson once a week. I don't know if it is helping much. Everyone keeps telling me that it takes time, it's a process, and I must be patient. I thought I'd notice something by now, though.

I read a blog once where they said finding a therapist that works for you is like trying on shoes. We need to try out the shoes to see how they feel before we know they will work. The great thing about shoes is that there are many different styles and sizes. Sometimes we are not going to find a shoe we like but we will eventually find the right fit.

My parents are still on edge since our talk. We are all trying hard to not let our relationship change, but the effort is changing the relationship. Dr. Branson says family therapy might help. I don't know if Mom will go for it though and to be honest, I wouldn't be going if they didn't make me. Dad's the only one who will take it seriously. It is not a surprise; he was really shocked to hear what Mom said and he wants answers.

The Paths We Travel

I remember that Ruby said we'd meet for coffee and tea on the way to school. That's a relief. I feel like I'm constantly holding my breath between my parents and my classmates worrying that I'm going to collapse every day. Ruby is the only break I get... I can breathe and exhale without holding anything back.

I choose a tie-dyed sweatshirt and my black jeans from the closet to get ready. I look at myself in the mirror as I brush my hair. The pattern on my shirt reminds me of the jumble of thoughts and emotions in my mind and dreams. The way blobs of each color dance around the others in somewhat circular patterns give a sense of order and chaos at the same time, just as my life seems to be at the moment. Still, I like the cheery colors. They remind me of Ruby. I pick up my backpack and head out of my bedroom.

As I walk through the hallway toward the kitchen to say goodbye to my mother, I realize that the house seems eerily quiet today. Usually, I'm greeted with the familiar scene of my mother sipping a cup of coffee (usually her third) and reading the newspaper or a blog on her phone. Today, it seems like she hasn't left her bedroom as the subtle humming sound of the coffeemaker and the smell of coffee are missing. Starting that fresh brew is a morning ritual my Mom's been performing for years now. My Dad's on a business trip and should be home by the weekend. Even when he is home, he always leaves quite early though.

A little confused by the unexpected silence, I walk toward my parents' bedroom and stop in my tracks as I hear periodic sobs coming from the bedroom. No doubt, my Mom is crying. This woman who always keeps a strong front is crumbling under the weight of something I don't understand. My first instinct is to walk inside, hug her, and ask her if she is okay. But I hesitate and stand in the same spot.

The truth is that I'm accustomed to and comfortable with the mask she wears every day. The mask of a strong, relentless woman who never gives up. Am I ready to see the vulnerable side she hides so seamlessly behind her mask? I think for a moment and turn to exit through the front door.

I hurry to meet Ruby at the coffee shop, eager to tell her everything that's been churning in my mind. What does the dream mean? Can it be some sort of warning? Does my subconscious mind know something I haven't yet realized? Is my brain honking a horn at me, warning me I'm about to crash? What does my mother know that she hasn't told me? Does she know something awful is about to happen? Could that be why she was sobbing? I have so many questions and so few answers.

I'm lost in these thoughts, my mind racing when I hear my name.

"Sid!"

I turn around. Oh, thank God. It's Ruby.

"Sid, are you okay? You walked right past the coffee shop," she says.

"Oh, yeah. I did, didn't I?"

"Seriously, are you okay?"

"Yeah, I'm fine. I was just thinking. There's just, well...I just have so much I want to tell you."

Ruby grabs my hand and says, "Well, spill then. I want to hear it all."

The Paths We Travel

She walks me back to the coffee shop and points to the table she has saved for us.

"Do you want to order a drink or some food?" she says.

I look up at the colorful menu and think about everything I want Ruby to know. I want to tell her about the accident, about my dream, about my mother — but more than anything, I want to tell her my history. I want to tell her everything I've never told a single soul before. I want Ruby to know my every secret, the very best and worst parts of me. And then I want her to love me — still.

I take a deep breath. I know that I need to tell Ruby, but I'm also apprehensive. What will she think of me? Will I have the courage to be as honest as I hope that I can be?

As we sit down, I'm transported back to that fateful night. I wish I could say that my memories of it are fuzzy, but they aren't; they are crystal clear in my mind. The sounds. The sights. The smells. I wish they were memories that weren't mine. But I know it's me. I was there.

Just as I'm starting to relive that conversation, all that I need to share, my reverie is broken by the sound of Ruby's voice.

"Sid? Sid? Hello in there? Come back to me." I blink a few times as I realize that Ruby is waving her hands in front of my face. "I asked what kind of coffee you wanted." She looks at me with a bemused expression.

"Oh. Right. Coffee. Um... Can I actually have lavender tea?" I know that some might feel that lavender tea isn't my style, but it's calming. I watch as Ruby goes to the counter to order our drinks, her hips swaying gently back and forth as she moves.

She turns back to me as if she's worried that I might be gone somehow. I see the relief in her eyes to find me sitting in our spot. Still here, still conscious, still with her. I love that she needs that reassurance, and it bolsters my courage. I can do this. I will do this. And I will trust Ruby, and who I know her to be – my love, my confidant, my other half.

She comes back to the table with our drinks and a chocolate chip cookie, my favorite dessert. I smile and take another deep breath.

"Ruby," I say. She looks up from her coffee, nothing but love in her eyes. "Ruby, there's something I want to tell you."

She looks nervous. She sits down and places her hands in her lap. I, on the other hand, am strangely calm and at ease. It is a busy morning in the coffee shop, but somehow, I'm unable to hear the customers, the coffee grinders, the espresso machine, orders being called out, or the ramblings of the other customers who seem to be seated unusually close to us. I'm hyper-focused on Ruby's face. Everything else is a blur, except for my phone. It keeps vibrating in my back pocket.

I take a deep breath and begin speaking my truth. Who am I right now? Who the heck do I think I am? Speaking freely about myself, my family, and my thoughts. This is new to me. "I have never been confident in who I am as a person, even more so now," I say in an almost whisper.

Ruby replies jokingly, "Of course not, you are a teenager! None of us are!"

"It's deeper than that," I continue. "I'm not who you think I am. I'm not who I think I am. I'll start at what is now the beginning for me, and I'm warning you, this sounds made up, like something from a show or movie."

"My parents aren't my parents. I was switched at birth."

I pause to take a deep breath as I'm sure I will be bombarded with a million questions at this point. But I'm wrong. Ruby sits quietly and continues to listen. I trust her, and her response is exactly what I need. I must talk for about 30 minutes straight, giving her all the details I know about my birth story. Unbeknownst to us, we have already missed our first period class.

I look around and am surprised to find that most of the coffee shop customers have cleared out. I look at my watch and it has been an hour, I quickly tell her that we're late. She interrupts me and says she has to use the bathroom. While she's gone, I check my phone to see who has been incessantly trying to get ahold of me.

"Hello, who is this?"

"Sid?" Mr. Alexander has been trying to call me. I don't recognize his number, but the repeated attempts and voicemail lead me to believe it's something more than a spam call.

"Hi, yes, it's me."

"Great. It's Joe Alexander. I hope you're feeling better."

"Yes, much." I wonder why he is trying to reach me. "Is something the matter?"

"No. Nothing's the matter. Well, not really." Mr. Alexander's voice is hesitant. "I noticed that Ruby and you are not at school yet. She mentioned this morning that she was grabbing coffee with you. I hope you both are on your way to class. However, I'm wondering if you could come by my room during lunch today."

"We lost track of time and are on our way. I was planning on having lunch with Ruby. Can I bring her too?"

"No," he says. "I'd prefer if we just have a conversation."

"Of course. I'll be there at lunch. Your room, correct?"

"Yes. Thanks. See you then."

Ruby sees me staring across the coffee shop, the phone still in my hand when she returns.

"Phone call?" she asks.

"Yes," I say, putting away the phone. "Just being the helicopter Mom she is."

Ruby and I don't say a lot after that. Given all that I've told her, I believe she feels it's better to allow me to direct the conversation. As much as I want to continue discussing my newfound revelation, I also wonder about her adoption. Does she ever wonder who her parents are? Maybe we can take our journey together, to find our true parents.

Back in his classroom, Joe hangs up with Sid, sets his phone on his desk, and stares into his empty room. He takes a deep breath and thinks about the list of tasks he needs to finish during his prep period, but he can't focus. All he can think about is the envelope burning in his back pocket, the one the private investigator gave him yesterday. He feels the breeze from the open windows across his face. Fifteen years and three different rooms at his last school, and he never had a window. So he vowed to always keep the windows open, rain or shine. While he misses his old school and town, they moved here for a reason. Ruby.

With resolve, he grabs his phone, takes a deep breath, and calls his wife. *Ring.* Silence. *Ring.* Another silence before he has to deal with her anger. *Ring.* "Hey, it's Andrea, leave a message, or just hang up and text me like a normal person!" *BEEP.*

"Hi, Ann, it's me, uhhh . . . he found her. Listen. I know you don't want this. She is still our girl, Andrea, nothing can change that. I just want her to know—"

"If you are satisfied with your message please hang—"

Joe sighs and hangs up. He drops his head into his hands. He wants to believe it won't matter, that she will still be his little girl – that despite not being blood, they will be okay. That day plays over and over in his head. The anger from his wife. It was a secret she wanted to take to the grave. Andrea pleaded with her husband, "Joe, please, she looks just like me. She will never know. You can't do this to me, to us!"

"Ann, we have to. She needs to know. What if she finds out someday? What if something happens and we never told her? Imagine how betrayed she would feel. I'm telling her."

"You want to tell her that her mom didn't want her? Do you want to tell her she just left her in the cold, crying and alone outside of a fire station? Go ahead. But you can do it without me."

As I think about meeting Mr. Alexander at lunch, I wonder why he wants to meet me alone without Ruby. Does he know about my feelings toward his daughter? I can't imagine what he wants to talk about, and I'm nervous.

Then, a sweet voice touches my ears. "Sid. Sid."

I look up and I'm back in reality with Ruby. It's so calming to hear her voice and see her expression. She puts me in a meditative state of mind, and I feel a sense of peace.

"I think we're running late for school," I say.

"Oh, wow! We better get going. I'll see you at lunch," she says.

How can I tell her that her Dad called me in for a meeting? I make an excuse to avoid uncomfortable questions. "Oh, I can't. I need to go to the library."

Later, I make a quick stop at the library, so my excuse has a veneer of truth. I pretend to seriously look for a book. Suddenly, a book about meditation flashes in front of my eyes. The cover page is interesting, and I put the book on a study table and turn the pages. It's about the mind, peace, and our thoughts. Basically, about the power of thoughts. How our thoughts dictate our feelings and even affect our health and well-being (with which I'm struggling).

This makes me feel a little hopeful. I decide to try to meditate and be present as I wait for lunchtime. As I close my eyes, I hear paper shuffling, smell the earthiness of old books, and feel a slight breeze coming from a cracked window. I try concentrating on my breathing. After a few minutes, I feel a calming sensation throughout my body. As I reflect on my thoughts, many of them become crystal clear and I feel the chatter in my mind settling. I'm a little more confident and feel ready to meet with Mr. Alexander.

"Sid, I'm so glad you made it. Please, take a seat."

Mr. Alexander, (or should I call him Joe?), motions for me to sit down next to his desk in a dark wooden chair. I hesitate for a second. My head is full of all that's happened in such a short period. The fainting spells, meeting Ruby, therapy, the revelation about my birth. But I've got this. What can Mr. Alexander possibly have to say that's more dramatic than what's already happened?

"Thanks, Mr. Alexander. So, what's up?" I say, with caution in my tone.

"Sid, I'm so glad you and Ruby have become... close. It means a lot to my wife and me. Moving, especially during a pandemic, can be destabilizing."

He pauses, and I can tell he's nervous. I mean, if this is just about a birthday surprise, he certainly wouldn't be so dramatic.

"So, the truth is, we moved here for a reason. You know that Ruby is adopted, right?"

I nod, and he continues. "Well, when we adopted her, we were not given a lot of information about her family. It's not that it wasn't an open adoption; they were very rare those days. But the details surrounding her birth were slim and unsubstantiated, and my Wife and I were curious. So about two years ago, we hired a private investigator to dig into details about Ruby's biological parents."

I take a deep breath. How is this story so close to my own? Ruby finds out that she's adopted. Me finding out that my parents are not my biological parents. My mind wanders and I think about my recent dreams.

The Celestine Prophecy's message that "Dreams come to tell us something about our lives that we are missing," feels particularly insightful right now.

"Okay Sid, be present," I tell myself, and try to shift from the thoughts clouding my mind back to what is in front of me.

Mr. Alexander looks nervous. He holds his hands tightly together and begins rambling on, asking about my parents. It looks as though Mr. Alexander is trying to do a complex math problem when suddenly he says "Ruby's real parents are your parents."

Like a crashing wave, it all hits me at once. Ruby is the child my Mom switched that night at the hospital. My parents are her parents. Wait! Am I the baby that got left at the fire station? As the wave roars in, out goes my consciousness.

I wake up and open my eyes. Mr. Alexander is sitting on the floor next to me with tears rolling down his cheeks. "What did I do... I didn't mean to say that out loud. I'm so sorry."

I sit up and am about to speak when I hear the bell ring. Students are being released from lunch. We have both lost track of the time and it is now time for the next period.

Mr. Alexander wipes his tears and says, "Are you ok?"

"I'm fine," I say as I get up to walk out of the room, feeling as though I'm in a trance. I realize as I walk out that this bombshell is too heavy for me to sift through while also trying to focus on class. I'm afraid I'll pass out again and instead decide to take a mental health day. I go to the nurse and tell her I'm not feeling well and need to go home. Mrs. Wilson knows what I have been through with my fainting spells this year and agrees with no questions asked. I call my Mom to come to pick me up and wait for her in a silent state of shock in front of the school.

I don't say much during the drive home, just that I'm not feeling well and need to rest. I walk to my room, shut the door, and lie face down on my bed. I allow the mask I've been wearing all day to fall as the tears and emotions pour out.

As students walk through the door, Joe Alexander skirts between them to see where Sid is going. He stops in his tracks outside his classroom. He feels like a cement statue, heavy with sadness, fear, and shame. The noisy halls are deafening, yet he doesn't hear a sound. He's not sure how much time has passed when he feels his arm being squeezed. Logan, the TikTok guy, is emphatically speaking to him.

"We're waiting for you. The bell already rang. Why are you standing out here? Mr. Alexander, should I get the principal?" Mr. Alexander hears "get the principal" and snaps his attention to Logan.

By this time, students from his sixth-hour class are at the door, trying to get a view of what is happening in the hallway.

"Okay, okay." He tries to be convincing while forcing himself to move closer to the classroom door. Every move seems like it's in slow motion. The sounds, his steps, and his voice.

"I was going to use the restroom before the bell rang," he says. The students laugh and begin to comment. "But I knew I didn't have time." He waves his hands, and the students go back to their desks. Relieved that Logan didn't call Principal Johnson, he turns his playlist on to distract the kids a bit longer.

After what seems like hours, he glances at the clock and breathes a sigh of relief. It's only been three minutes since the bell rang. He pushes the last 30 minutes out of his mind and begins his lesson.

After shifting his focus to welcoming students, he decides to do something a little different in class today. He's glad to see from his attendance sheet that everyone in this class is present, and no students are learning virtually while quarantining.

He asks the kids to take out a notebook and pen and look at the whiteboard when they're ready to begin. After a moment of confusion, they search their backpacks frantically for writing utensils and paper, as most of their assignments are typed on laptops. Thuds from backpacks, clanging metal water bottles, zippers, sliding chairs, whispers, and muffled laughs quickly fill the room.

As a veteran teacher, Mr. Alexander is excited about this assignment – a pre-planned question to empower students to think like sociologists. He turns to the whiteboard and realizes a question like this might even help Sid process the life-altering news she's just received and could help build a foundation for a healing journey ahead.

The potent aroma of the blue dry-erase marker fills his nostrils as he writes on the whiteboard. "What happened during the pandemic that helped you better understand the reciprocal influence among individuals, groups, and society?"

Mr. Alexander decides to complete the assignment too. This purposeful, open-ended writing activity turns out to be extremely therapeutic for multiple students, as well as himself. A few kids compliment him as they head out the door, thanking him for creating a classroom environment that empowers students to "speak their truth."

Eleven: The Challenges We Face

The Challenges We Face

I wake up to the sound of my morning alarm and check my email. I see an email from Charles about Mr. Alexander's assignment question and I decide I will write all my truths on paper too. After all, I have learned a lot about my life during the pandemic. It's been tragic for both the world and me personally. A million thoughts run through my mind. I must tell Ruby about my parents. I don't want to pile stress on my Mom after hearing her sobbing in her bedroom. I don't want to cause further distress to my Dad with him being away. I need to talk to Ruby before she finds out. A million questions run through my head. Should I be the one to tell her? Should Mr. Alexander tell her? Will Mr. Alexander be upset at me if I tell Ruby?

After school, I go to Mr. Alexander's classroom to finish our bombshell talk. We agree that he'll tell Ruby, but I insist that I be present. I don't want her to think that I knew about all this and left it out while telling her my own truths.

As night falls, I head over to Ruby's house. She meets me at the door with a hug. I pull back and she immediately knows something isn't right. We sit down with Mr. Alexander, and he tells her everything. When he finishes, she cries uncontrollably. I hug her and leave for the evening. Now, we're both devastated.

I wait until my Dad comes back from his trip and ask my parents to read my assignment, revealing my truths and what I've learned about my parents. My mother is devastated, which now makes three of us. But my Dad is furious. He storms out of the house and goes to Ruby's to have a man-to-man discussion with Mr. Alexander. He feels that Mr. Alexander should have discussed all of this with him and my Mom before involving me and Ruby.

The Challenges We Face

Now there's silence between me and Ruby. I think people notice, but no one says anything. When we pass each other in the hall, all I can say is "I'm here if you need to talk."

By Friday, I'd had enough. I pass Ruby in the hallway at school, and she tries to give me another brush-off. As she turns to walk away, I grab her by the arm. She looks down at my hand, and I let go.

"Can we talk later?" I say, regretting having squeezed too hard.

"I guess," she says. "Lincoln Lake at 4 p.m." To my relief, she throws me a grin. "And don't be late."

She disappears into the crowd. I wonder why I don't feel faint because the rest of me is shaking. The idea of Ruby and I drifting apart because of a new awkwardness surrounding her adoption has been unbearable all week. I can't lose her. Not after I've finally found my person. The one I don't ever need to wear a mask for. And yet, if my parents are her biological parents, what does that make us? Stepsisters? Nothing at all? We certainly aren't blood relatives. The whole situation is insane, and my health issues aren't helping.

The rest of the day at school is a bit of a blur as my mind goes over and over what I want to say to Ruby. What I still want from our relationship. How can I just forget the attraction I feel for her? And yet this new information is distancing us. Maybe if I can find out who my biological parents are, everything will make more sense.

As the last afternoon class ends, I decide that I need to speak with Ruby. I need her to be straight with me about how she feels

The Challenges We Face

about me now. We need to be honest and trust each other. I've had enough of this fifties-style comedy of errors.

I hear every minute and every second ticking away as the time moves closer to 4 p.m. The physical walk to Lincoln Lake isn't bad, but my thoughts are causing my heart to race and my brow to perspire. I talk to myself while I'm walking, practicing what I will say. But as I approach the lake path, my mind goes blank. All I can think of is how I feel about Ruby.

Before I know it, she's here. The sun shines behind her and reflects off the lake. She is beautiful and I feel like a frazzled mess. As I approach, neither of us makes direct eye contact. Awkwardly, we both say, "hi" at the same time. We break into a fit of giggles and finally look into each other's eyes.

As quickly as the laughter begins, it ends and there's silence. Suddenly, Ruby pulls a piece of paper out of her pocket. She can barely hold on to it. Her hands are shaking so violently that I want to reach out and hold them, but I can't. She softly says, "Sid, can I go first? I think I need to get this out or I may not be able to later."

A moment goes by, and I take in our surroundings. It is such a beautiful evening, the clouds appear to be on fire and are reflecting off of the calm water. It is an absolutely stunning sight to witness. I'm grateful to be here, grateful to be here with someone I love.

I turn my gaze toward Ruby; she is loud without even saying a word. With my mask firmly in place, I smile, nod, and she begins to read.

The Challenges We Face

The sun fights through the blue-gray haze lingering across the sky. I sit quietly and listen to Ruby read her carefully crafted thoughts via the letter she has written to her parents. It is devastating; one part touching, one part crushing, with a full spectrum of emotion sprinkled throughout. She has found exactly the right words to amplify her heartbreak. I close my eyes as she speaks, so I can really focus on the words, and not on what is going on in my mind–the inevitable and impending conversation that I still need to have with my parents.

They learned what I knew by reading my assignment, but after my Dad left for Ruby's house, we haven't discussed it again. My Mom has tried to talk to me, but I'm not ready. She has been extra-present, alternating between trying to insert herself into my schedule and giving me space, but I just feel so weirdly betrayed. I try to think about things rationally—if I were the parent, what would I have done? Would I have done anything differently? Probably not, I surmise. But that isn't enough of a resolution. I need closure. For me, and maybe for Ruby. Maybe they will tell me something that can fix everything. And then it occurs to me—the only thing to do now is to have a joint family meeting. The secret is out. We may as well make a party of it.

As Ruby finishes her reading, tears begin streaming down her cheeks. She lets the paper drop to the mossy rocks beneath where she stands, and I bend down to pick it up.

"That's beautiful," I say. I stand up and kick at the green clutching to the rock she's standing on. I'm nervous to tell her what I have in mind, but she's just emptied all her deepest emotions to me. It's the least I can do.

The Challenges We Face

"Ruby," I said, "I have an idea."

"What's your idea?" Ruby asks, taking a few deep breaths so she can hear me out.

"We need to be the ones who decide what happens next. You were right in what you said. All of this has been too much at once. Our lives have been turned upside down and we feel like we don't know who we are anymore. But we've also been there for each other during this, and there's no reason we can't continue to be there for each other.

"Our parents are not the people we grew up with, they're the people who tried to care for us and help us even if they didn't know how. I agree, they could've, no, they should've been upfront with both of us from the start and communicated with each other before talking to us about it like that. But they didn't, so we have to decide now, what happens next?" I hold my hands out to her and she takes them tentatively, a few stray tears rolling down her cheeks.

"We move forward," she smiles softly. "Our lives will never be the same, or normal, again." She nearly laughs at that, which makes me smile. "But they're not just going to switch us suddenly. We're their kids."

"Exactly!" I say, a bit too loudly. "Sorry. I care about you a lot, and I don't want you to disappear from my life. I think we can find a way to move forward together and be with our parents, our parents who raised us. We can't change the past, but we can all support each other in the future." A few tears run down my cheeks as well, but as Ruby smiles, I realize they're not from sorrow.

The Challenges We Face

"I care about you too." She nods and sighs. "We should go talk to them about this. Tell them it's okay and that we want to try and move forward together. Although, my Dad isn't in a great place right now. Someone reported that he was crying and that you rushed out of his classroom. The school is concerned about what's going on." She glances down, anxious about this new complication on top of everything else.

We walk back home together with the sun on our faces. A gentle, reassuring breeze is filling the air. Still, though, we're viscerally concerned about everything that's happened to us but determined to find clarity. Jack is playing in the front yard as we approach Ruby's house.

We walk through Ruby's door, and after hearing her Dad on the phone, I wish we hadn't. "Mr. Johnson, please let me explain!" Mr. Alexander's face is flushed. Ruby loosens her gentle touch from my hand and covers her mouth, trying to manage her emotions. "There must be something I can do!" I catch a glimpse of myself in a mirror, and I wonder in disbelief how all of this can be happening. "An investigation? Mr. Johnson, is that necessary? I can explain."

Ruby turns to me as if to find answers about what is happening. I take a step closer to her and whisper, "Remember, it will be okay... we're in this together." More tears run down Ruby's face. Mr. Alexander hangs up the phone and seems overrun with emotions and uncertainty. He says he's fine but needs to leave. He heads out the front door and gets in his car.

"Ruby, I'll explain to Mr. Johnson what happened. I'm sure we can figure this out." Her reaction is subdued. I try to understand. "Trust me; I get it! So much has happened to us."

The Challenges We Face

"Sid, I don't know what to do! I want to help my Dad, but I feel so overwhelmed right now." Ruby has been there for me, and I decide nothing will stand in the way of figuring out how to make this right. After all, Mr. Alexander is only trying to protect Ruby, and now I'm going to do the same.

We decide that I should go home, even though I want to stay with Ruby. Walking home, I think, "Monday, I'll go to school early and meet with Mr. Johnson." I'm feeling confident, something I haven't felt in a while. I change the song playing through my headphones to "Fix You" by Coldplay.

As I turn onto my block, I quickly become confused. Why are the police at my house?

A policeman is standing in our living room, holding my Dad's arms as he screams threats at Mr. Alexander. Mom is crying quietly in the corner. I instantly feel lightheaded and know I need to walk away from this, take a deep breath, and head back to Ruby's on this night of high emotions.

When I get there, I tap on Ruby's windowpane.

"Ruby," I call. "Meet me at the park on the edge of town."

"Okay," she says. "I'll just sit with Jack for a little while to make sure he's okay."

I get to the park first and wait for Ruby. Is she the other part of myself? Born of my mother's womb? This must mean something.

What if she doesn't come? The new moon smiles, assuring me that I'm not alone. The drumbeat of my heart lifts at the crunch of leaves on the path. Ruby approaches ever so closely. I can smell her salty tears like the sea and feel the heat of her body. She's carrying a small pack on her back.

"Sorry it took me so long to get here," she says. "I waited until Jack calmed down. My parents were discussing something about your Dad and how he's trying to ruin my Dad's career." She pauses.

"Our Dad," I say, and she cracks a smile.

We walk hand-in-hand toward the sound of the stream and stop at the rock with a cave-like entrance. I used to play here with Autumn when we were kids. Ruby places a breathy kiss on my neck, then on my lips. We lay down and watch the stars, moon, and sky above, feeling blessed and grounded at this moment.

"We'll get through this together," I say.

We talk and kiss throughout the evening and decide to head home before it gets too late.

When I get to my room, I decide to work on an assignment I need to finish for Dr. Branson. I don't usually enjoy the homework Dr. Branson assigns me following our weekly sessions. I just can't get into it.

But tonight is different. I feel purposeful. I'm determined.

I take out my journal that's buried at the bottom of my backpack. Breathe.

I pause to contemplate Dr. Branson's question that I had quickly scribbled down. "To whom are we accountable?"

My thoughts linger on my evening with Ruby. The moon. The magic. Only, it's reality. Then, flashback to my car accident with Ramon. My mind is racing. Natasha Bedingfield's "Unwritten" is blaring through my headphones. The lyrics seep in. That's it.

The Challenges We Face

There are endless possibilities, just fleeting moments in time when people make decisions that have consequences. These consequences have no limits and can be intertwined with our connections to other people. The question is, will I let them be my calm or calamity?

My meeting Ruby in the bathroom at school was no coincidence. She's brought some clarity into my world, but not without consequence. I interrupt my thoughts and stare at the five words that Dr. Branson posed. Accountability. That's a heavy word but its load is lightened by one realization.

Me. I'm accountable to myself. I can be angry. I can hurt. I can heal. I can choose. My words float on the page. I read them aloud and repeat them.

On Monday morning I will talk to Mr. Johnson.

I'm on tenterhooks, expecting to be called for a meeting to explain my side. Nothing. I convince myself that if I make the first move, I can slow any investigation in its tracks, and make Mr. Johnson see it's all a misunderstanding. The twisting in my stomach jolts me so that I need to catch my breath. Once, I would have spoken to Mr. Alexander or Dad if I was in a tight spot. Now, it feels as though Ruby is all I have in this world. I wonder if she feels the same way about me, and I can smell her cherry lip gloss and see her smile as if she were here. Even though she has been brave, the life she once knew has been snatched away. We walk together when possible and have talked endlessly during the past few days, but she is suspended between moments, rootless.

Another deep breath. I realize I have not prepared or collected my thoughts in a way that makes sense even to me. What should

The Challenges We Face

I say? Before I knock, Mr. Johnson opens the door and leaves it ajar. He ushers me in, making a show of asking his secretary to chaperone us. She peers at us over old-fashioned glasses, then returns to work. I'm ashamed; the situation's unfairness trails like a bad smell. Which reminds me that I haven't forgiven my Mom. What kind of mother does not look for her own flesh and blood, and settles for a substitute? If you love somebody like I love Ruby, you fight for them with everything in you. Mom did not fight for her child, she settled for me, like the barter system Mr. Alexander taught us. Why am I dealing with these consequences while Mom lives on Xanax? I understand now that love can co-exist with rage; I will tell Mr. Johnson everything. I'm accountable to myself.

I'm standing on the edge of Mr. Johnson's small office. Staring at his secretary, Ms. Shaw, I wonder if I want to do this. Should I take a bit more time and consult with Ruby? With Mom? With Dr. Branson? Shouldn't I give it deeper thought and consideration? No, I'm not fazed, neither am I confused nor diffident! I'm confident and determined to tell my story. My full story.

Ms. Shaw looks at me and reads my mind. She excuses herself and walks out of the room, leaving the door slightly open behind her, but not before she looks at me with a motherly smile. Oh God, how much I've missed that!

"Come in, Sid. Grab a chair and sit down," Mr. Johnson says. He sits in a chair behind a desk loaded with books and papers.

One book on the desk catches my eye. "The Theory of Communicative Action" by Jurgen Habermas. I remember Mr. Alexander recommending this book to us during sociology class. "In his book, Habermas tries to find the way to ground the social sciences in a theory of language, to establish a concept of communicative rationality," he had told us.

"Communicative rationality." How desperately I need this NOW!

I gather myself, or what remains of me. "Mr. Johnson, I think–"

He interrupts me, saying, "Look, Sid, I'm sorry for the police and all that mess with your father, but he left me with no reasonable choice."

I didn't come here to hear him. I will not let him confuse me with this. There's no way he's taking over and turning my story aside.

"Mr. Johnson, I came here today, with a heavy heart and soul, to spell out my point of view on this madness. Please let me go first," I say confidently.

"Go ahead," Mr. Johnson replies.

I tell him. I tell him about how I fainted in Mr. Alexander's office, and how he helped me wake up. I explain that our families are connected, though I don't say how. I don't think that's something Mr. Johnson should know or care about. I tell him that nothing Mr. Alexander ever did was immoral or inappropriate.

"I appreciate your concern for me and my family, Mr. Johnson," I say, concluding my account. "But there is no need to involve police or social services in this... incident."

"That remains to be determined," Mr. Johnson says. "Even assuming your account is correct, you can't account for what happened while you were unconscious."

"Mr. Johnson, please," I reply. "There's no reason to suspect Mr. Alexander. He's been nothing but respectful and forthcoming to me and my family ever since I've known him."

"Could you explain to me the nature of your relationship with Mr. Alexander?"

I want to storm out. I want this probing of my heart and soul to end. But even if it does, other issues are still waiting for me, outside of Mr. Johnson's office. I can't let Ruby's peace of mind be ruined by this intrusion into her life. I can't allow that, so I just bite my tongue and give a brief reply: "Family friends."

"Could you be more specific?" Mr. Johnson asks.

I sigh and then answer: "I befriended his daughter. We've visited each other's homes, and our parents have talked to each other. My trust in him is well-founded" I say. I hope my anger doesn't show in my words.

"I think I've heard enough," he says. "I assume you have classes to attend today, so I'll dismiss you now."

"Thank you, Mr. Johnson," I say as I stand up.

As I walk out of his office, I can't help but wonder if what I said has made any difference. With everything that's happening, Mr. Alexander does not need this. And Mr. Johnson doesn't even know half the story. Half of my story. Half of Ruby's story.

I adjust my mask and head back into the hallway. The bell rings loud and clear and the halls are bombarded by students trying to get to their next class. Some are following every single arrow, line, and marking on the ground; others plow through the hallway. Some seem to be walking as if they notice nothing and want to be noticed by no one.

I feel like for the first time this year, maybe even ever, the faces of my peers register in my mind. What is really happening

The Challenges We Face

in their lives? Behind their masks? I feel like my own life has been such a mystery up to this point. If I don't know myself, do I really know anyone?

I glance around the halls while trying to navigate the hustle and bustle. I notice Charles animatedly talking to his friends. One would think he was a happy-go-lucky guy, but what goes on in his life after he hops off the bus each day? Or Autumn Jones? She seems like she always has it together. She's a cheerleader. It's been a long time since we were friends, but what is under her mask?

I start to think of myself and my own mask. In some ways, I feel like I've been wearing one my whole life. The joke being, of course, that my life has been masked. It's a life I know nothing about. I, Sidney Simpson, have been masked for so long. Who even is Sidney Simpson? Thankfully, Ruby Alexander seems to know me better than I do. Then it hits me.

Sidney Simpson *is* Ruby Alexander. Ruby Alexander is the *real* Sidney Simpson.

So, who am I?

Twelve: The Seeds We Plant

The Seeds We Plant

I am nobody. I am everybody. I am myself. I am the other.

I come from nowhere. I come from everywhere.

I'm the tomboy; the unicorn; the jock; the nerd; the shy one; the prom queen.

I'm the masked; the compliant; the obedient. I'm the rebel; the defiant; the warrior. I'm both the ship and the waters into which it sails.

I'm an 18-year-old dilemma—no longer a child but not yet a woman.

I dream of walking down a crowded street and ripping off every physical and metaphorical mask I've ever worn. I want to show every faint line of my inexperienced complexion, of every smile and every tortured tear I've ever cried.

I'm both the storm and the blue skies from which the gentle rain feeds the Earth. I'm the abyss of my darkest thoughts and the colorful lush meadows of my blissful dreams.

I'm nothing. I'm everything.

In the chaos of my silent thoughts where I want to melt into nothingness, I know that without me, the world ceases to exist. So, I continue.

I want to experience all my tomorrows. I want to meet the bright souls who are there to teach me the way. I want to see the soft light of the moon reflecting on the dark streets. I want to bask in the steady sun that always rises again. I want to feel my heart beating to the pulse of the beautifully imperfect humanity that surrounds me. I want to feel myself in it—even as an outsider.

The Seeds We Plant

In this, I know we are not alone. I know—in this—we are all together. I will forever ask myself: What will the future bring? With this lingering question, I sit back and close my journal wondering if I will find the answer. That question alone is worth living for.

I sit underneath a beautiful weeping willow tree and contemplate. What is my real name? If I'm not Sidney Simpson, who am I? If I shed the mask, what protects me? What are my defenses? How do I go forward?

Confused doesn't even begin to describe my feelings. I could sit and ponder my existence and become paralyzed by the magnitude of events, however, there is another part of me that understands deep in my being that I'm powerful beyond belief. Energy shines inside of me nurtured by the love in my heart, the perseverance in my mind, the strength embedded in my soul, and the passion to persevere toward a new day, a new me, a fully empowered confident woman who doesn't shy away from living her life.

Perhaps, I think, I've been evolving for some time, much like a butterfly who transforms through metamorphosis. Has my mask been evolving too? I wonder, is my change due to some magical synthesis of Covid, my illness, emotions, anxieties, relationships, choices, actions, my entire life? As I mash it all together, I see that the true mask I wear is that of a warrior.

It is my future. A future, not based on the past of Sidney, Ruby, a taken child, or an adopted girl. My future is now under my control. I know the pain I experienced will not heal itself and I must seek support to truly heal. I must decide not to be tormented by my past. I will seek to reconcile the issues that have impacted me to my satisfaction, without being captured by the past, or second-guessing. I will seek the relationship I deserve with Ruby, aside from the circumstances of our lives, but rising out of the love that deeply binds us. I will seek to move forward toward my destiny.

It is my life, and I'm closer than ever to putting all the pieces together to fully heal and become whole.

But before I move forward, I must solve the mystery my life has become. Again Dr. Branson's question comes drifting back to my mind accompanied by a new sense of determination and confidence. "To whom are we accountable?"

I hear the bell signaling the start of the next period, but I don't move. Lying down on the cold and damp grassy field, behind the science annex, I'm lost in my thoughts, but in control of my destiny.

I owe it to no one other than myself to dig deeper into the past to liberate the trapped person I have become behind all these masks. I, whoever I am, am worthy of a future filled with potential, feelings, and emotions – the kind of passion that has infiltrated my body since I met Ruby.

If we don't tell people how we feel, how will they know... I must get rid of this last mask, the one I've been wearing since birth without even knowing it. I know it won't be easy, but then again, what about life is easy?

I have an unimaginable urge to know who I am. Where did I come from? Who was it that carried me in their womb and brought me into this world? How did I end up at that fire station? As painful as it may be, I need to find out the answers to these questions whirling around in my head.

The Seeds We Plant

I made my decision... Before the school year is over, I need to go to that fire station to hopefully gain some information.

I start to feel that ever-so-familiar feeling from within. Despite my pounding heart and my heavy breathing, this time I'm not going to faint. I'm grounded, I'm here. I'm strong.

The spring tulips are nestled between the trees and dotted along the grass. The sunshine feels warm against my skin. I admire the way nature is unashamedly itself, whatever weather and hardships come its way. The sunshine makes me squint and blink, the colors behind my eyes a reminder that this world is not all it appears.

To whom are we accountable? The question still rings in my ears as I blink into the sun. Are we our names at birth or those that are hidden from us?

If any good has come of the past few months, it's that sunshine and rain make rainbows and that kindred spirits like mine and Ruby's are destined to meet and put right ancestral wrongs.

Perhaps this is because we are accountable to our souls and star families that align in the night sky and are present in human form. Maybe it's The Celestine Prophecy that has awakened my desire to know more, to ponder if there is more out there than just this. But this. This here and now is beautiful. Spring has rebirthed a change, the seedlings into flowers. When the masks finally come off, maybe we can see who we really are and are meant to be.

Bumping into Ruby that very first day of school was no coincidence. That "accident" was no accident. It was all written in the stars and as Shakespeare once said: "It is not in the stars to hold our destiny but in ourselves."

I feel like I truly understand the meaning and value of our entwined lives. Even the simple act of sitting in English Literature class gives me an insight into how the world turns and shape-shifts.

It occurs to me that destiny is more than The Celestine Prophecy but also a product of geography. I know that geography may not be destiny, but it comes awfully close. In ways large and small, our surroundings shape our lives. Our productivity, happiness, and creativity are all functions of place.

Simply put: Where we are affects who we are. Lost in my thoughts, I become fixated on the stubborn persistence of geography. I realize this is something to celebrate.

So, yes, place matters, but what exactly do I mean by place? At the most basic level, I'm speaking of topography, the lay of the land. This matters. Ancient Greece sprouted hundreds of distinct cultures and city-states largely because the hilly, rocky, terrain created natural barriers that encouraged a potpourri of cultures. Meanwhile, the clear and sharp Athenian light inspired philosophers and artists alike in the most successful of city-states. What truly makes a place, though, is not topography but culture. Culture is the sea we swim in. So pervasive, so all-consuming, that we fail to notice its existence until we step out of it. It matters more than we think.

Take happiness. With our words, we subconsciously conflate geography and happiness. We speak of "searching for happiness," or "finding contentment," as if these are locations in an atlas, actual places that we could visit if only we had the proper map and the right navigational skills. The power of place gives life to one of the greatest myths perpetuated by the self-help industrial complex: namely, that our interior lives are all that matter. We can be happy (or productive or creative) anywhere, and this is my place to unveil the person that I have worked so hard to be.

But happiness, itself, must be molded. We cannot simply just find it within us, we become it. I think about my name again and how my nickname is Sid. Short, but not my full name. Sidney is my full name and I've always just been Sid; a personal term of endearment of sorts. Whoever it is I'm becoming, she will embrace everything, even her full name. Sidney....

Sidney....

Sid... no!

SIDNEY!

Ruby has always been Ruby, her most authentic self. Gravitating to her that first day was more telling than I ever thought it could be. How many of us teenagers, even 18-year-olds at that, truly know who we are? Not many, I would assume. We're still in high school and there is a whole world out there that lies beyond school. That is where I think most of us begin to embrace who we are. We need to live.

I just want to be. Be me, be everything I've ever wanted or nothing at all. It's a privilege to have that capability, without fear, to simply be; to exist. I think about the word "exist" which usually has a negative connotation. They say, "Oh they're just existing, not living." In my case, to exist would mean freedom.

All of us have had to adjust to the significant changes Covid dumped on us, but they were mostly social changes. Up to this point, I'd say it was one of the most difficult things I've had to adjust to. However, now I believe everything that's happened recently takes the cake. We are constantly morphing and changing, and I'm reminded yet again, that this is my butterfly moment.

I think more about how I just want to be "me." Unmasked. My coming together with Ruby was no random act, nor were any of the recent events, devastating as they are.

I feel a shift inside me, and I make a resolution, an intention. I rise to my feet, mouth dry, head clear, heart steady. I make the choice to live my life on my own terms. I'm Sidney now, and I want Ruby to stay with me. I know that I'm only in charge of myself and not in control of others but I hope Ruby feels the same way.

Covid has shown me that life is precious and cut short for many, like my Uncle Joe. A clear message from the universe. My story almost ended that dark cold night. No longer. I resolve to live my life to the fullest each day. I'm not going to let a "career" eat up my life energy. For what? So, I can go into debt to live in a big house full of *stuff* I hardly use? I've watched my Mom and Dad struggle like this for as long as I can remember.

I will buy a tiny house and leave a simple footprint. I will focus on my relationship with Ruby and take each day as it comes. I can even learn to grow my own food and live off the land. I will find work that is fulfilling and brings me joy.

This makes me feel powerful and immensely happy. But a little voice of doubt creeps in as I wander back to the school entrance.

Thirteen: The Connections We Seek

"**N**ice work, ladies! Get a load of all those weeds!"

Skylar Huang, a middle-aged woman wearing dirt-stained, slate-gray, overalls and a straw sunhat, gives me a thumbs up. She's the director of the community garden Ruby and I have joined.

At first, Ruby didn't want to do this. With so much chaos swirling around us, she thought it'd be too stressful. I said I understood, but that I was thinking about the kind of future I wanted for myself – for us, whatever that meant – and that I needed to start building skills if I hoped to realize that future. For now, that means learning how to grow my own food. With that kind of framing, Ruby decided to give it a shot.

"We can always go home if it gets too stressful," I tell her.

"I'm bolting the instant I see any type of bug that bites or stings," she says.

"Fair. I don't know how I'm going to put up with bugs either."

But now that Skylar has us settled with garbage bags and a laminated sheet with pictures of plants to help us identify weeds, neither of us cares about bugs anymore. We also don't care about the sun beating down on our necks or the aches in our shoulders or the dirt on our jeans. We have a job to do - clear the weeds so the plants can grow unencumbered. It's easy work, but it matters whether or not it gets done. It feels good to be the person to do it.

I think that Ruby feels the same way because once we finish the job, she says she wants to take a selfie with our bags full of weeds. I lean toward Ruby, smiling with my fingers in a peace sign. Ruby poses with me, but her smile quickly fades. Her phone displays a notification from her father that says: "I need to speak with you."

My breath catches in my throat as I forget how to breathe for a moment. I can hear my heart beating loudly in my ears, and the familiar feeling of lightheadedness returning.

I remember a grounding technique Dr. Branson taught me. I force myself to swallow and quickly try to center myself. I focus on the rough seam of my socks rubbing against the tops of my toes. The brim of my sun hat where it presses against my forehead. The hot sun warming the back of my neck. The tiny bead of sweat coursing down my back between my shoulder blades. The scent of the moist soil. The smell of sunscreen mixed with our sweat. The soft perfume of Ruby's floral deodorant. My breathing slows, and my head feels like it's part of my body again.

"Are you okay?" Ruby asks, a look of concern spreading across her face.

"Yeah... I'll be okay." I manage to get out.

She hesitates for a moment, looking me up and down. Satisfied that I'm not going to collapse, she smiles.

"Okay... if you're sure you're alright... I need to go."

Her eyes sparkle in the sunlight as she looks at me. I drink her in for one brief moment, storing this image of her in my heart.

Then she turns and rushes away.

I know we will talk later.

With a smile on my face, I breathe in the fresh scents from the garden and lounge on the grass in the shade of a beautiful tree.

The Connections We Seek

In my determination to understand what is happening to me, to truly know myself, without the mask, and to be able to know and speak my truth, I've forgotten to think about how all of this is impacting the people I care about most. I've been angry at my "Mom" for not telling me what she did and upset at my "Dad" for not telling me when he found out our blood types weren't a match. But wow, what they've been going through must be devastating, shaking them to their cores.

Until now, their identity as my parents has never been questioned. It's been a large part of their identity as a couple and as individuals. No wonder my Dad has been so angry. No wonder my Mom has been so emotional. I can see she cares deeply for me as any mother does for her child—that she's worried about me. And I've been mad at her for lying to us and for not searching for the baby she birthed. But I haven't thought about my parents' point of view on all this.

My parents have loved and cared for me as if I were their own – because that was the only truth they knew. And they continue that love – never wavering. What can it be like for them, being told that Ruby (my Ruby!) is their biological child? How do they feel about her? They don't even really know her yet. I wonder if they will like her, and how she will feel about them. I wonder how Ruby will feel about what my Mom did. Will she be able to forgive, accept, or understand?

And Ruby! Our paths have brought us together in this present time, but our destiny was connected eighteen years ago before any of us knew. My family, her family. We are entwined in ways we are only now discovering.

The Connections We Seek

My head starts throbbing as I slip inside the front door and make my way to my room. Ruby left the garden in a hurry, going home to her family. Lying in bed, I catch a glimpse of my neighbors through my window. They're planting seeds in their garden. A wave of peace washes over me.

I close my eyes and think about the community garden. For the first time in a long time, today I felt light. The weight of my life dissolved into the soil as I cracked jokes with Skylar and worked side by side with Ruby. I didn't think pulling weeds from the ground would feel like a meditative practice, but it was just that. Cathartic. Purifying. A breath of fresh air.

The soil we worked today reminds me of myself. On the surface, it appears dirty, messy, and out of control. It is plagued with weeds growing through blistering cracks left by an unquenched thirst. Winter has not been kind, but spring is making amends. I have been through a lot in the past month with no reassurance that spring will thaw the ice for me. As I plucked the weeds from the garden today, I thought about their bravery and how they dared to occupy sterile, neglected soil. They pave the way for the beautiful flowers that will come after them, but the truth is, they must go. There's not enough space here for them to coexist.

My life lately is a collection of weeds. Suddenly, it dawns on me that I need to pull out the weeds for flowers to begin growing and thriving in my life. Instead of mourning the reality that my parents aren't my biological parents, I should celebrate being living proof that love is more powerful than blood. Perhaps the truth will help me find the piece of myself that I've longed to uncover for as long as I can remember.

The Connections We Seek

Despite my giddy confusion, road signs are slowly emerging through the fog. I need an honest motif I can proudly own. As much as I love Coach Taylor's idea about believing in ourselves, I don't want to be a Macbeth "dressed in borrowed robes" and wearing a stolen crown. Truths don't depend on my belief in them. Now that I'm surer than I was before that I don't know who I am, I desperately need a way – my way – of being myself without succumbing to selfishness. How can anyone find happiness if, like the Phantom of the Opera, we need hideous masks to hide our imperfections from those we love? I'm sure Ruby cares about me - so did Autumn. We were a pair. Did we each unpeel a mask too far, bite into each other's apples and carelessly drift apart? I'm starting to realize that the hardest part of finding happiness isn't just the incredible difficulties of working out our accountability to ourselves; we also need to live alongside others whose agendas are so different from our own. It's okay to be solely accountable to myself, but we can never be islands unto ourselves because true love is reciprocal. Selfishness sparks the fires that turn great beauty into ash.

I am who I am, and I want to be free to discover new parts of myself. I want to love freely and feel my love accepted and returned without judgments and conditions. I need to uncover my roots that run deeper than I know. It's like my destiny and identity were untimely ripped from my unsuspecting mother's womb and tossed into a vast stormy sea, to drift forever on waves of unknowing.

A sudden silence comes over my thoughts, something I haven't experienced in a long time. It makes me feel uneasy at first, like there's a static disruption in my mind, but after a few moments, it becomes soothing. I can hear the subtle sounds in my room, throughout the house, and even faintly from outside, like an orchestra tuning their instruments before performing.

I let this newfound calmness seep from its starting point in my head to the rest of my body, confusing my subsiding tenderness from bending over to pick weeds all morning with a psychologically induced hyper-sensation. I've never done any drugs before, but what I'm feeling now is almost a kind of high, a release from the day-in and day-out awareness we're all so tightly bound to. But when it ceases to be, it's something novel, yet distantly familiar that we experience. I close my eyes and take in all the sounds around me, dare I say – a brave new world. Maybe it isn't new, and certainly not brave, but to me, at this moment, it needs to be heard. Though I hear cars surfing outside of my house, there's beauty within and beyond it. Knowing that each person has their own story, life, and connections. Not to mention the harmony that can surely be made from it if we learn to simply be present.

At that instant, my phone rings. It's Ruby. I answer anxiously, seeing how late it is. We talk about our families and how we are doing. I'm trying to listen to Ruby's words, but I'm distracted by the sudden sirens and flashing lights of emergency vehicles rushing past my house.

Ruby's voice is still hovering in my consciousness, but I can feel my focus slipping away. Thoughts of her and the sirens meld together in my mind. I find myself imagining the worst. I feel the phone slip out of my hand and my head hits the pillow.

Fourteen:
The Space We Hold

The Space We Hold

I imagine Ruby on the side of a road, flashing lights and sirens all around her. I'm picturing the last moments Ruby would remember before the airbags went off. Her parents arguing in the front seat of the car, her Dad's face, streaked with tears, staring over his left arm in shock and terror, and glass breaking.

A paramedic touches her shoulder and tries to talk to her, but Ruby can't understand anything he's saying. He gently begins placing her left arm in a splint, as Ruby watches him blankly. She's sure she should be crying or something. Suddenly, the scene around her comes sharply into focus.

"–need a stretcher over here!"

"IV!"

"Next of kin–"

And she finally hears the questions being thrown at her.

"Miss, what is your name? Who was in the car with you? Do you have any family or relatives that live nearby?"

She nods, numbly, to the questions. "It's Ruby. My Mom and Dad. My brother, Jack, is at tennis practice."

She looks down at the shattered glass and metal fragments on the road. The flashing red and blue lights reflect off the wreckage, turning this gruesome scene into a beautiful mosaic.

I must be having a nightmare. My two worlds, past and present, are colliding.

In my mind, Ruby's imagined crash turns into my memory of what happened with Ramon and I that night. We were arguing, I wanted to break up, "Sid, we need to talk!" he yells.

The Space We Hold

I glare at the stretch of asphalt before me. Everything around me is a blur. Are we going too fast? I try to make sense of my location, wondering how I ended up back here. How can one embody an entire spectrum of emotions at the same time? Hot and cold. Empathy and apathy.

"Sidney, please tell me why. What did I do wrong?"

There is a pleading tone in Ramon's voice. He wants this relationship to work, but I've made my decision. I just want to be honest with him and go back to being friends.

I reach for the dash and turn to the first radio station I find, "Every Rose Has Its Thorn" thunders from the speakers, and at that moment, I feel at peace. I follow along, drawing power from the lyrics. I finalize my decision, I am going to tell him the truth. He thinks he's seen my thorns and loves me anyway, but he doesn't. I look up just in time to see a curve in the road. Slowing down is not an option, we are going way too fast to correct. I close my eyes as I hear metal crunching against a tree. The crash was inevitable just like the end of our relationship.

"Sidney?" The sound of Ruby's voice jolts me back to the present. I snap open my eyes and gasp, suddenly transported back to my room. Ruby is beside me. I almost don't recognize her. Sadness has contorted her face, and her eyes, normally the color of the ocean on a clear day, have darkened into a stormy gray.

"What happened?" she shrieks, and her words cut right through me.

"You're here?" I ask.

"Sidney, we were on the phone and you stopped responding. I tried calling you over and over again. I drove over here when

The Space We Hold

you didn't pick up and your Dad let me inside. You were having a nightmare."

I curse the divide between my conscious and unconscious mind - the confusion left in its wake, the moments forever lost to the space between.

My mind fights to close the gap, to fill the space between past and present. With a cold, hollow, and pressing feeling, I realize it's not only in these recent bouts of illness and fainting that I'm subject to this shadowy space. I've been living in the space between my whole life. Ever since that fateful night at the hospital, I have lived in the space between the life I've been living and who I should have been. And each day I walk in the space between who I was, who I am, and who I will be.

Perhaps that's all life is - the space between.

The space between self and other.

Dreams and disappointment.

Pain and pleasure.

Right and wrong.

Love and hate.

Truth and lies.

Masked and unmasked.

Life and death.

How much space lies within such voids? An infinite expanse, separating the East from the West? Or a minuscule, imperceivable, speck that tips the scales ever so slightly, yet more than enough, cascading us to the other side?

How close do we come to ever occupying one space over the other? Do we exist, forever and only, trapped in the space between?

Ruby's concerned face hovering over me interrupts these inner thoughts. I shake my head trying to clear the fog away. "I'm half sick of shadows," I murmur.

Ruby gives me a quizzical glance.

"Tennyson," I say. "From *The Lady of Shalott*." A sudden wave of elation fills me. Ruby's arm is not encased in a splint. Hopefully, her mother and father are still alive and kicking. The horrible car wreck never happened. These last few visions have been entirely in my head.

I take a deep breath and push all philosophical thoughts and quotes from Tennyson from my mind. "Yes, I'm OK. You're here. I'm here. We're both alive, despite the avalanche of events that have conspired to send us spinning." I reach out, taking her hand and she quickly sits down next to me.

"Are you all right?" she asks again.

I pull a tissue from my pocket and press it against the single tear running down my face. I'm lucky I was lying down and didn't hurt myself this time. I'm wondering if I should start wearing a helmet. Start a new fad at school or something. My grimace turns into a grin. Time to develop a sense of humor. Laugh so we don't weep.

Ruby still looks concerned. I take her hand again and squeeze it. "Sweetheart, have you got your gardening gloves on you?"

Ruby colors with pleasure at my term of endearment. "No, I think they're back at the house. Do you need them for something?"

I nod my head and smile. "We've got some weeding to do."

It's getting late in the evening now, but I manage to convince Ruby to go back to the community garden with me. Something about everything that's happened – with our parents, with our families, with my health, has given me an unexpected sense of clarity.

I still don't have clarity for what's going on, of course, and to be honest, I don't know that I'm quite ready for it anyway.

I thought I wanted to know. I thought I would be bursting at the seams with impatience actually – but I'm not. Whatever it is is going to permanently change my life, or how I look at it at least.

Having a full-blown identity crisis with all these changes... Finding out my love interest is, in some weird twist of fate, very closely tied to my family, is enough to send anyone on a downward spiral.

I'll find out why my Mom did what she did eventually. Maybe tomorrow. Maybe next week. Just not now. Right now, I just want to be with Ruby. Just Ruby.

We reach the garden and are completely alone. The remains of today's work are scattered on the outskirts and some tools lie in the corner.

"Sidney, when you said we had some weeding to do, I didn't think you meant it literally."

I have to laugh at the way she says it. She's adorable.

"I sure did. I just want to be here. It's so peaceful and quiet. Something about working with nature is just ... therapeutic." It sounds silly I know. Like I should be some health and wellness spokesperson, but it's true.

Ruby gives me a lopsided smile.

Mia leans against the community garden gate.

When she was 18, alone and pregnant, Mia often came to the garden for refuge. She didn't know how to keep herself alive, much less a baby. But the plants? She always loved the simplicity of what grew from the ground. After aging out of foster care, she found herself growing her own little seed. She recalls the blur of those last months.

Without family or faith, she stood trembling, exhausted, and confused on the firehouse steps. The baby, her baby, lay silently in her arms. Mia had wrapped her in her old cross-stitch blanket. One with faded flowers. The one her mother had made for her birthday months before she was gone. And now Mia would be the one to leave.

Mia knew her baby deserved a better life than she could provide, but she also never stopped believing one day she would tell her truth. Truth became her passion. She worked hard and graduated with top honors, counseling women at the local hospital, advising and guiding them with words she wished she could've heard. Two years ago, when Lora Simpson came to Mia with tear-streaked confessions about a daughter switched at birth and a fire station baby, Mia knew she was consoling the mother of her daughter. This gift of chance sparked a flame that turned into a wildfire. Mia needed to see Sidney.

A counseling position opened at Sidney's school, and Mia took it. What would she say to her "secret" daughter? How could she keep her distance? When Sid fainted the first day of school, a worried Mia stared into her daughter's eyes. There was an instant understanding and connection. Did Sidney feel the same way, she wondered? Could she feel her heart as they sat across from each other in Mia's office? My eyes speak a lot but so do hers, she thought.

"Ms. Rose?" Mia snaps to the present and stares into the garden. She masks her urge to embrace both girls and tell her truth.

"Ms. Pep in Your Step" is looking at me with her sparkling, caring, eyes. Something about how lost she seems in thought feels familiar.

"Ms. Rose," I call out to her again. I can tell she's coming back to the present as she softly shakes her head.

"Hi, girls," she says, with the same warmth and authenticity she always seems to have.

"How are you?" I say. Ruby is next to me, her arm wrapped around my waist.

"I... uh... am doing well. Thanks for asking." Ms. Rose appears to be struggling to collect her thoughts.

Mia's mind is racing. She wants to tell Sidney that she's her mother. That she's the one who loved her enough to let someone else love her. That she didn't know how to raise a baby then. She had been a child herself! That she wanted Sidney to be cared for in a way that she couldn't do herself. That she thought about Sidney every moment of every day. Mia thinks now might be the time.

"Ms. Rose?" Ruby asks. "Are you feeling okay?" Ruby and I share a look of confusion.

Ms. Rose seems to be holding back tears, and her gaze moves between us.

I break the silence. "Ms. Rose, I'm really glad you wrote a pass to check in on us. There has been so much going on. I'm not sure we can handle one more thing. And Mr. Salvatore announced a quiz on a reading passage he just assigned!"

And just like that, Mia knows her moment is gone.

What did she think she was going to say anyway?

What was she thinking?

Later that night, Mia is still thinking about Sidney. How can she tell her the truth? How will Sidney react? Should she just stay quiet?

No, I can't do that, she thinks. She needs Sidney to know. But she knows she needs to be careful and find the right time.

She wonders if what she's doing is right. She knows this secret will change lives forever.

With her mind still racing, Mia starts to get ready for bed. She drinks a glass of water, walks her dog one last time, and takes a melatonin pill to help her fall asleep. She hopes maybe in the morning, she'll be able to think more clearly.

"HELP!"

Mia shoots straight up in bed. She's fighting for breath and feels confused. The nightmare seems so real. Her dog looks at her nervously and begins licking her face, trying to reassure her human that she is okay.

"Coffee, I need coffee," Mia tells Harper, her 3-year-old Cavapoo. Harper cocks her head as if she understands. They both jump out of bed and head to the kitchen. As the coffee is brewing, Mia's mind returns to her problem. There must be a solution. Will Sidney even want to know the truth? This one secret will change so many lives. And once it's out, there will be no going back.

Ding, Dong.

As if the doorbell isn't enough, Harper jumps into action to let Mia know someone's at the door.

Who would be here this early? Who goes to someone's house anymore without texting first?

Fifteen: The Cracks We Find

The Cracks We Find

Ruby's hopeful eyes lock with her father's. She can see his face is vacant, and he's rapidly searching for words to express his feelings. He tries to think of the right way to describe his emotions. But he only finds an all-too-familiar nauseated feeling in the pit of his stomach, accompanied by a desert-like sensation in his mouth.

"Dad? Earth to Dad!" Ruby moves closer and waves her raw, red, hands beneath her father's sunken eyes.

"Sorry darling, it's just. Hey, could you grab me a glass of water? Where's your mother?"

"I think she got a phone call from work this morning."

Mr. Alexander lifts his head, closes his eyes, and takes three deep breaths that seem to last an eternity while his daughter pours him a glass of water. Ruby waits patiently before tentatively extending her arm with the glass toward him. His breathing returns to normal as his eyes open again, and he reorients himself to the situation. He nods in gratitude at the offered glass, and Ruby watches him drink it in gulps.

She glances at Jack, who is clutching his chips to his chest; he's never seen his father like this before. Jack's unease makes Ruby hasten her inquiry. "Dad?"

"Thanks, Ruby. Have you finished your homework? Where's your mother again?"

"My homework? Yes, whatever... nearly! Mom? I just told you. Are you and Mom okay? Dad, tell me what's on your mind," Ruby demands. Her eyes fix on her father's lips, awaiting his response.

Before he can reply, the telephone rings.

The Cracks We Find

"Can't someone stop that from ringing?" he asks fretfully.

"I'll get it, Dad."

After Ruby leaves, Joe Alexander stares in bewilderment. He thought his life had come full circle. He has always survived by his wits, believing his instinct when it hinted that he would get nowhere on his physical strength. Years ago, as a budding real estate agent with a steady income, he should have counted himself fortunate. But he was bored. His boredom led him to pursue a master's program studying education with a special interest in sociology. There he met Andrea, who was studying psychology and sociology. They spent the little free time they had talking about their similarities and differences. They both found the brain fascinating, and both of them shared a love of watching people, especially at the local coffee shop.

He snaps back to reality when he feels a tap on the shoulder. He finds Ruby standing beside him with another glass of water.

"Are you okay, Dad?"

Joe looks at her dully, taking the glass of water from her hand before replying.

"Yes, I'm all right," he says. "Who called?"

"Mom. She says she's going to be late."

"Why?"

"She has a work emergency."

He sighs, fixing his gaze on Jack, who is still munching his chips.

"Dad, do you want me to get you some tea instead? We can talk later."

The Cracks We Find

Joe shakes his head. It's been hard for him to keep his mask on this long.

Ruby worries about her parents, but mostly about her Dad.

She has never seen him like this before. With everything that has been going on, she feels like they are all hanging on by a thread. She's scared about what is going to happen to her family, to Sid's family, to Sid, and to her.

I need to talk with Sid, she thinks. But she knows she can't. If all of this is a lot for her to deal with, she knows it's even more for Sidney. Sid is dealing with so much right now, Ruby thinks. I just want everyone to be okay.

She decides to make some tea, hoping it will make her Dad feel better. At least that's what tea is supposed to do. She makes two, one for him and one for herself.

When it's ready, she gives a cup to her Dad and sits beside him.

"Thanks, sweetheart. You're so kind."

"No problem, Dad."

"I see you made one for yourself too."

"Yeah, I wanted to give you some company."

He gives her a smile and a nod. She knows that being present and sitting next to him is going to be more meaningful to him right now than anything she might say. Silence can be a powerful form of communication, just knowing you aren't alone, she thinks.

As they sit together, she wonders how her Mom is doing with all of this. Since the beginning, Ruby hasn't felt the need or desire to speak with Lora or Bill. Ruby has felt at peace with

The Cracks We Find

her decision. "My Mom and Dad are the ones who raised me, the ones who chose me and I chose them." she thinks.

The person Ruby wants to check in with is Sidney. Her past relationships weren't like this. She didn't mind there being space between them. It's different with Sidney. She wants to spend every waking moment with her. Hearing her voice. Holding her. Kissing her. It dawns on Ruby; is this how it feels to be in love with someone? She smiles at the idea.

She needs to call her.

Ruby gets up and says, "Dad, I'm going to go upstairs to my room and finish my homework."

Her Dad takes a sip of his tea. "Okay. I'll let you know when your mother gets back."

Ruby nods, pushes in her chair, and heads upstairs. Once she's in the comfort of her lavender walls, she pulls out her phone and taps Sid's name.

I pick up on the first ring. "Hey. I was just going to call you too!"

"Yeah? Well, I did it first." Ruby chuckles into the phone. "I just wanted to check up on my favorite person. It's funny. I can't help but need to know that you're doing okay."

"Oh, trust me. I know the feeling." I pause a minute. "But not much is going on. I just ate and am listening to music and doing homework in my room. How about you? What are you doing?"

"Oh, I am okay... I feel a little overwhelmed to be completely honest with you. My Dad is acting weird and my Mom is at work."

"Okay. Would you like to come over?" I ask.

How could anyone - anything - ever explain the desperate ache in the pit of my stomach every time I happen upon the eyes of Ruby Alexander? From the moment of our first meeting, I could see her. Every inch of me craves to be near her, to know who she is, and what possesses her to live for more than just life itself?

Every inch of my body wishes that things were simpler. I cherish the moments of happiness that I've had throughout my life and in my senior year, but at the same time, I feel as though I'm not and have not been living my life. I constantly feel as though I cannot take a full breath, as if I'm continuously bracing myself for the next change or challenge.

As soon as I open the door, I see her mask become translucent and I feel all the overwhelming emotions her face shows. And I feel a sadness creeping into my bones. A sadness I can't begin to comprehend. We are both hoping to convince ourselves that everything is okay, when in reality it is not okay. Ruby's life has been impacted just as much as mine and I think it has finally caught up to her. She has been so strong for so long and in this moment when I look at her, all I see is grief.

Meeting Ruby changed everything. Meeting Ruby made me realize that love is possible. She saw the light shining through the cracks in my mask. What kind of vicious game is this world trying to play? I didn't consent to be used as some sort of guinea pig. How can my heart feel so worthless, tossed aside like it's nothing? Like I'm nothing.

The entire world feels like it's burning to the ground. The only thing I know for certain is this gnawing pain. She stands in the doorway, hands deep in her coat pockets, shoving a similar ache downward, I presume. Grief is a huge part of life that isn't talked about enough and perhaps at this moment, all we have in common is this grief.

Because, when it comes down to it, do we truly know each other at all?

Sixteen: The Feelings We Share

The Feelings We Share

"It's Lora Simpson," says Sid's mother as she waits impatiently for Mia Rose to open her front door. Finding Mia's address is not difficult in a small town like this one.

Mia wrestles the front door open as she holds a barking Harper in her arms. "Hush, Harper." She sets the dog down and looks quizzically at Lora. "Lora, what a surprise!"

"I'm sorry for showing up unannounced," Lora says, still on the front porch. "I need help, and I don't know who else to turn to," she says as she bursts into tears.

Mia feels an irresistible urge to hug Lora, to thank her for raising her daughter, and to tell her everything. But what if Lora rejects her? Mia's fear becomes suddenly overwhelming. Harper, sensing her fear, barks even more furiously at Lora, still standing petrified on the front porch.

"Please come in!" whispers Mia, lifting Harper into her arms and making space for Lora to come in.

"I'm so ashamed!" whispers Lora.

"Please have a seat!" says Mia. "Let me go put Harper in my bedroom. I'll be right back."

The moment has come, Mia thinks, to reveal the truth. She collects herself as best as she can, pours iced tea into two identical cups, walks back into the living room, and sits across from Lora.

"My husband is trying to ruin Joe Alexander's life!" confesses Lora. "He's projecting his anger onto Joe, and I don't know how to make him stop. It's killing Sid. I know that you and Joe work together, and you're a counselor. You know things about human nature I don't. What should I do?"

The Feelings We Share

The sudden presence and pleading face of a person sitting across from her asking for help snaps Mia into the mask of professional mode. Her education and training immediately sweep aside her own concerns. "What are you feeling?" she responds. "Take a moment and think."

Lora's face goes wide and white with shock. A pregnant pause of silence fills the room, before the thunderous roar of pain, shame, and guilt explode from deep within her. Layers of masks are washed away by the torrent of tears. It takes her what seems like hours to rewind her life and silently choke out her truth. All those years ago, as a young bride and expectant young mother, she wanted to build a good life. But she didn't even know what that meant. She was determined to be the best version of what everyone expected of her. Her deep insecurities grew as fast as her belly. How could she be sure this baby would love her?

The baby's birth came before Lora felt ready. Bill was always less than present. Out of town, out of the room, outside of the conversation. Lora was lonelier than she had ever been, with no friends or family by her side. And then there was Sidney. Alive. Real. That evening, as she rocked Sidney in the nursery, surrounded by other babies, she was surprised by how calm and content Sid was. Her eyes were just like Bill's, with that same faraway look, in a world all her own despite the wails from the newborn next to her. Lora leaned over and looked at the other infant, who was crying with eyes wide open. She felt a sudden bond and she placed Sid in her bassinet and picked up baby "Pickle." When a nurse had been by earlier, she explained that was the code name they used for abandoned babies in the nursery. Pickle folded into her and cooed as she latched on. Lora gasped as she felt this precious creature connecting to her. Tears of joy rolled slowly down onto the tiny head.

"At last, my love," she whispered to the baby in her arms. Decision made, she picked up Sid, and placed her into the bassinet labeled Pickle.

Lora forcefully snaps back into reality, realizing that she is deep in thought, ruminating about the day she gave birth to her daughter. Mia, too, has slipped into her thoughts, thinking how bittersweet it is to sit across from the woman who might reject her if she speaks her truth. How can she not take a moment to bask in the opportunity to engage in a conversation with the very woman who is raising her daughter? Mia is elated to know that Sidney is being raised by a woman who seems to dearly love and care about her.

"Are you okay, Mia?" Lora asks gently.

"Yes, I am. Your presence somehow took me back to the day I had my daughter," Mia replies. As soon as the words leave her mouth, she immediately regrets them and realizes she can no longer ignore the feelings alive in her heart and mind. She badly wants to reveal her truth to Lora, but at the same time, dreads the outcome. She knows in her heart of hearts that what she unveils could bring her and Lora together or tear them apart. Or maybe worse, she thinks, Lora might be very angry to learn that Mia has kept her true identity secret.

"You have a daughter? I thought you didn't have any children?" Lora says.

Mia remains silent, her fear preventing her from uttering a single word. It's as if she's stuck in time and can't get her mouth to speak what she so desperately needs to get off her chest.

She starts to stand up, but quickly faints, and drops to the floor at lightning speed.

Lora cannot believe her eyes. She's had plenty of experience with Sid's fainting spells and knows to call 911 immediately. Her mind races as she dials the numbers. What caused Mia to faint, she thinks?

Lora is surprised at how quickly the paramedics arrive. Two women and one man head straight over to Mia, and begin taking her pulse and blood pressure, while asking Lora questions.

"Her pulse is thready and dropping," the man says suddenly. And then, "We need to place a line. Get me an IV kit, now."

Lora thinks the man seems unusually nervous. Isn't this something he does all the time? Why is he behaving like this?

The two women spring into action, pulling tubing and an IV catheter out of the red bag they brought into the house. The younger woman kneels over Mia and applies a tourniquet, wiping the crook of her arm with an alcohol swab and feeling for a vein. The other paramedic pulls out an IV solution. Mia is still lying on the floor, the color quickly draining from her face. Meanwhile, Lora finds herself shaking at the sight of Mia, despite the fact she has dealt with this scenario numerous times with Sid.

As the paramedics work on Mia, Lora begins to wonder if this was a mere fainting spell or something more serious. Mia hadn't clutched her chest or called out any words. Lora replays the scene in her mind, comparing it to what happens when Sidney faints. The incidents seem familiar.

Seventeen:
The Impacts We Have

The Impacts We Have

I step aside to let Ruby in the house. We look at each other and she moves into my arms. We hold onto each other for a minute.

"I'm a bit worried about my Dad," she says.

"What are you worried about?"

"It's probably nothing, but my Dad doesn't seem to be himself as of late."

"I'm sure he is trying his best. Ruby, I forget this at times myself, but this is our parents' first time going through life too."

"You're right... Thanks," she says with a weak smile.

"Maybe he's just having a down day and trying to sort some things out." I say, trying to make her feel better.

We settle in my bedroom, both just looking out the window, deep in our thoughts. My shoulder is touching Ruby's, but my body feels a thousand miles away. What's going on in the world and why does it all feel so unsettling? What can I do to support Ruby?

It seems like the walls are closing in on us. "Let's go for a walk," I say. "How about the community gardens?"

"A walk sounds good, but let's go to my house," Ruby says. "We can do some homework there and check on my Dad. And I want to be there when my Mom gets home."

I'm happy to oblige. I just want to get some fresh air. My Mom has gone to visit a friend, so I'm not worried about her.

On the way to Ruby's, it begins pouring rain which does nothing to improve Ruby's mood. She's now absolutely wracked with worry. Both girls are drenched, but that is the last thing on their minds. Ruby grabs some dry clothes for Sidney to borrow.

The Impacts We Have

They undress in Ruby's lavender-walled bedroom with a dodgy lock on the door. Time slows as each girl spins around to face the wall while the other changes. The rain is loud, but their thoughts are screaming.

Until about two years ago, Ruby Alexander's life seemed idyllic. A calm, stoic child of calm, accomplished parents. Ruby always strove to excel and to please, and at both she succeeded beyond expectations. Even for a teenager, she was always pleasant and self-assured. Family and friends would describe her as wise beyond her years. But how long can one avoid the heady combination of teen hormones, one's circumstances, and fate?

Cracks were beginning to show in her parents' marriage long before Ruby became fully aware of them. She was not necessarily one to take on blame where none was warranted, but then her parents dropped the truth bomb about her adoption. Correlation or causation? First came the muffled fights, then silences, and then the absences. Ruby's anxiety slipped in through these cracks in an attempt to fill the gaps with something tangible, something actionable.

Right on cue, life presented her with another insurmountable challenge – the pandemic. Ruby's anxiety jumped at the opportunity and manifested itself in the form of compulsive hand washing. Did the pandemic create this OCD or merely tease an existing nervous tic out into something more substantial? Correlation or causation? Is she washing the virus off her hands or the guilt and worry that she wants to be rid of? Scrubbing seems right; it feels good, even if it bleeds.

The Impacts We Have

With a jolt, Ruby feels Sidney take hold of her shaking hands as the doorbell rings.

Ruby tries to remove her hands from mine, but it seems we are both lost somewhere. Gazing into each other's eyes, silent tears fall on Ruby's face. We're both going through the same phase of life and juggling with self-identity. I try to help Ruby feel calm and relaxed, but she seems lost somewhere and is murmuring to herself.

Is this the life I'm destined for? Ruby thinks. Why was I adopted? What would my parents say if I left the house? What will my name be, Simpson or Alexander or something else entirely?

The bell rings again, and I open the door, even though it's Ruby's house. It's Autumn Jones. I haven't spoken to her in forever.

"Full transparency... I might have stalked you a little bit. I saw you leave your house with Ruby and followed you here," she says. "I wanted to check on you."

Autumn says she's been wanting to see me in person, to make sure I'm okay. She tells me she's been checking in with my Mom on and off over the past few months to see how I'm doing. But she hasn't gotten a satisfactory response.

"So, I finally worked up the courage to talk to you," she says. "I thought I had a lot of questions, but I guess I only have one."

She looks at me searchingly. "Did you tell your parents what happened that day?"

"Let's talk outside," I say, and motion to the covered porch.

We stand in silence, the only noise coming from the rain, which is still falling.

"I have been meaning to tell you how sorry I am. Please know that I care for you, Sid," she says.

"Jeez, Autumn, what the heck? You stopped hanging out with me, don't you remember?"

Autumn shies away from me as if I'm about to attack her. She's wearing a pale-yellow dress, sprigged with tiny purple flowers. Her hair has been teased up into a topknot, several strands hang wet to the side of her face. We are so different; it's almost incomprehensible how we were ever best friends. Yet we were. For years. The kind of friends who held hands in the street and confided everything to each other. And more, so much more.

I breathe in slowly, toning down my voice. "Sorry, but you can't just come here after what happened, Autumn. I appreciate you saying you care for me. It's sweet but…"

"Can we please start over?"

"What?"

"I still think of you as my friend, Sid. Even though it is not the same as it was, I need to know you're okay." She gazes at me with such sorrow in her eyes. I'm momentarily stunned into silence. The sound of the rain, pelting down onto the vegetation around the porch, sparks a memory of the last time we were together like this, except there was no rain then, just a cascade of tears.

"Is everything okay?" Ruby appears through the open door, a questioning expression knitting her brow. I don't know how much she's overheard, but, quite frankly, this whole scene is starting to unnerve me.

The Impacts We Have

'Sure, we're good.' I stretch out my arm, beckoning Ruby to come to my side, which she does. I squeeze her shoulder as I drape my arm around her.

Autumn gives Ruby a nod of acknowledgment before shifting her gaze back to me. As I stare into her eyes, I'm reminded of all the ways it is not anymore... I think about the last day we were friends, just before the start of high school. The bond we had and the crippling shame come flooding back, like an avalanche into my soul, chilling me with icy waves of sharp pain.

"Why now, Autumn? You stopped talking to me. I thought I could trust you, how wrong I was. You were my best friend and you left me that night alone crying so hard it felt like I was suffocating. You were the first person I had ever told." My voice cracks as I raise an accusatory finger to Autumn Jones, my one-time best friend.

Autumn winces, her eyes looking like the weather. Her pupils train on the floor as she answers weakly, "I'm so sorry. If I could go back in time, I would have said what my Mom said to me recently – 'Thank you for letting me in and trusting me. I'm so proud of you.'"

The ice in my soul melts, now boiling with my anger. "And you thought showing up at the door, in the middle of a storm would somehow make it better? That it'd change the fact that you've ignored me ever since? I thought I had experienced grief before, but I learned grieving a person who is alive is so much harder thanks to you."

I get up to go into Ruby's house, but as I move, Autumn stands and blocks my way.

The Impacts We Have

"Hate me if you want. It's fair, I messed up. I just wanted you to know, to understand that I'm sorry." Tears start to well up in her eyes. As the first streaks run down her cheeks, she begins again. "After what has been happening these past few months, I needed you to know. Life's too short to carry around all this hatred, all this animosity. I want you to understand that I still love you and miss you deeply." Autumn raises her other hand, wiping her eyes. "I miss us. I made a terrible mistake and for that I am sorry. You were the best friend I ever had."

The white-hot anger fades away, cooling into surprise. I raise an eyebrow at her, half-struck by her confession. Why now? I wonder. Autumn and Ruby are here in this place with me. It seems like worlds are colliding, like two different times and worlds have met.

I can hear the sound of Autumn's voice, but my thoughts block the words. I feel this sudden fear. What if Ruby leaves like Autumn did? Is my fear of being abandoned rooted in my past, in what happened to me long before I can even remember?

Perhaps this is something I need to work on. I need to get to a place where I love myself enough that I don't doubt myself and I know my worth. Or perhaps, every person my age is leaning in and wondering who they are and what their place is in this world.

"Sidney, Autumn asked you a question."

I'm drawn out of my internal dialogue. "Sorry, what did you ask?"

At some point, Autumn must have gone from apologizing and saying she cared for me to asking how my family is doing and how this school year has been going. These days, even answering the question "how are you?" seems taxing. And now I'm being asked how my family is doing and what I think about school. I can't help but feel my notion of home, family, heritage, and legacy are all being disrupted and challenged.

I used to tell Autumn everything. A trust, a bridge between us that seemed indestructible. I don't know if honesty is what this type of colliding calls for, or if keeping myself guarded is what is right. On one hand, I need to speak my truth. On the other hand, I still need to figure out what is going on.

At the moment I'm finding myself lost in the eyes of someone I once trusted and cared for deeply. Shifting my gaze, I see the beautiful blue eyes of someone who wants to be a part of my life… Someone I'm falling for.

"Family's fine. The school year's okay." That's what comes out of my mouth. Plain and simple. It invites fewer questions and gets what I want to say across—that I'm not ready to forgive her just yet. Not when I'm still trying to forgive myself, to be less harsh on my faults, and find my worth. To forgive everything that has happened in my life outside of my control. Autumn nods understandingly, but I see Ruby look at me as if I've made a mistake.

"I see. I'm glad to hear that," Autumn says, almost whimpering. She scratches the back of her calf with her other foot. "All right, well. That's pretty much what I wanted to say. I'm sorry to have bothered you, Sid. I'm sorry for everything. I am one text, phone call, or house away if you want to chat." She then leaves without a second glance, without a departing look toward me or Ruby. I feel a sudden pang in my chest, and it's doubled when the girl I truly love nudges me to look at her.

"Why did you do that?" Ruby asks calmly.

"Do what?" I coyly reply. I know exactly what I did.

"Lie. You lied to someone genuinely concerned for you."

I hear the raindrops soften to a patter and I desperately want to go back inside. I want to tell her about my past with Autumn and explain to her that I said what I said for a reason. It was not just to defend myself, but Ruby too. Our worlds are both intertwined now. Does she want me to open up about my situation when it potentially involves her life as well?

"I didn't know what else to say. If I said things have been complicated, she would've tried to pry every detail out of me. She would've tried to get it out of my Mom." I take her hands, trying to make her understand. "Why would she come here, and now, of all times to talk? Why does she suddenly care?"

Ruby opens her mouth to say something but closes it again.

I'm glad Ruby stays quiet. I don't want to say something I'll regret. I have always found that friendships and relationships are complicated and seldom easy. Who knows why things happen the way they do? We are not psychic or clairvoyant. We may want to predict and control actions and feelings, but sometimes we just need to go with the flow. Every choice we make has an impact – good or bad. That's what makes life interesting and unpredictable.

"What do you think I should do?" I ask.

"Stay calm, but I want you to put yourself in her shoes." Ruby says.

I appreciate this advice. But whenever someone tells me to stay calm, all I can think is that it is unbelievably hard to do in times like this. The torrential rain feels like a sign, a washing away of pain and sadness. Maybe now we can make some sense of this madness.

While trying to calm down, I realize that Autumn's very brave for coming over here today. But I hope she gives me some space. Our paths might cross, but I need some time to think and process everything. I want to move forward. I want to feel whole again and happy. I don't want this stress and turmoil to fester. I want to be present.

"You know," Ruby says, "sometimes we just want to wake up in the morning and find that things are back to normal or that it was all just a bad dream, a nightmare of sorts. But I don't think that's going to happen here. So, we have two options. The first is to put in the work and figure out what has happened. The second is to pretend that everything will be okay. So, what do you think? Are we too busy to stop and take the time to figure out this situation?"

"I want to put in the work and figure everything out with you," I say.

"Good," she continues with an upbeat tone. "And let's try not to judge Autumn. We're all going through something and trying to deal with it the best way we know how. So let's just breathe deeply and take the first step forward together."

Eighteen: The Truths We Uncover

The Truths We Uncover

Hoping for a little normalcy, Ruby and I decide to play a board game. Suddenly, there's a knock at the door. I look out the window and see my Dad standing on Ruby's porch.

"Joe," my Dad yells, still knocking on the door.

I have never heard or seen him like this before. I make a desperate dash for the door, but Mr. Alexander is already reaching for the handle.

"Wait," I plead. Mr. Alexander nods and takes a few steps back.

I take a deep breath and open the door.

"I need to talk to Joe." My Dad asks as he steps forward. I have never felt so small next to him. I feel all the confidence leave my body. I look down at my toes, but I can't make out if I'm really here, or if this is actually happening. I take a step backward, as everything turns upside-down and goes black. My limp body drops to the floor like lightning.

I'm back almost immediately and scan the room to see where I am. Ruby is already by my side. With tears in her eyes, she asks if I'm okay.

All the anger on my father's face has drained to concern. Mr. Alexander looks confused and unsure. Time feels suspended.

Someone must have called 911 because now there's an older firefighter by my side and a paramedic checking my blood pressure.

They offer to take me to the hospital, but I decline and promise to take it easy.

All I want is to be with Ruby. Dad reluctantly agrees that I can stay over tonight and grabs his phone to call my Mom.

The Truths We Uncover

While my Dad is on the phone, Mr. Alexander assures us everything is okay. "Do you girls mind going upstairs? I need to talk to Sid's Dad."

As I climb the stairs, I see them sitting quietly in the living room, waiting for Jack, Ruby, and me to go to sleep. I realize my Dad is drunk. I'm sure because of the way his hands are tiredly hanging from the chair. This is not the first time I've seen him sitting like this. When I was a little girl, I used to think his resting hands looked like two dead fish, and I would laugh at him. Now I'm just glad he's not mad anymore.

As night falls, I think about my parents and how they deal with problems. I'm flooded with memories of my Mom bottling her emotions and reaching in the drawer for a pill to calm her nerves. My Dad deals by being mostly absent. Even when he's sitting right beside us, his mind seems elsewhere. He's either running from his thoughts or trying to drown them with alcohol.

At this point, I realize I have a choice. I can use my parents' coping mechanisms to deal with life, or I can figure out my own path. I know I will choose the latter, but I still haven't figured everything out. Even when my life is going well, I have this intense feeling of impending doom and fear that something terrible will happen. Like I am in constant fight or flight and it's exhausting. And Ruby might be feeling the same.

Perhaps I should stop thinking about what could have been and figure out what I can do now to heal. I need to speak with people who will ask the right questions and help put all the puzzle pieces in place. I need to go to the fire station where my journey began and I need to eventually talk with my parents.

The Truths We Uncover

Soft rhythmic breaths let me know Ruby's finally asleep. I pull away slowly, trying not to disturb her. I roll off the bed and stand up. My life is spinning wildly out of control and the only person who can ground me is me. I watch the gentle rise and fall of Ruby's chest. Our future together is uncertain and I contemplate in this moment—taking in every breath—every sweet sound. A moment of peace before I venture into the turbulent storm.

I slip my shoes on quietly and leave through the front door. I need answers that no one in this house can provide. I'll have to seek them out myself.

The fire station, just a few blocks away, will be my starting point in finding out who I am. There's a stillness in the air as I walk with solid purpose toward the simple brick building. I've passed by it hundreds of times, thinking nothing of it until now.

An eerie electrical charge settles around me as I feel the hair on the back of my neck rise. I hunch over, sucking in deep breaths and fighting against the tightness that begins creeping around my ribs.

White, fluorescent, light filters out the bay windows, lighting up the pavement in front of me. It's now or never. Determination settles in my jaw as I stride up to the door on the left and ring the bell.

Nausea wells in my knotting stomach. I take a deliberate step back from the red door, forcing back down the bile crawling up my throat. What am I going to say? "Hi, does anyone remember me? The discarded baby?"

There isn't time to think it through further. The heavy metal door swings open. A broad silhouette stands in the doorway;

his shadow looming toward me. It's time to wade through the depths of the unknown — alone.

    Mia bolts up, gasping for air with sticky perspiration oozing from every pore. Her forehead is cold and clammy. A familiar tightening in her chest steals life-giving breath as coldness creeps in. She is determined not to faint this time. She shrugs her shoulders to establish control of her body. She doesn't have time for grounding, her brain argues as she feels her breath quicken. Her rational side fights back. Mia looks at her hand, her Mom's ring, the memory quilt lovingly sewn by her grandmother, Sid's great-grandmother. Tears well. She knows she needs to stop and focus. Breathe. She holds for five and slowly pushes the breath out, making a whistling sound as she forces carbon dioxide-rich air out through her nose. She breathes in again and feels her pounding heart slowly as thudding blood begins to ebb away. Her chest relaxes as vital organs return to natural rhythms and respiration resumes.

    She can't believe she fainted in front of Lora. It was the first time she had in over a decade. After her grandmother taught her to control her fainting, it rarely happened. She knows she should have learned those skills from her mother, but she was long gone by then.

    The doctors in the hospital had told her to rest and try to stay hydrated. A nurse joked that there must be something in the water. As Mia heads to the bathroom to splash cool water on her face, familiar features gaze back at her. How has no one else noticed? The eyes... the same color and shape. Only mine are edged with experience-earned wrinkles, Mia thinks.

Quietly, so she doesn't wake up Harper, Mia pulls on her dark purple hoodie, beanie, and shoes, Mia creeps out the door. Her feet know the way, having made the pilgrimage most nights since she moved back. Sitting on the bench at the cemetery, she begins talking to her mother and grandmother. She glances up toward the neon glow of the fire station and catches a glimpse of a shadowy figure crossing the bay windows. Is that Sidney?

And it would happen now, Mia thinks. She rises from her seat, weaving between cemetery stones, seemingly weightless as if a ghost herself. She's sure that's Sidney in the distance, standing in the open doorway, bathed in the glow of the lights. Her daughter.

In the cemetery, wild and overgrown, Mia hides behind a winding old bay tree that strangles the fence, and through wrought iron bars, ensconced in leaves, she watches..

The silhouette comes into focus and it is an older male firefighter.

"Can I help you?"

I'm shaking under the light. I feel small, fragile, and childlike.

"Uh. I... yes. Maybe. I don't know." I look down at my hands.

"This is probably not going to make a whole lot of sense. Nothing's been making sense lately, and uh—I might need your help. I need help."

The Truths We Uncover

"Is there an emergency? Are you lost? Are you in danger?" says the firefighter.

"I'm lost," I say, tears welling up. "I just have this powerful feeling inside me right now. I know I was left here. At this doorstep. Years and years ago, as a baby. I know, and I'm feeling it all right now. I feel, somehow, that someone didn't want to leave me, but... they sort of... had to. Someone had no choice but to give me up. I feel it so powerfully, and I'm so close to them right now, in some way—and it's killing me."

I wipe away tears as he escorts me into the station.

Leaning back in his battered leather chair, Kevin Slaywood wondered how he went from doing the dishes to being interrogated by a teenager during the middle of the night.

"That's all I know," I say. "Can you help me?" I lean back into the battered leather chair, exhausted.

Capt. Slaywood examines me closely, his mouth set into a grim line. He leans forward, fingers steepled. "Well, I've been here for twenty-five years," he begins. "I've seen my fair share of incidents. Can't recall half of them."

I sigh. It's a dead-end. Most people can't remember what they had for breakfast, let alone something that happened 18 years in the past.

"However, we've only had three babies left here in my time. Looking at you narrows it down." He chuckles.

"How come?"

"Well, one little fella arrived just last year. Before that, a little girl, she would be about ten now. Then there was our Quilt Baby about eighteen years ago."

"Quilt Baby?" I'm immediately curious.

"Yeah, hold on," he says. He rummages in a filing cabinet, producing an ancient photograph album. He flicks through the pages. "Yup," he says, "there you go."

I look at the yellowed newspaper clipping stuck on the page. "Fire Station Miracle" reads the headline. The picture shows a much younger Slaywood, holding his fire helmet toward the camera. Inside the helmet lay a tiny baby, cozied up in a cross-stitch quilt.

He smiles, pointing at the picture. "If the story you were told was accurate, then that must be you," he says. "Don't tell anyone, but once we realized you were okay, we put you in the engine, turned the lights on, and gave you a four-pump salute." He laughs.

I feel another piece of my jigsaw slot into place. Because she loved me, my Mom had taken me to the safest place she knew. Maybe I can be the hero in my own story after all.

With a light heart, I thank Capt. Slaywood and leave the fire station. It feels like I'm floating on a cloud. I finally have some of the answers about who I am. My body feels calm for the first time in a long time. My breath is smooth and peaceful.

As I enter the quiet night, I instinctively look up at the night sky. The stars wink at me, and the moon is full and glowing white. Autumn used to say that the full moon is special. The energy can be harnessed for good or bad – let go of any dark energy and invite in the light.

The Truths We Uncover

Amazed at how these words have folded into my subconscious, I breathe deeply and open my eyes. The moon is so beautiful. A warm wind is at my back, and at this moment, I feel wrapped in love. Can this be a signal that I'm heading in the right direction? I tear up at the thought. Is a new journey waiting for me? One in which I can drop my mask, know who I am, where I come from, who cares for me, and maybe even who loves me still?

My heart swells to the point of bursting. I feel a connection enveloping me. In awe by the wonder of it, I breathe. "Could my biological mother or father be looking at the moon right now? Are they thinking of me?" Breathing deeply again, I experience a body memory of what could only be my earliest thought: it was one of safety.

I close my eyes and sigh, letting the old Sidney go, no masks in sight.

I feel a tap on my shoulder and turn around to see Capt. Slaywood with a joyful smile. He's holding out a worn cross-stitch quilted blanket. He asks if I live nearby. I nod, and he asks to walk me home. While we're walking he recalls that night. He took me to the hospital, saved the blanket from being thrown away, and hoped one day for this moment. To him this blanket with little flowers represented something special; he saw the care someone had taken to wrap me.

With a tear in his eye, Capt. Slaywood turns toward me and thanks me.

I know in my heart and body that I'm loved.

Frustration floods Mia's veins. Drat! The firefighter is walking Sidney home!

When she saw Sidney at the station, Mia was so set on telling her the truth and about being her mother that she ran to hide behind a bush near the door. Now waiting for Sidney to come out, she has been planning to call to her, ever so gently. She will then reveal everything, and they can begin their relationship together anew.

At least, that's how she envisioned it playing out in her mind. She didn't anticipate that when Sidney left the fire station, she would be accompanied by the firefighter who had let her in. He seems to be walking her home. Well, so now what, she thinks. She puts on her hoodie to conceal herself and follows behind them at some distance to avoid being noticed, feeling like a total creeper and at the same time feeling like she has no other choice.

The pair approach Sidney's house, pausing outside the door to exchange a few words. Mia crouches behind another bush, watching them, the anxiety of anticipation bubbling up within her like a witch's brew.

The firefighter waves goodbye and walks away with a smile on his face.

When the door closes, Mia realizes this is not the time or place for this discussion. She decides it's time to go back to her own home. She looks up at the moon and breathes in deeply to collect her thoughts.

She knows that she needs to talk to Lora, mother-to-mother.

Nineteen: The Cycles We Break

The Cycles We Break

Mia heads over to the teachers' lounge and makes herself a hot cup of ginger-lime tea. To her relief, someone has already started heating the water. While waiting she takes a seat, thinking about the past few days and how unbearable it has become to keep the truth from her "secret" daughter. Mia's planning how to speak with Lora when she feels a tap on her shoulder. "Ms. Rose?"

She snaps to attention and stares at her principal.

"Ms. Rose, you have Sidney Simpson waiting for you in your office. Will you please check on her? She's been going through a lot this school year."

When Ms. Rose opens the door, I try to hide my tears. "Hi, Sidney! What's going on?" she says. She gives me a hug, which feels reassuring.

"I just had to get out of sociology class. There's been a substitute in Mr. Alexander's class this whole week, and I don't know where he is. Is he sick? Has he spoken with you? Did he get fired because of me?" I'm trying to compose myself but it's hard. So many thoughts are swirling in my head.

"And also, this fainting has become a real problem. I need to learn how to control it. I just don't know how. I need help."

Ms. Rose smiles. "I learned a technique for that from my grandmother," she says. "Hold for five and slowly push your breath out." She signals for me to try. After a couple of practices, I seem to be getting the hang of it.

"Ms. Rose, thank you! That helps," I say, feeling a little more hopeful. "But what about Mr. Alexander?"

She says she doesn't know anything about Mr. Alexander's absence and suggests that, after a few more breaths, I return to class and ask Ruby.

Once she's alone, Mia picks up the phone. "Ms. Simpson? It's Mia Rose. I know our last conversation ended a bit abruptly. Would you be able to come in to talk this afternoon?"

Lora arrives about an hour later, confused and concerned. "Is everything okay?" she asks.

As they sit down, Mia's mind races. Where do I begin, she thinks. The firehouse? The similarities between Sidney and me? Losing my mom at seventeen?

"Listen… I don't know where to begin. I know you've had a lot going on. Sidney's fainting, learning about Ruby, their relationship, wondering about Sidney's biological mother." Mia chokes up and her eyes fill with tears. She looks up from the floor and meets Lora's eyes. "When I was seventeen, my mother passed away. My life was turned upside down. I had no one. I was alone and numb." Mia mumbles through the details and stares at a confused Lora across from her. "I got pregnant and didn't know what to do. I was a child and so confused and angry at the world. I took my baby, my little girl, to the safest place I knew of – the fire station…" Her voice trails off as she hears Lora gasp.

"You?" is all Lora can muster. Processing what has been said, she wonders how this can be true and if Mia has known all along. A rush of heat runs through Lora's face. And she's been playing the tender loving guidance counselor, taking Sid under her wing, pretending to suddenly care for her like her own, she thinks. Tears slowly drip down her pink cheeks. Without saying a word, she stands up and leaves. She walks to the office and asks to take Sid home.

"Mom? What's going on?"

She doesn't answer and grabs my hand without a word.

"Mom?" I'm getting no response, but her face is brimming with answers. Her tears — it's a convolution of anger, confusion, sorrow, pain, and betrayal.

I glance down the hallway, realizing in an instant that something is very wrong. I break free from my Mom's grip and run back to the office as quickly as I can.

"Ms. Rose! Can you explain to me what just happen—" I think I'm going to get answers, but instead I have a million more questions when I see the state Ms. Rose is in.

I rush out of the office and follow my mom, trying again to get some sort of answer from her. As I catch up to my mother, I realize her thoughts are becoming too heavy for her mask to conceal. Behind her fracturing mask, I begin to see her in a way I never thought I'd see.

With all the running and confusion, a familiar sensation comes over me. I stop abruptly and touch the wall for support. Then, I notice my Mom snap out of her turmoil. Seeing me about to faint, worry has drowned out all the other emotions on her face, and she rushes to me.

"Sid? Sid. I'm here. Mom's here. I'm gonna call Ms. Wilson."

I don't think it's right to be thankful for this fainting episode, but I am since it has caused my Mom to put her mask back on for now. I realize this is the opportunity to apply my newly acquired technique from Ms. Rose.

"5...4...3...2...1... breathe out." I'm half-expecting to see black at any moment but wow, it worked! "Mom," I say tentatively. "I think I'm fine. I don't think I'm going to pass out."

I point to Ms. Rose, who is slowly walking our way and whose face is full of compassion and concern. "She taught me this technique and it seems to work."

"Thank you," my Mom mutters in Ms. Rose's direction, but avoids eye contact.

Ms. Rose reaches for my arm and steadies me.

I watch their exchange with curiosity as we walk toward her office.

"Why don't you take a seat? Both of you." Ms. Rose says, glancing at my Mom. She takes a deep breath, closes the door and sits across from us. My Mom puts her hand protectively on my leg.

I turn and search her eyes. Sadness, worry, regret, resignation. "Mom?"

My mother looks up and stares at Ms. Rose.

"Sweetheart, we have something to tell you," Mom says as she hugs me.

I turn towards Ms. Rose, hoping she can clear up my confusion.

Time stands still and all I can hear is my heartbeat.

The Cycles We Break

I watch as Ms. Rose clenches her hands and looks at a sign on the wall that says, 'You can do hard things.' She seems to be deep in thought, but then looks up and focuses on us.

It looks like something has been weighing heavily on her mind.

"Sidney," she says as she clears her throat. My Mom's grip on my leg tightens.

I look up at Ms. Rose, taking in the light hazel color of her eyes for the first time. How have I never noticed them before?

Ms. Rose's eyes are filled with a sea of memories and her mask is overfilling with a spectrum of feelings and emotions.

"Sidney," she utters softly. "I…..I have to be completely honest with you."

I lean forward on the sofa. All the haziness of my near-fainting episode is gone.

I glance at my Mom and instinctively grab her hand.

Ms. Rose's voice echoes in my ears. "Sidney. Sidney, I'm your biological mother."

"You're what?"

"I'm your biological mother."

I can't believe those words don't make me faint, but they don't. I certainly don't feel clear-headed though. A memory pops into my head from an old Christmas movie, *The Bishop's Wife*. Cary Grant plays an angel named Dudley, who works incognito for a pompous bishop. Dudley decorates the Christmas tree by waving his hands up and down, and all the garlands, lights and ornaments fall into place where they belong. That's how my brain feels, racing a mile a minute, bits and pieces of information wildly rearranging themselves into connections I'd been unable to see until now.

With a shaky hand, I reach for my backpack on the floor and pull out the cross-stitch blanket. I'd stashed it there to keep hold of the joy I found at the fire station. Ms. Rose - Mia? Mom? - gasps and looks like she might faint. I hand it to her and she rubs it against her cheek, but it doesn't seem to calm her.

"Breathe," I whisper. Together we count down as she taught me, and her grandmother taught her. At some point, I realize I'm holding onto her with one hand and my Mom with the other. I hear Mom's voice softly counting with us. The secret between us is out in the open. Revealing this is not going to kill us or destroy what sanity we still possess. Instead, the truth proves that we deserve love. All of us.

I realize that the masks we had been wearing to protect ourselves prevented us from truly connecting with others, being our authentic selves, and believing we were worthy of love from ourselves or others. Because if we truly believe we are worthy, there is no need to wear a mask.

As I sit, arm in arm, connected to both my mother and my biological mother, the encroaching blackness fades from my vision. With each passing breath, and each pulse of warm hands on mine, my vision clears into a new present.

In the past, I have imagined myself a cork boat thrown to the wild winds, each event throwing me off kilter and into more mayhem. But here, now, I feel like I'm where I belong.

"I'm the fire station miracle. This was the blanket Captain Slaywood found me in, and you, Ms. Rose, are my mother who left me there…" I stammer, as though waking from a dream.

"Yes," Ms. Rose blurts out. "I thought you would be safe there. I couldn't, not then…"

"You couldn't care for me, I know. But what about now? Is there space in your life for a daughter?" I wonder aloud.

"Darling, perhaps now is not the best time for this." Mom, Lora, cuts in.

"No, please, it's fine. Let's get it out into the open," Ms. Rose, mom, replies. "I want to make up for all the years I missed. I want to right my wrongs." She concludes authoritatively.

My masks are strewn across the floor. I have two mothers, the one who raised me and the one who left me. The intentional care shown to the blanket and the fire captain's words slide into place. I'm a miracle, forged in the hardship of abandonment within a firehouse.

Ms. Rose grabs something from her purse and hands us a picture. I stop and stare at the photograph. It's Ms. Rose as a child, smiling at the camera while clutching the blanket. The cross-stitch with little flowers. The very blanket that is sitting between us – connecting us.

I glance up from the photo to Ms. Rose.

My eyes say a lot, but so do hers.

"M-Mom," I stutter, though I'm unsure if I got the whole word out before tears stream down my face and a sob chokes out. My heart breaks as my mother next to me, Lora Simpson,

squeezes my leg and lets go. I walk over to Ms. Rose, who stands up and greets me with a hug.

So silent, so spontaneous, but the choreography is perfect, as if we've planned this

moment our whole lives. Like an invisible string that has tied us for the past eighteen years.

I close my eyes because I don't dare look back at my mother, the woman who raised me. Not yet. For the first time since the truth of my past came to light, I feel capable. I feel strong.

Ms. Rose squeezes me tighter, and I do the same. Neither of us wants to let go.

When we finally pull apart, I realize I've draped the blanket in my hand over Ms. Rose's

shoulders during our hug. I leave it as we part, as if to say, 'Thank you for trusting me with this.

You can have it back now.'

Finally, I steal a look back at my Mom, but her chair is empty. I hurry over to the door

and peer outside. Nothing. I turn back to Ms. Rose, whose eyes are closed, her breathing even.

She's still wearing the blanket.

"I'm sorry," I say, my eyes darting from her to the door. "I have to—"

Her eyes open and she offers a small smile. "Go. I'll be here when you're ready."

I nod and jog out the door, heading toward the parking lot. My Mom's car is immediately

evident — the only orange Prius in a sea of beaters and hand-me-down cars typical of high

school students.

"Hey!" I call out. "Don't leave!" I can't bear to say, Mom.

When I reach the car, I see my Mom sitting in the front seat, her forehead to the steering

wheel, her hands on either side, sobbing.

I've seen her cry before. Of course I have. Movies where a dog dies, after stubbing her toe on the dining room table, in times of frustration, anger, and sadness. People grow up and live together, celebrating and mourning every moment. We've been through so much. I'm eighteen years old, of course, I've seen her cry; just as she's seen me sob, weep, bawl.

But this is different.

I'm frozen in place while watching her cry. I see her pain and I feel it too. There is this weight on my chest that reminds me of people in my life whom I care for, and who have made this moment possible. We will all have to fight through this pain to find the answers we are seeking. No family is perfect, we all have made mistakes and we all deserve second chances.

"Mom," I say quietly, tapping my fingers gently on the car window.

She doesn't look up.

"Mom," I say it louder. The word passes through my lips so easily, with no strain, no hesitation. Mom, Lora, the woman who raised me, the woman who knows me like no other, the woman who I know loves me.

She looks up at me, her face flushed and smudged with mascara. I can only offer her a small smile, a bit of bravery. She's been by my side my whole life, and I will stand by hers. I wave, and I gesture for her to open the car.

There's a moment where I can see a whirlwind of emotions cross her face: confusion, hope, regret, love, fear, and guilt. The things we let ourselves feel, the masks we hide behind. But there's no hiding here, not with my Mom. At this moment, looking at my Mom's red eyes, I feel her love. I hear the car unlock and make my way to the door and slide into the passenger seat.

"Can we go home now, Mom?" I ask, grasping her hand tightly.

Twenty: The Person We Become

The Person We Become

As we arrive home, I rush upstairs to my room. I collapse on my bed and the room starts spinning from the emotions and revelations of the last few days.

I have so many questions and get lost in the possibilities. What would my life have been like if I had not been switched at birth or if Ms. Rose hadn't left me at the station house that night at all? I barely recognize myself anymore. Has it all been a lie?

Would I have the life Ruby now has? Would Ruby have the life I now have? If the Alexanders had not been looking for my parents, would mine and Ruby's paths have ever crossed? All these questions are building up and making it hard to concentrate.

"5... 4....3... 2... 1... breathe out."

I can do hard things... I can't live in the "what ifs" anymore. I need to live in the "what is." I need to focus on the here and now and be in the present moment.

We learned about nature versus nurture in school. I cannot imagine life without my Mom and Dad, Lora and Bill. The Mom and Dad who have raised me my whole life, the ones who molded me into the person I am today.

I decide that I'm going to have a conversation with my parents tonight about the night of the accident with Ramon. They have been keeping this secret from me since my accident. We all need to tell the truth. Though I don't want to imagine a life without them, I do want to learn more about my past so I can build a future.

I go downstairs to ask my parents if we can invite the Alexanders and Ms. Rose over for dinner tomorrow night so we can all talk. Luckily, we had the same idea, and they were already in the process of organizing the dinner. I begin to imagine us all sitting under one roof. Me and Ruby, Mom and Dad, Mr. and Mrs. Alexander, and Ms. Rose.

I feel happy as I call Ruby. She picks up and I immediately spill everything.

"I can't believe it! Ms. Rose is your mother?" she shouts. "I do see the resemblance now. You have the same hazel eyes and you both smile the same way. How did I not see it?"

I laugh at how disappointed in herself she sounds. Never would I have expected that my birth mother was just around the corner. I had imagined a lot of possibilities. Maybe she was passing through town, maybe she moved away, or my worst fear, maybe she was dead.

"I wanted to ask you, will you all come tomorrow for dinner? I think it would be great having everyone around," I say.

"Like a party?" Ruby asks.

I giggle. This year has altered my life so drastically that I forgot what a party is.

I'm reminded of a show Autumn's mother used to watch with these crazy plots. Autumn and I pretended to be characters in the show and we would laugh for ages. I never thought my life might look like one of those shows… Which reminds me that I still need to talk to Autumn.

"Sort of like a get-together. But I like the sound of a party" I say.

"I'll talk to my parents. My Dad is not as mad as he was with your father. Sid, I'm so relieved he calmed down after your Dad almost ruined his career." Ruby sighs.

The Person We Become

"I know, Ruby. I'm so sorry. My Dad was totally out of line. I hope to see you tomorrow. I think this will give us all an opportunity to talk and hash everything out. I miss you."

"I miss you too! I'll make sure we're there. See you tomorrow, Sidney."

After I hang up, I text Autumn an apology and an invite to tomorrow's gathering. I know we can't get the wasted time back, but it would be nice to heal and move forward.

I head downstairs toward the living room with the same hope in mind.

"Mom, Dad. Can we please have a family meeting? I think we all need to talk." I say.

Ms. Rose is the first to arrive at our dinner. I notice she's wearing a silver-gray shirt with a burgundy rose printed diagonally across the chest.

"I like your shirt," I say as the evening sun shines through the doorway.

"Thank you! I thought it was fitting," she says as she passes the threshold.

"I'm glad you're here, thank you so much for coming tonight," I say.

"I wouldn't miss it for the world." Ms. Rose says in a genuine tone.

I'm happy that the weather is nice enough to have dinner on our back patio, and my Mom gestures for us to head back there.

The Person We Become

"You can sit out there and I'll handle the door and the food. I see the pizza pulling up."

My phone rings and I can feel in my gut that it's Ruby.

"Hey, Ruby. What's up?"

"Just calling to let you know we're running a bit late, but we'll be there. The party won't start until then!"

"Ha. Ha. Very funny," I say.

After I hang up, I hear the sound of my Mom's voice greeting Autumn.

"Well, hello. Am I early?" Autumn says as she steps onto the patio.

I watch her glance over and register Ms. Rose, who is sitting in front of our cement ledge, a garden variety of plants and flowers drooping behind her. Autumn's eyes meet mine as they have so many times before and I realize how much I have missed her presence.

"Right on time," I say. I give her a quick hug and a half-smile. "Can we talk?"

After a slightly awkward welcome, Autumn and I sit on one of the benches. The sun is starting to set behind the horizon, painting the sky with blazing hues of orange and pink. I've been so blinded by all the things going on with my life currently — my health, the pandemic, my family, and my relationship with Ruby — that I've forgotten to stop once in a while and watch the sunset. The masks I have worn for so long have been keeping me blind to the beauty in this world, but not anymore. I think I'm finally ready to let go of the past and move forward.

The Person We Become

I turn towards Autumn, who's sitting next to me, her eyes closed as she basked in the last sun rays of the day.

"Autumn, I-" before I can continue, she interrupts me.

"Don't say anything, I'm the one who should apologize" she begins, turning towards me and placing her hands in her lap "I'm sorry, for what I did, it was selfish of me to leave you. I took my pain out on you and I hurt you. Then I barged back into your life when you were at your lowest. I don't blame you for what you said, I kinda deserved it, if we're being honest."

She looks down and then meets my gaze. The words struggle to flow out of my mouth, but after what felt like an eternity, I finally say "Thank you, Autumn, it means a lot."

"So, do you think we can still be friends?"

Tears start swelling in the corners of my eyes, "I would like that." Before I know it we are hugging and my pain slowly washes away while taking in her so familiar smell of lilacs.

"So," she says "I must admit you and Ruby are adorable together."

I playfully smack her arm, and for a moment, I feel like when we were kids once again. My laugh fades away and I begin to tell Autumn everything that has been happening this school year. Autumn's face is unreadable. A few moments pass before I find Autumn's arms wrapped tightly around me.

Things are finally starting to look up. It's been an emotional rollercoaster of a journey, but I know so much more about myself. And if anything, I've gained a family.

"Pizza's ready!" Mom calls out.

The Person We Become

I stand and Autumn and Ms. Rose follow me into the house which seems to glow under the light of golden hour. I hurry into the kitchen and fold the lids of the pizza boxes back down, the smell of fresh dough warming the room.

"We have to wait for Ruby before we start." I say.

"You're right." Mom smiles, running her hand comfortingly across my shoulder.

We stand around in the kitchen with our backs to the countertop, making small talk as we wait. In the end, Dad stole a slice, the cheese stretching itself away from the rest of the pizza.

It feels right having Autumn join us tonight. I have missed her friendship and humor.

As we are waiting for Ruby, Autumn is cracking jokes to ease the tension.

Finally, the doorbell rings. I hold my breath, they're here.

My Dad opens the door and there is a moment's silence as Mr. Alexander stands awkwardly on the porch. They look at each other suspiciously, before my Dad extends his hand, offering a truce. I wait with bated breath. Mr. Alexander takes his hand and grins. Mrs. Alexander gives my Mom some flowers. At last, we can move forward into our new beginning.

Jack's eyes light up when he spots the pizza and I give him a slice with a wink. It feels strange having dinner with so many people. We have almost forgotten how to share, how to hug, and how to laugh together. The evening drew on with pleasant conversations and stolen glances between Ruby and me, until, at last, it was time to do the dishes.

The Person We Become

I stand next to Ms. Rose with the tea towel in my hand as she rests against the counter with her arms in the sink, up to her elbows in fresh white bubbles.

I stare at her washing the dishes for a long moment, thinking about how often this would have happened had things been different. How many evenings would we have spent washing the dishes together as mother and daughter?

She notices me looking and gives me a small smile. "Tonight was nice," she says.

"Yeah," I say, leaning against the counter. "It almost felt like we were a real family."

Her smile widens a little and she turns her attention back to the dishes. "We are a real family, Sidney. We may look different than other families, and it may have taken us a while to get here, but that doesn't mean we can't... try. This feels like a fresh start."

I nod.

She gives me a little nudge with her hip and hands me a plate, soap suds sliding off the rim. "Thank you for inviting me to dinner."

"Ruby kept calling it a party."

She laughs. "It kind of felt like one." She slowly washes a glass, looking meditative. "I wonder how different things would have been if..."

"If things had been different?" *If we hadn't hidden behind our masks all this time*, I think but don't say.

She smiles. "Yeah. It feels nice to do stuff like this. Dinner together was great but...I almost like this time together with you better."

I take the glass from her hands and wipe it clean. "Yeah, I know. But what were you just saying? It's a fresh start, right?"

"Right," she says, with a bright smile. She picks up a spoon and dunks it in the water.

"Tell me if I'm out of line in asking this, but I've been wondering… What have the doctors said about your fainting?"

My mouth opens to respond straight away, to share some snippet of a diagnosis from Dr. Miller perhaps. But then I close it. It's not that I'm shutting down. It's the opposite. I used to answer questions like an automaton, that's if I answered them at all. But that was the old me: pre-pandemic, pre-Ruby, pre-having a whole new birth mother. Now I'm not the me-behind-a-mask any longer. Now, if I could just figure out who I've become.

Maybe we would all like to be butterflies, emerging with kaleidoscopic grace from our gawky caterpillar-teen years. But I'm still in my chrysalis. Looking at the plate in my hand, I see soap bubbles effervescing into nothingness, and that's a better metaphor for where I am right now. My old world, my old life is disappearing, and it isn't clear yet what will replace it.

"Sid?"

I blink and wipe away the bubbles.

"Sidney?" Ms. Rose backtracks from the shortened version of my name.

"Nobody seems sure yet," I reach for another plate, more froth. "Concussions could be a factor, but Dr. Branson has this theory about the physical impact of anxiety. Like the car crashes in my head might be a bigger problem than the real one I was in."

The Person We Become

I continue to blurt my thoughts. More than I have revealed to Dr. Branson. Things I haven't fully articulated in my talks with Ruby. Or even admitted to myself. Words fall out of me - panic, pressure, pain – and I find I'm not thinking about what I'm saying at all, just staring at Ms. Rose. Mia. Mom. And that's when another realization bombs my brain.

We have the same eyes. The same smile. We have the same genes. Her eyes are fixed on me now, and she isn't smiling or frowning, she's concerned. Something in her face prompts me to ask:

"What do you think about my fainting?

Ms. Rose says as she sets down the dishes and turns to face me and says, "Of all the cycles we can't break, this hereditary and health issue is one we have some control over. I know what is happening to you because it happened to my mother and it was happening to me." she pauses and then adds, "I know you have many questions, and you deserve answers. I too had many questions after my mother was already gone and it was too late to ask them. I want you to know that I will help you through this."

With optimism in her voice, she takes my hand, "Over the years, I've learned to cope with the health issue and embrace the moment. I also began enjoying those around me which is why I began searching for you. What I found to help me is to become aware of our unproductive thoughts, change unhelpful thoughts, and reshape the negative thoughts we have. We also have to start letting go of the high expectations we set for ourselves."

She continues, "Sidney, I want you to know that you are surrounded by so much love and support. I'm thrilled I have this time with you, the moments and feelings we shared, the truths we uncovered. You are so much stronger than I ever was. You've learned to be YOU regardless of what others might think or say. I'm proud of the brave young lady you've become."

I start to tear up as I'm filled with newfound hope. I look at Ms. Rose and give her a hug that releases all the bottled-up worry I have had. I hear some footsteps approaching and turn to see my Mom who has overheard what Ms. Rose said. Mom asks to have a moment alone with Ms. Rose and as I'm walking away, I turn around to see that my Mom is hugging Ms. Rose.

I find Ruby and sit next to her as she's talking to Autumn. I look around the house, filled with the people who matter, and take in this moment. I know there is a long road ahead, but I can finally take a deep breath and that is enough for now.

I hold Ruby's hand and know that everything will be okay.

Sidney + Ruby Playlist

"Sweet Dreams (Are Made of This)" by Eurythmics

"Love You for a Long Time" by Maggie Rogers

"I Will Always Love You" by Whitney Houston

"Treat People With Kindness" by Harry Styles

"Love Will Tear Us Apart" by Joy Division

"Baby Can I Hold You" by Tracy Chapman

"Shake It Out" by Florence + The Machine

"Don't Get Me Wrong" by The Pretenders

"When You're Gone" by The Cranberries

"Sweet Disposition" by The Temper Trap

"Don't Worry Baby" by The Beach Boys

"Just Exist" by Eliza & The Delusionals

"Somewhere Only We Know" by Keane

"Shadows of the Night" by Pat Benatar

"Every Rose Has Its Thorn" by Poison

"everything i wanted" by Billie Eilish

"This Charming Man" by The Smiths

"Lost Without You" by Freya Ridings

"Time After Time" by Cyndi Lauper

"Unwritten" by Natasha Bedingfield

"If That's Alright" by Dylan Dunlap

"Take A Chance On Me" by ABBA

"Keeping Your Head Up" by Birdy

"When We Were Young" by Adele

"Heaven For Everyone" by Queen

"Off My Mind" by Hazel English

"The Funeral" by Band of Horses

"The Promise" by When in Rome

"Upside Down" by Jack Johnson

"Time In A Bottle" by Jim Croce

"Breakaway" by Kelly Clarkson

"Voices Carry" by 'Til Tuesday

"Don't Kill My Vibe" by Sigrid

"I Like That" by Janelle Monáe

"Grow As We Go" by Ben Platt

"Landslide" by Fleetwood Mac

"Ghost Town" by The Specials

"Love Song" by Sara Bareilles

"Aquaman" by Walk the Moon

"Call You Up" by Viola Beach

"Blue Monday" by New Order

"Mess Is Mine" by Vance Joy

"William" by Graveyard Club

"Brazil" by Declan McKenna

"Don't Speak" by No Doubt

"Kyoto" by Phoebe Bridgers

"Dreams" by Bishop Briggs

"Hold Out" by Sam Fender

"Hard Times" by Paramore

"Imagine" by John Lennon

"Someone New" by Hozier

"What About Us" by P!nk

"No One" by Alicia Keys

"River" by Leon Bridges

"Lovesong" by The Cure

"Good as Hell" by Lizzo

"Dandelions" by Ruth B.

"Perfect" by Ed Sheeran

"Fix You" by Coldplay

"Naive" by The Kooks

"Marathon" by Rush

Who We Are

Samantha Pearlman, 24

St. Louis, Missouri

Hello! I am the creator of The Next Page Book Project. I'm so honored to have connected with 174 individuals around the globe. My bio has changed numerous times throughout this multi-year project. It started when I was 22 years old and has been a part of my life for the past two years throughout my undergraduate and graduate school studies. A little bit about me... I am currently 24 years old and a Licensed Master Social Worker (LMSW). By day, I am a school-based mental health therapist and by night I am a concert photographer. I want to thank you for reading The Masks We Wear, and therefore, becoming an integral part of this project and family.

Nicole Landwehr, 33

St. Louis, Missouri

I'm a Licensed Clinical Social Worker, Registered Expressive Arts Therapist, and Certified Sex Therapist in private practice in St. Louis, Missouri. In my free time, I enjoy spending time with my partner and our pets (we have 2 dogs, 3 pigs, 1 cockatiel, and 5 ducks); tending to our garden; playing tabletop board games or D&D, kayaking with my stream team @TheDirtyOars, practicing yoga, and creating art. I'm also completing my Ph.D. in Clinical Sexology where I'm studying the intersection of expressive arts and sex therapy treatment modalities.

Vianney Gonzalez, 30
Arvin, California

I'm a full-time high school counselor and adjunct counselor/professor for my local college. I have worked in the mental health and counseling field for over 10 years. I'm passionate about working with children, young adults, and their parents/guardians to provide them with the needed support and services to be functioning members of society. I enjoy reading daily and traveling as often as possible. I'm a first-generation college graduate and both of my parents immigrated to the U.S. with the American dream in their hearts. I have 3 amazing sisters and we have all pursued higher education; obtaining both our bachelor's and master's degrees from our local State University. Giving back to small rural communities is my true calling and passion.

Anita A. Brown, 56

Taylorville, Illinois

I'm the Director of Curriculum & Instruction and Federal Grants in our school district. I began my career in education with primary students, teaching Kindergarten, 1st, and 2nd grade. After several years as a building principal, I moved to the district office in my current position. I guess you could say... kids are not only my business but my passion. I live in Taylorville with my husband, Ronald, who is a coal miner, as was my father. I have one daughter, Heather, a son-in-law, Kyle, a stepdaughter, Jordan, a son-in-law, Ross, and four grandchildren (Monroe, Parker, Grayson, and Tatum). None of them live around us anymore; so, traveling to visit is often on our agenda. My latest passion is being a NiNi to those grandchildren. If there is down time, we like to venture out on the Harley and find new places to stop.
"The expert at anything was once a beginner." Helen Hayes

Sheila Diaz, 43
Coalinga, California

Throughout my career, I have been blessed to work in a variety of roles within the educational field: teacher, school counselor, instructional coach, and am currently in administration. Additionally, I'm proud to say that my journey in education has allowed me to work at my alma mater, Coalinga High School. I'm passionate about spreading positivity (This past year, I created a wellness site and a positivity site, links are below), building relationships, and making a difference while helping others reach their fullest potential. A goal that I have on my bucket list is to someday write a book, and this experience has been an amazing opportunity to get my feet wet and spread my creativity wings. There is nothing more that I love to do than spend time with my loved ones, including all of my animals. I enjoy traveling and exploring, but equally love my quiet time at home.

Seema Bhatnagar, 61
Delhi NCR, India

I'm first and foremost a mother of two lovely grown-ups and a doting grandmother. Professionally an educationist and have been a school teacher and Principal for a major part of my life. I have authored several textbooks during my professional journey. As a teenager, I was a good student but not very focused on anything beyond college books, and never imagined that I would end up being what I'm today. I have travelled extensively in India and across the globe in professional as well as personal capacities. I'm still learning a lot from life experiences and will remain a lifelong learner. My present is occupied mainly with spiritual leanings which make me a better human being with each passing day. I strongly believe in being kind and calm under all circumstances.

Susan Jachymiak, 26

Orland Park, Illinois

I currently teach 6th-grade mathematics, and I view myself as a lifelong learner. In my spare time, I enjoy crafting on my Cricut and listening to music.

Sophie Brookes, 28

Melton Mowbray, United Kingdom

I'm Sophie, a writer, and poet based in the UK. I write gothic and LGBTQIA+ fiction, and I'm also a published poet. I'm currently working on a poetry collection centered around my struggle with insomnia. When I'm not writing, I enjoy reading and listening to heavy metal, and I'm also an amateur cosplayer! You can find me on Twitter at @ladyxesphio or at my website sophiebrookeswrites.com (I wasn't sure whether we were including socials or not, but I added them just in case)

Linda Amici, 53
Westerville, Ohio

I'm an educator from Westerville, Ohio. I have taught middle-grade students for 15 years, and also serve as a part-time faculty member of Otterbein University. I graduated from the Ohio State University and hold a Master's Degree in Curriculum and Instruction.

My passion is to empower future leaders to "be the change" the world needs. I have had opportunities to work overseas on projects to bring health and clean water to remote locations of Papua New Guinea, Indonesia, and the Amazon river basin. In 2019, I was selected as the Inspirational Teacher Award winner for the state of Ohio through Sanford and the National University System.

I'm a mother to six children, one dog, and a small herd of guinea pigs. In my free time, I enjoy reading, biking, kayaking, and keeping myself and my community strong and healthy by teaching fitness classes to all ages. Connect with me on Twitter @LindaAmici

Bonnie Servos, 44
Welland, Ontario (Canada)

I'm a freelance writer based in Welland, Ontario (Canada.) A lover of the written word from an early age, I have been fascinated by reading and writing for as long as I can remember. It took me many years to gather the courage to pursue my passion, but since 2015 I have been using my skills to help others pursue theirs. In addition to my current work in social media, my resume is extremely well-versed and includes everything from archaeology, belly dance, and wine & hospitality management. I currently have several of my own works in progress including a collection of short stories based on the antics of rural life I experienced while growing up here in the heart of Niagara's farming community. I live in Welland with my husband, daughter, and our 2 bulldogs, Violet and Daisy (AKA Violence and Destruction.) I'm about to switch website hosts, but my address is www.bonnieservos.com

Will Malone, 37
England but very proud Irish!

I'm a lucky father of 4, on which my first published children's book was based. I like to sing, swing and work in an office Monday to Friday! Not the most exciting part of life but I find it fulfills the small things like food and shelter. My dream is to write and sing professionally and I'm thrilled to have been lucky enough to be a part of this wonderful project.

Nicolas "The Withdrawn" Correa, 27

Buffalo, New York

I'm a multi-talented artist from the Lower East Side of Manhattan. I have been writing for about 17 years, believing that creativity in the arts serves as my truest form of self-care. I started as a kid writing raps, poems, and comic books, and still have a lot of the art saved in a safe place thanks to his mother. There's no sign of imagination slowing down anytime for this creative, especially since I write every single day. In my writing, you will see that I'm a heavy supporter of mental health, vulnerability, and self-awareness. If you know me, you'll know that I'm also ALL for not taking life too seriously! The Withdrawn has been published in various works including POETRY in the TIME of CORONAVIRUS: The Anthology, BeautiFUl Ways to Say, and I Can't Breathe: A Social Justice Literary Magazine. You can connect with me on my website "thewithdrawn.com" or via social media @thewithdrawn.

Stacy Ann Parish, 54

Appleton, Wisconsin

With a BS degree in art education from UM Mankato and 11 years in broadcasting—as a professional disc jockey, voice talent, and copywriter—I've been professionally involved in education and communication for over 25 years. A working local artist, I'm currently employed by Pinot's Palette as an art instructor and corporate trainer, and my original paintings have been taught to tens of thousands of people nationwide. Also a working actor, I have several professional film roles, commercials, and industrial credits to my name. I revel in nature, movement, and in promoting the arts as tools for healing.

Judy Seitz, 66
Chesterfield, Missouri.

I have three grown children. One lives in New York and is going to make me a grandmother in November. The other two children live here in Missouri. My youngest will be getting married in October. I'm a retired Speech and Language Pathologist that has worked in the field for 17 years. The majority of those years were spent in the school setting grades Kindergarten through 12th grade. I worked in the hospital setting as a PRN where I enjoyed doing cookie swallows the most. That is where you can follow barium down through the esophagus. I like traveling and now that I'm retired, I'm hoping to be able to do more. I have also found out that I enjoy sewing, crafting, and decorating/remodeling. My passion has been with an organization for 50 years and continues to be volunteering with this organization called Job's Daughters. This is an organization created for the purpose to promote young girls to become leaders in their communities, devote their time to charities, respect their elders and each other, and grow to become upstanding citizens. If you know a girl between the ages of 7-19 that is shy and needs some encouragement or just wants to have a lot of fun contact us at mojdi.org.

Chris Fancher, 63

Round Rock, Texas

I'm a retired math, science, and engineering teacher. I co-authored the book series Project-Based Learning in the Math Classroom and have led project-based learning training for more than 10 years. I have gotten to live in various states in the US and have lived in two countries outside of the US and I enjoy meeting people who are very different from myself.

Veronica Valles, 57

Dallas, Texas

I'm a magical, mystical lover of life. I'm an Ordained Minister for the Centers for Spiritual Living who weaves secular mindfulness and the arts in an innovative, original program to empower children to live fully in every moment. I offer beauty to the world through photography, poetry-writing, inspirational services, spiritual workshops for adults as well as retreats. My dharma is to awaken people to Love and Wholeness

Jesse Wren, 20

Kirksville, Missouri

An adventure enthusiast, conversation connoisseur, dreamer, first-generation student, marathon runner, and world traveler currently studying education at Truman State University.

Carly Spina, 36

Palatine, Illinois / Chicagoland area

I have 15 years of experience in Multilingual Education, including service as an EL teacher, a third-grade bilingual classroom teacher, and a district-wide Multilingual Instructional Coach. I'm currently serving 8 schools (EC-8) in a linguistically rich community of over 60 languages and over 800 active EL students. I'm an active member of the multilingual ed community on social media and I enjoy networking and growing with teachers and leaders across the country. I'm currently working on my first book with EduMatch Publishing, tentatively titled Moving Beyond for Multilingual Learners.

Alexandra Crawford, 20
Champaign, Illinois

I'm a student at Truman State University. I'm pursuing a major in English and a minor in Theatre. I've dreamt of being an author my whole life. Writing has always been something that has given me an escape from the world, and I turn to it any chance I get. I hope that I have the opportunity to write throughout my whole life.

Melanie Luebbert, 46

St. Louis, Missouri

I love books and reading, so this was such an amazing project for me! My educational background is a B.A. in psychology, and I have a varied work life. I'm married to my husband of 23 years, Bryan, and our son Nate is currently in college. I love exploring nature through hiking and biking, as well as traveling with my family. We love to experience different people, places, and cultures. It may sound like a very typical, middle-aged existence, but I love it and am passionate about experiencing as much as I can in life! Thanks so much to Samantha for this one-of-a-kind opportunity!

Rachal Gustafson, 48

Rapid River, Michigan

I'm the mother of 3 teens/young adults and have been married for 24 years. I was a special education teacher for 24 years and had the honor of being Michigan Region 1 Teacher of the Year 2019-2020. I'm currently a K-12 Principal in my hometown district and I love my job. I also love spending time outdoors in the beautiful Upper Peninsula of Michigan. My favorite activities are kayaking, camping, snowshoeing, and spending time with my family whenever I can. I'm passionate about advocating for students and families in the school setting and I'm proud to be an educator in Michigan. #GoRockets!

Cheryl Mallicoat, 52
Union, Kentucky

I have two Masters's degrees- one in Social Work and the second in special education. I've been in the social work field for almost 30 years and in special education for 27 years. At the present, I'm strictly a therapeutic social worker in a local middle school. Blessed to love the work I do!
My long-term plan is to write more about my life experiences
as well as about what I've learned while working in the
special education and mental health fields.
I'm by no means an expert in anything, as I believe we
are always learning however I have survived and thrived
through some very difficult life situations, and I long to share
with others in hopes of helping future generations.
In my downtime I enjoy spending time with my dad as we recently lost mom, my two adult children, my pets, gardening, and being outside in general and I look forward to a life of travel during my retirement years. Thank you for this opportunity with The Next Page.

Lizzie McLaren, 57
Lincolnshire, United Kingdom

I have had many occupations, such as librarian, van driver, civil servant, door-to-door salesperson, project manager, and painter to name a few. I have moved about a bit over the years, inside and outside the UK as I can't seem to settle down anywhere for too long. I'm also a parent to my four adult children. After a writing gap of 30-odd years, I finally decided to gather up my amassed life experience and plunge back in at the deep end: one book published in 2020, and more on the way.

Dr. Gina Pepin, 47
Upper Michigan

I hold an Ed.D. in Teacher Leadership and a MA in Reading, Literacy, and Assessment. I'm honored to share that I was the 2018-2019 Upper Michigan Teacher of the Year and am currently an elementary reading teacher in a fabulous rural school. I recently became a national author and co-wrote a professional learning book with the amazing children's author Eric Litwin! #JoyfulReadingApproach - I'm an online instructor of graduate literacy courses for two universities; Grand Canyon University and Northern Michigan University; I also am a university supervisor for student teachers. And this year I'm continuing to serve as a commissioner and board member for AAQEP - teacher preparation accreditation.

Mary Hui, early sixties
Ontario, Canada

I'm semi-retired, living in Sault Ste. Marie, Ontario, Canada. I have been interested in literature and writing for as long as I can remember. I have kept journals most of my life as well as writing for local newspapers and a meditation blog. I also play flute and teach piano. Music, writing, and meditation are my passions!

Corina Oana, 51
Cambridge, Massachusetts

I'm Corina Oana, thrilled and honored to be part of The Next Page project! My immigrant struggle is the source of my memoir, Second Chance Revolutionary. I'm currently pitching it to agents, please share any agent or editor recommendations. You can find my published stories, poetry, and reckonings in online publications such as The ManifestStation and Medium. My daughter is my life's turning point. Cliche, I know! Her arrival, in 2004, dwarfed my American acculturation which started in 1991 with $70 in my pocket and one friend. I raised her by myself by going in and out of the gig economy and steady salaried jobs. Her presence demanded I shed my fiercely independent ways for interdependence, authenticity, and collective liberation through grassroots organizing. Personal turned political over decades in which I witnessed a revolution (1989 Romania), was on location for September 11, 2001 (working for Lehman Brothers) and now during Covid, I help shift our world through Mutual Aid and Grass Roots Organizing. I called Boston, NYC, Providence, Andover, Worcester, and Cambridge home towns. Not bad for arriving with $70, right? I'm aware of my privilege, I want to laugh more, and I'm a trained conflict mediator. I love plants and crystals and the many ways to create fiber art.

Ms. Nyesha James, 40
Ohio

I'm a middle school teacher, specifically, I work with students with special needs. My two teen children are my world, and I would be remiss not to mention my third child, my fur baby, Frenchie. I'm currently in school completing my license in Clinical Mental Health Counseling. In my free time, I enjoy traveling, teaching yoga, crafts, and spending time with family and friends.

Chandra Battles, 47

Checotah, Oklahoma

I have worked in public education for more than 20 years. I'm currently a School Psychologist working in a school district in Eastern Oklahoma. I love working and collaborating with teachers, students, and their families. I believe being trauma-informed and promoting social and emotional learning is important.

I'm a wife, a mother to two young women, and "Nan" to four grandchildren. I love the outdoors and spending time with my littles. I live on a small farm and enjoy the peace and quiet of country living.

Jyotismita Das, 39

Hyderabad, India

I'm a Social Studies teacher for Middle School at Sancta Maria International School, Hyderabad, India. I have a passion for knowing about different people and cultures around the world. My curiosity lies in who they are in other parts of the world, how they talk, how they react, how they lead their lives. The world is such an interesting place after all. I watch, hear, read and love to write down my thoughts and observations. This Next Page Book initiative gave me control to shape the future, even though fictional and I grabbed the opportunity. I reflected upon how I see people in this world and tried to create the best possible options for character development.
I love exploration. It's unbound and infinite.

Heather Nizzio, 33
Wichita, Kansas

I'm a personal injury attorney and military spouse. I have two young daughters. My husband and I are originally from central Illinois, but we relocated to Wichita, Kansas (McConnell Air Force Base) nearly ten years ago. My mother was a teacher, principal, and now a curriculum director, and was the driving force behind my passion for reading. This love of books has now been passed down to my daughters as well.

R. Jason Wallace, 50
Tuscola, Illinois

Principal at North Ward Elementary in Tuscola, Illinois in Tuscola CUSD 301 School District. I'm beginning my 20th year in education this fall. However, I'm the artist formerly known as a television producer and on-air talent (local TV) as well as a salesman. My wife, who is an artist formerly known as an engineer, and I both returned to school after getting married to become educators. So we started life together with a house, two cars, and more college debt. It was the best decision we ever made. She has been a math teacher since graduating in 2002 and I have been a principal since 2007 after being a kindergarten teacher to start my career. My goal moving forward is helping people understand that relationships and people are more important than any data we can ever produce. Students and adults will remember how they have been treated more than any lesson ever will. As I write this, my family and I are on a 23-day vacation. We love to travel and will always find ways to see more of our world and have more time together. Blessed!

Larry Laraby, 70s
Green Bay, Wisconsin

I'm a retired language arts teacher. I taught creative writing and sponsored writers' groups for many years. I own Spirit Mountain Press and am a member of a local writer group "Hippies in the Attic." I have a wilderness camp in the upper peninsula of Michigan and like to spend time in the quiet of the north woods.

Aadila Tilly, 51
Johannesburg, South Africa

I'm a Muslim female and treasure my spirituality and faith, and respect my fellow human beings with different belief systems. I value family connections. Teaching chose me. Being a teacher enriches my life in ways I'm unable to express in words. Children under my care are instrumental in my ongoing growth as a human being. Supporting children to progress academically and encouraging them to believe in themselves is immensely rewarding. I love traveling, animals, and meeting people from different walks of life. Aspiring to be kind pervades every facet of my life, and I appreciate this important trait in others. When I was a student in school, I enjoyed creative writing so when the opportunity to join The Next Page Book was presented to me, I embraced the idea wholeheartedly. To say that being a part of this global project is exciting is an understatement. My wish is for every person to enjoy peace, be loved, and cared for, and to prosper in every way

Dr. Julie Ramirez, 46

Lisle, Illinois

I have been a special education teacher since 1998. I'm married with two sons. I enjoy writing, creating curriculum, reading, and helping advocate for individuals with intellectual disabilities.

Nancy Buonaccorsi, 71
Northern California

I'm a retired 71-year-old special education teacher who lives in Northern California. I have always liked to write since I was a child and have thoroughly enjoyed a writing workshop for the last few years, here in the East Bay Area. Retirement has afforded me the time to write, keep bees, and hike in the Bay Area hills as well as the Sierras. I write essays mostly about my experiences in nature and my travels in Central and South America, Europe, Africa, and the US. I love animals, including snakes and insects, and am constantly picking up slithering or crawling creatures. I'm also attempting to paint a 24' mural on our back fence.

Amorina Carlton, 35
New Orleans, Louisiana

I'm a Southern fiction writer, currently editing my first novel. My blue-collar, single mother read to me every day as a baby, instilling a love of stories so strong that I started telling them as soon as I could talk and writing as soon as I could hold a pencil. Inspired by generations of strong, sassy, Southern women, I knew I had to have the means to take care of myself before finding my happily ever after. So, I earned a degree in journalism and an MBA. My primary job is taking care of and homeschooling my own sassy, strong, little girl. I squeeze in editing, writing, and serving as the PR/Marketing Lead for Ravens and Roses Publishing in between. When I'm not working, I enjoy spending time with my family, reading, watching movies/television, knitting, cross-stitching, and playing board games.

Katja Philipp, 41
Montreal, Canada

I'm an artist, designer, and writer living in Montreal. If not bending on a yoga mat, I'm out in nature or cycling around the world. Extensive travels enriched my life. My last trip to Japan was a culinary and artistic highlight. Foreign cultures, languages, art, and nature invigorate me to create and write. My favourite food is matcha ice cream.

Anonymous Contributor

Naomi Harm, 52
Cave Creek, Arizona

Naomi Harm is an EdTech influencer, women in leadership strategist, and entrepreneur. I have a passion and drive for instigating STEM innovation and future-proofing educational leadership into all of my professional learning offerings. I welcome every opportunity to share my researched-based expertise on brain-based teaching and learning instructional strategies, personalized learning techniques, and student choice and voice activities through innovative design thinking and technology integration projects. I'm dedicated to providing ALL students of every ability access and equity to STEM teaching and literacy resources and hands-on learning experiences, as to continue to motivate our #CreativeIntellectualHumans with building their lifelong learning confidence and to represent their best selves each and every day.

I'm very proud to share that I'm the CEO and founder of my own Innovative Educator Consulting company. We design and implement innovative learning experiences of professional development for k12 educators and administrators worldwide. Our women-led facilitator team of master educator consultants from around the nation is best known for helping k12 organizations collaboratively build solutions focused on measurable learning outcomes with technology literacy, while supporting and meeting the needs of today's diverse Generation Z and Alpha students and dynamic K12 educators.

To continue the learning conversation, feel free to reach Naomi Harm through Twitter: @NaomiHarm or Email: Naomi@NaomiHarm.org or Webpage http://NaomiHarm.org

#TogetherWeAreBetter

Beth Romines, 51

Kansas City, Missouri

I'm a wife, a mother, a dog mom, and a school counselor...in that order. My husband and I have two boys who are seven and a half years apart. I love animals and have two big rescue mutts, a fluffy old cat, and a Russian tortoise. As an elementary school counselor in an urban district, I'm lucky to have 600 students I also call my "kids"! In my spare time I like to hang out with my family and my pets, read, further my education, enjoy watching KC Royals baseball all spring and summer, and obsess over Chiefs football all fall and winter.

Laura Anna, 26

Dublin, Ireland

I'm a writer hailing from Dublin, Ireland. Following an undergrad degree in English & Classical studies, I somehow became an accountant, but in (all of) my spare time I write poetry and fiction about memories and love.

Dr. Paul Blair, 48

Kingsport, Tennessee

I'm the assistant principal at Happy Valley High School in Elizabethton, TN. My passion and research surround underserved students and those at risk for drop-out. I desire to continue to promote the idea that students don't quit because of a lack of capability, but a lack of hope. Educators must attempt to provide avenues of hope for all students, and they need to be prepared to start filling the "hope meter" of students every day.

Melissa Jane Knight, 40

Berlin, Germany

I have written two novels, Since the Riots, delving into the lives of London-based teenagers set during England's 2011 riots; and Cracking Up (forthcoming) about what happens to Poppy Rivers after finding her partner with an underage schoolgirl. He has the perfect alibi and a witch-hunt ensues as Poppy becomes a hate figure after the schoolgirl tries to kill herself. Between writing two further books, I run the Alt-Stralau Writers Group based in Friedrichshain, Berlin, where I live with my husband and our two children. I'm currently looking for a representation after spending 18 months being personally tutored by author Damian Barr (Maggie & Me, You Will Be Safe Here) who runs The Literary Salon at the Savoy Hotel, in London England.

Dr. Jennifer Fuller, 51

Garland, Texas

I'm a lifelong educator serving in the field of public education for 20-plus years. I recently earned my doctorate in education administration and serve as a director in the SEL & Well-Being Department of Uplift Education. I'm a champion for social-emotional learning, restorative practices, and mindfulness in education. I'm a foodie, and an avid sports fan, and love to read, write and dabble in photography.

Angela Tee
United Kingdom

I'm a child of the 60s and I was born in the month of November. My mother always said that the sun shone on the day that I was born. This is something I try to remember even on the cloudiest of days. I like to share messages of hope and encouragement through my writing and my stories. My creative writing journey began through journaling following a bereavement. Writing was a way for me to process my feelings and some of the pain. It still is! Later on, journaling became blogging as a way to share some of my experiences in the hope of helping others. I enjoy encouraging people and trying to make a difference.
"Happiness can be found even in the darkest of times, if one only remembers to turn on the light"- Albus Dumbledore

Tesa Standish, 47
Warrenton, Virginia.

I'm originally from Kalamazoo, Michigan. I have a wonderful husband named Michael, and three wonderful children. We have our 6 cat and dog children as well! I have been in the education field for 22 years. I'm currently a reading specialist at the elementary level. My job is challenging, but it is my passion to help students learn and succeed at literacy! I also like to travel, watch movies, garden, and eat good food!

Megan Ladwig, 32

Burleson, Texas

6th grade ELA teacher

Jerry Toups, 55

Richmond, Texas

I started teaching in 1990 when I made my first classroom rule: Always Believe in Yourself. Over three decades later I'm still using this rule and changing the lives of my students for the better. My passions are traveling, photography, and videography. In 2018 I became a published author with the release of "The Story of Always Believe" which is an autobiography that tells the story of how I became the educator that I'm today. I'm currently working on my second book, "The Art of Inspiration" which will be published by EduMatch Publishing. This book teaches the reader how to use non-verbal communication skills to become a source of inspiration.

Rajaa Abu Haya, 43

Brussels, Belgium

I'm a mother to three amazing kids, Tamir, Adi, and Norah.
I work online, as an English language & Literature teacher,
besides my job as a coach for life and a coach for ADHD.
What is interesting about me is that I'm an Israeli Druze (a small
community in Israel) woman, speaking Arabic, Hebrew, and English with
a bit of French since we have been living in Brussels for three years.
I love reading, writing, and traveling. I loved the idea of my first
book page, so I was among the ones who joined. I'm very much
involved in social media and volunteering in the community.
Recently, I'm trying to adjust to living with our new cat,
as for me, it's the first time in my whole life raising a cat.
Hopefully, it will be a great experience for both of us!

Joanna Gillespie, 51

Buffalo, New York

Writing has been my lifelong compulsion, though my output is limited to press releases, excessive Facebook musings, indignant letters to the editor, and random memoir excerpts foisted onto unsuspecting friends. I've studied creative writing since childhood, inspired by the tutelage of Dennis Loy Johnson, Pamela Des Barres, and the many talented mentors of Gotham Writers. I attended Allegheny College and the University at Buffalo, studying English and Art History, before working in the music and arts industry for several decades. Presently I'm a project manager with West End Interiors. I enjoy reading, redecorating friends' houses, and snuggling my three-legged cat, Jude Hamloaf.

Mark Saenz, 56
Austin, Texas

I'm currently a middle school social studies teacher in Austin, Texas, I have been teaching there for six years, prior to that I worked in private industry. My favorite things to do are spend time with my wife and family, read, watch movies, and go to sporting events (although we have not been to a theater or stadium since all of the current health events started in March 2020). This is my first attempt at a writing project outside of academia, but certainly not my last.

Katie, 32

St. Louis, Missouri.

I'm a healthcare professional by day but at night I fulfill my love of writing (or, at least, I try!) I live in St. Louis with my son and enjoy art fairs, hiking, and reading as many books as I can.

Maren Kelly, 41

Tehachapi, California

Hi. I live in California, with my husband, Tracy Kelly. We have two sons living at home, Grayson and Austin, and one, Rutger, who had his own children, our grandchildren. We currently have three dogs and two cats. I have been teaching in Special Education classrooms for 15 years. I teach students with Moderate/Severe disabilities for our local school district. I have taught Pre-K to Middle School. I earned my B.A. in Political Science, Pre-Law, and Psychology. I have a Clear California Credential in Special Education, as well as an M.A. in Curriculum and Instruction. I love to paint, take photos, and ride horses, as well as support my sons who are in Scouts and like to play soccer.

Andrea Sánchez Aguirre, 40

San Antonio Texas & The Metaverse

As a mother, entrepreneur, and abolitionist educator I'm here to create diversity representation with strength and conviction. I'm an Educational Consultant that resigned from public school education in the name of being an anti-racist in Texas. I produce multimedia to benefit the LatinX community. My passions are responsible historical reconstruction and equitable futurist construction by means of the metaverse ecosystem and cooking meals for those that I love.

Melissa Rathmann, 46

Austin, Texas

I'm a Texas educator, servant leader, and the founder of #CelebratED weekly Twitter chat/learning community. I'm most proud of my role as mother to my beautiful college-bound daughter who never ceases to amaze me with her wisdom, strength, and courage. I'm a lifelong learner with a passion for people and Starbucks coffee. And, I'm honored to be a contributing author to this book!

Jennifer McShane Barrett, 57 years young

Wantagh, Long Island, New York

My career has taken me from sports television to public schools. I'm an avid reader, TV watcher, and die-hard NY sports fan, especially baseball. The most important things in my life are my family, friends, and my golden retriever, Buddy.

Dr. Tracy Kelly, 54

Tehachapi, California

I live in California, with my wife, Maren Kelly, and our two sons, Grayson and Austin. We have an older son who is on his own and has his own children. We have three dogs, at this point, and two cats. The number of animals in our house fluctuates often. I have been teaching Special Education as a second career for 13 years. I have taught all grades K-12 and aspiring Special Education teachers at the University level. I have earned a BA in Economics, an MA in Special Education, two clear Credentials in Special Education, and an Ed.D in Educational Leadership. I did not earn my first degree until I was 39 years old. I enjoy reading and writing. I don't devote enough time to either.

Dr. Joanne Fullerton

County Down in Northern Ireland, United Kingdom

I'm a Specialist Clinical Psychologist and a Mummy to 3 young children. My work and home life mostly revolves around attempting to apply a trauma and attachment-informed therapeutic perspective to relationships. I'm interested in art and love to draw. I'm very interested in polyvagal theory and how it drives behaviour. I'm interested in making this accessible to everyday situations and individuals. I love books and reading and sharing that love with my children fills me with joy.

Kelly Hantak, Ed.D., 52

Saint Peters, Missouri

Throughout my career, I have worked with young children as an early interventionist, early childhood/early childhood special educator, and higher education faculty member. I'm currently a researcher focusing on studies and the development of strategies to improve the lives of individuals with a disability in aspects of their life. When I'm not conducting research, I enjoy spending time with my family and friends, traveling, and cooking.

Megan Cannella, 35

Reno, Nevada

I'm a Midwestern transplant currently living in Nevada. My debut chapbook, Confrontational Crotch, and Other Real Housewives Musings, is out now and available at https://linktr.ee/mcannella. You can find me on Twitter at @megancannella.

Paula Rawson, 49

Charlotte, North Carolina

I'm a former newspaper reporter and editor. I love reading, walking, and going to flea markets and antique shops.

Christel Norwood, 46

Bolingbrook, Illinois

I'm a Special Education Teacher, currently co-teaching Middle School students within Inclusion classrooms, but have taught grades K-8, in a multitude of settings throughout my 11-year career. I'm a single parent to an amazing 21-year-old son who happens to have Autism, or Awesomism, as we refer to it in our home. In December 2020, I self-published a book on Amazon titled "The Journey from Autism to Awesomism: 30 Stepping Stones Along the Path" depicting our journey from diagnosis to acceptance and ultimately to embracing 30 wonderful gifts Autism brought into our lives. One thing I love most about teaching special education is the relationship I get to develop with families. I love helping them learn how to navigate the ins and outs of a very complicated system as well as assisting the students in learning how to advocate for themselves while not being ashamed of who they are. I enjoy spending my free time with family and friends, listening to music, both live and on the radio, reading, writing, watching true crime television shows, self-improvement, playing cards, and board games, and exploring various walking trails with my son and our Australian Cattle Dog, Tulip.

Caroline Chase, 57

Austin, Texas

I'm a recently retired educator after 31 years of service. Writing was my first passion; I earned a B.A. in English Writing from St. Edward's University with a double major in Social Work. My education career came as a result of an alternative certification program at the University of New Mexico. In 2014, I completed my M.A. in Education Leadership at Concordia University in Austin. I was a founding member of the Austin ISD Social and Emotional Learning (SEL) Program in 2011 and served my last 10 years as an educator building and nurturing that work. I continue to love the art of writing and hope to pursue many opportunities as a writer in my retirement years.

Rebecca Alexandra Knight, 23

England, United Kingdom

Hello, I'm Alexandra Knight. For most of my life, I have been in love with stories and the process of writing amongst many other things in life. I'm very fortunate to have been brought up around the arts and creative activities from a very young age, since the age of 5 I have been incredibly lucky to have had the influential legacies of great writers such as J.R.R Tolkien and C.S Lewis in my life. It is because of these experiences with books and many other forms of writing that I have become motivated to create my own work and collaborate with others on theirs. Aside from stories I have a great love for animals and being in nature. This part of my life has lead me to study ecological sustainability with the Cambridge University Institute for Sustainability Leadership (England), as well as this I also have an interest in politics and am currently learning about how civilisation is built up from anarchy with Oxford University's Blavatnik School of Government (England).

Michael Kidd, 30 years

Texas

I'm a professional copywriter and Bella author. Most days I can be found playing with my two kids and concocting schemes with my beautiful wife.

Charlotte Rodricks, 29 years

Thrissur, Kerala

I'm a veterinarian, currently pursuing my Ph.D. in Animal Genetics and Breeding in Thrissur, Kerala. While I enjoy my profession, I use reading and writing to escape and destress. In my free time, I love experimenting with new dishes and exploring new places. I have an online webcomic on the site Tapas and upload my flash fiction and short stories on the site Simily. My brother and our mom are my biggest supporters and the only reason I can pursue my profession and hobbies simultaneously is because of their encouragement.

Ashley Auspelmyer, 37
Columbia, South Carolina

I'm a new stay-at-home mom, having left teaching after 14 years to take care of my newborn son during a global pandemic. I have lots of experience designing, teaching, leading, and coaching project-based learning and interdisciplinary design thinking in the high school classroom. I now spend my days caring for my son and leading guided kayak tours in Congaree National Park, a dream come true in so many ways. Much like this project, I have no idea what comes next! I love kayaking, traveling, camping, hiking, yoga, college football, craft beer, local festivals, and assorted adventures.

I live with my incredibly talented husband, our baby boy, and my two teenage step-sons in my hometown of Columbia, South Carolina. SYOTR!

A.L. Breggen, 48

London, United Kingdom

I'm an Author originally from Stockholm, Sweden that lives in London since 1996 and writes in English. I'm also ambassador for the Swedish charity Do Good Now and a proud business owner and founder of Alpiece Ltd. (www.alpiece.com)

From as early as I can remember, I have always loved the creation of stories. As a child, my stories were mainly created through Lego or playing with Barbies, dressing up, pretend play, drawing, or painting. Not a day went by when I didn't create a story in my head, and I still do it; on the tube, in the car, and at work, there are no limits to how much you can spice up everyday life!

I wrote my first book as a four-year-old "The Birthday Party." The second book got written together with my best friend as an eight-year-old called "The HighJackers" which hopefully entertained the classmates at "fun hour" a little.

Then a busy life happened, building a career, moving to London from Stockholm, travelling the world, getting married, and having children. For a short while, I got into Stand up Comedy and photography, never with the intent to work as a comedian or a photographer but as a way to be creative and learn something new.

Storytelling kept being part of my life, in the form of customer case studies and presentations, daily good night stories to my two girls, comedy material, or to cheer a friend up with something fun.

My inspiration comes from everything around me, such as my own experiences, people I meet, relationships, news/fake news, leadership styles, and different cultures and religions I come across. The arts, music, books, observations, debates, cultures, films, and life's other magical moments are also powerful sources sparking my creativity. Injustice in the world, entitlement and all kinds of abuse makes my blood boil which inspires significant parts of my darker writing.

I strongly believe in doing good now and that every contribution, however small, helps to make a positive change.

From 2012 until now, throughout a breakup, divorce, and family court, I started to write a fictional story - The Secret of the Crying Minds. It wasn't until 2020, during the Coronavirus lockdown, that I finally challenged myself to become a published writer by sharing this story.

Folasade Olayemi, 38
Nigeria

Professionally, I'm an Early Childhood Educator with over ten years of teaching experience also in career Fine Art as well as a homeschooling educator who now privately works with young children using developmentally appropriate practises
I have a passion for writing and I have been a freelance writer "ghostwriting" and proofreading works from other independent authors. I have worked with authors like Dele Andersen, author of "The healing Mendez" from the Vitrian Secrets on captions and proofreading.
I'm an incurable romantic and as an independent author writing under the pseudonym Victoria Goldstone (Goldens) with Smashwords, my two previous books "She & I," and "When Love Fades" have received multiple free downloads. I have recently just completed my third book "Secrets, Sins and Desires" which is being queried with another publisher, and the fourth book, a historical fantasy, which I'm just starting is underway.
I'm a mother of two boys who love to eat so I cook a lot. When I'm not writing, I'm reading for my own pleasure, painting, or drawing.
I love listening to music, singing, and taking long nature walks.

Gina Antonia Nepa, 29

Seattle, Washington

I'm a social worker, middle child, and published poet who leans on writing to showcase trauma, identity, liberation, mental health, relationships, and shame. Having lived and accumulated stories in Minnesota, Pennsylvania, Washington D.C., Florida, Illinois, California, and Washington State, I believe we all can only learn and grow in the community. I'm deeply grateful to get to be a part of such an innovative community-driven project.

Smriti Iyer, 24 years
Mumbai, India

A creative writer, published poet, and aspiring filmmaker,
I'm deeply interested in psychology and human behavior.
Currently, I work as a copywriter at a digital marketing agency.
Personally and professionally - writing is how I process things.
When not writing, I roam pet cafes or bake up storms.

Tri Ngoc Minh Nguyen, 23

St Louis, Missouri

Hello everyone, my name is Tri Nguyen and I'm currently working as a Paramedic with the county's ambulance district! I was born in Vietnam and have traveled to many places in the world. I absolutely love traveling and experiencing new cultures and food. I'm passionate about helping others in any way I can and I believe that's the best way to have a fulfilling life. I'm very fortunate to have had the opportunity to be one of the authors of " The Next Page " and can't be more excited to share this masterpiece with the world.

Sam Campbell, 29
Fayetteville, Arkansas

I'm a writer and teacher from Tennessee, although when people mistake my accent for Cockney, I don't correct them. I earned my English M.A. from East Tennessee State University, where I was the Editor-in-Chief of The Mockingbird. I serve the Arkansas International as Assistant Managing Editor, and I'm the fiction editor and co-founder of Black Moon Magazine. I'm currently a second-year fiction MFA candidate at the University of Arkansas, living in Fayetteville with my favorite person (my mom) and my 47 houseplants.

Noelle Chandler, 38

California

I'm an educator, performer, poet, arts advocate, and mama to the sweetest 5-year-old boy.

Jo-Anne Oakley, 58
Ottawa, Ontario.

I work in a project management office of a federal government department to make a living, but in my off time, I prefer to be working on multi-media art, writing projects, or just trying out a new craft. I'm passionate about the planet and I love animals of every kind. Yes, I'm vegan. I currently live with a handsome beagle/black lab named Flynnigan who just turned 11, and a beautiful rescue pup from Barbados named Winnifred. I'm also mom to a grown son and daughter. I have big hopes of retiring in the next five or ten years (less if I can ever win the lottery and not just a free ticket!) to pursue all things creative on a full-time basis.

Lisa Whitten, 45

New York City, New York

I have been helping people find and share their stories for more than twenty years. I'm an improviser and storyteller originally from North Carolina. I studied performance at Appalachian State University and currently am making final edits to my gothic memoir *Burning Barbies*. You can see my storytelling show *Becoming a Noble Gas* on Socially Distant Improv's Instagram or several of my short films on *The Sequestered Film* Festival's website. I have truly enjoyed being part of The Next Page Book Project.

Amaziah Shalu, 45

Birmingham, Alabama

I'm an educator and lifelong learner who stands on the foundation of faith. I work tirelessly to advocate for the success of all groups of students. I believe in the important and life-changing power of seizing opportunities with every student in every moment. I also believe that we are all success stories in the making.

Elyse Hahne, 33

Grapevine, Texas

I'm a K-5 Functional Life skills teacher who has moved from just supporting students to also supporting teachers and staff as well over the past few years. I graduated with my Master's in Leadership in December of 2021 and am constantly wanting to support educators who support students. As a society, our educators need as much support as students in the work we do. From consulting on behavior and social-emotional support to strategizing and making plans, my heart is in it for the success of teachers and students. My passions are public education, special education, teacher support, and improving school culture with collaboration. There is good in every day and I'm grateful to see it. Professionally, I love Twitter chats, reading books, and engaging in discussion. I enjoy nature photography, my family, downtime, and our dogs. It was so fun being a part of this project.

Cassie Soliday, 34

Los Angeles, CA

I'm a writer and cartoonist, working in the film, tv, and games industries. I've worked on projects for companies like Disney, Cartoon Network, Warner Bros Animation, Nickelodeon, and more. I love road trips and the ocean- especially road trips that lead to the ocean.

Paula Januzzi-Godfrey, 62 (May, 1959)
Durham, North Carolina

I was born and raised in northern Ohio in a large Italian family. I have an Associates Degree in Design Merchandising, but I found my true passion when I returned to college to become a teacher. I have been working in public education for over 35 years, first as a special education teacher, then a fourth-grade teacher, a Literacy Coach, and now the librarian in an elementary school. I moved to Durham, NC in 1992, and in 1998 I founded and then directed a children's museum for five years. I'm a lifelong advocate for social justice and equity, especially in public schools. I'm the proud mom of a son, age 29, and a daughter, age 25. I have been married for sixteen years to a now-retired school social worker. I love writing, photography, swimming, hiking, and working on visual journals. My long-term hope is to write a book that acknowledges the strengths and gifts that all children and families bring to our world, and that weaves in my many experiences with children, teachers, and families and my deep concerns about equity. Being a part of The Next Page book is an opportunity I could not pass up. It has been a pleasure to co-write about topics and issues that are near and dear to my heart.

Kelly Esparza, 24
California

My name is Kelly Esparza. I work as a book editor and am also a writer. I hold a B.A. in English and a B.A. in Creative Writing from the University of Arizona. My poetry, short stories, and personal essays have appeared in various literary journals, and I have self-published a poetry collection. In early 2021, I co-wrote a screenplay for a feature film. I'm working on a few novels and hope to get them published someday!

Susan Jane Lowe, 66

St. Louis, Missouri

My name is Susan, sometimes Susie, and sometimes just Suz! I enjoy the love of family and friends, teaching and learning, creativity and new experiences, animals, and nature. I'm blessed over and over with each passing day for opportunities to grow and experience God's grace. I'm an adoptive mom and retired special education teacher who taught and learned with children in grades K-8 throughout my 25-year career. I continue to find ways to be with children as I delight in their spontaneity and growth. I also delight in being a pet owner and just love my fur babies. I'm currently writing and illustrating a children's book and am enjoying the flexibility in my schedule for many passions such as painting, walking outdoors, simplifying my home environment, and giving back.

Kanwar Sonali Jolly-Wadhwa, 45
San Francisco Bay Area (California, USA)

I'm a poet and writer of fiction and creative non-fiction. Writing in English, Hindi, and Punjabi, I have published poetry collections in all three languages. Growing up in India and moving to the US 25 years ago, I'm a wife, and mother living in the San Francisco Bay Area. A member of the Diablo Writers Workshop, I often find myself writing about the intersection of my Indian and American lives. My poetry has been published in *The Pine Cone Review* and *Eucalyptus and Rose*. I have published a collection of essays, *Gender: A Cross-Cultural Perspective*. My Doctoral thesis "Women Writing Women's Worlds" is currently under publication. I love gardening, writing with my kids and of course, reading, reading, and then some!

Paul LaTorre, 34

Newark, New Jersey

My name is Paul LaTorre, also known as Paulconqueso in performance poetry circles. I'm a poet, professor, publisher, advocate & activist. I was born and raised in Newark, NJ and my love for hip hop / music led me to poetry at a young age. Having studied poetry as an undergrad, I found my calling in publishing my college's literary magazine and realized I wanted to teach at a college level. Thus, I received my MFA in creative writing and returned to my Alma mater of Bloomfield College, where I'm the Lead Editor of BC Underground. I try to use my writing as a means to advocate for mental health, social justice, body image, eating disorders, and sexual assault survivorship.

Maggie Lee McHugh, 38
La Crosse, Wisconsin

I wear many hats, all of which make up the many sides of me (Maggie McHugh)- teacher, advisor, innovation specialist, PBL consultant, reader, writer, picture taker, stand-up paddle boarder, friend, wife. I spend most of my time wearing hats at school as the Innovation Specialist for La Crosse Polytechnic, a secondary charter school specializing in project-based learning (PBL), personalized learning, and community-based learning. My inspiration in life remains my students, continually finding ways to meet their needs through creativity and joy.

Matthew Gilbert, 32

Tri-Cities, Tennessee

I'm a writer, artist, and teacher from the Tri-Cities, Tennessee. I'm the current poetry editor and co-founder at *Black Moon Magazine*. I work as an accessibility coordinator and cook in a local nursing home. I enjoy writing about social issues, meditating, and chilling out with my cat on weekends. I publish across all genres and appear or am forthcoming in several online and print journals along with *The Southern Poetry Anthology Vol IX: Virginia* and the *I Thought I Heard a Cardinal Sing* anthology. Learn more about me at matthewgilbertwriter.com.

Patricia Darien Cope, 72

I'm a Canadian writer who resides in the province of beautiful B.C.

As a graduate of UBC (Vancouver) and SFU, I have taught in K-12 classrooms since 1974.
My love of writing began early in life growing up on a farm in the Fraser Valley. As soon as I could grip and grapple my first HB pencil, my story began. There were only 8 colours of wax Crayola crayons in a box when I started school, but to this day I liken crayons to the smell of a wildflower bouquet where my imagination took me to faraway places beyond the green hillsides and grey gravel roads. And what is a story without pictures?
Apart from the excitement of writing and drawing, I attribute my greatest "success" always to having been the moment I gave birth to my daughter, Nevada. It is she who inspires me every day to "stay gold" and "do what makes you happy."
At 72, I continue to enjoy teaching part-time in public schools. I believe that all of us have learned personal stories of courage, strength, and endurance. Through listening and observing, I join the dots to better understand myself and others. I stay connected by writing.

Kaitlin Kilby, 24
St. Louis, Missouri, USA

As an elementary educator, life-long learner, and lover of stories, books have been a part of me for as long as I can remember. As Cath Crowley so beautifully writes, "We are the books we read and the things we love." I would add that we are the places we've been and the people we've met, too. When I'm not teaching or taking graduate courses, you may find me singing, reading, writing, or spending time with my friends and family. Some of my dreams include receiving my doctorate, coaching field hockey, traveling abroad, and maybe even writing a book!

Mark Nechanicky, 48
Albert Lea, Minnesota

I grew up in rural Minnesota, studied physics in college, and materials science in graduate school, and was an electrical design engineer in the automotive industry in metro Detroit before going back to school to become an elementary teacher. I teach back in my hometown. I have a wonderful wife of 21 years and an amazing 12-year-old daughter. When not busy, I enjoy reading and taking nature photography. It's a gift to learn that everyone around you is stumped at times, that others have different ways of looking at things, and that you can be a leader. The best opportunities are available when you surround yourself with amazing people. A long time ago I learned to enjoy being out of my comfort zone. Collaborating with the other Next Page authors has been a fun and rewarding experience.

Gene Glotzer, 47

Newington, Connecticut

I'm a father, writer, and teacher from Connecticut. I play a little bit of bass and have a cat. I write fiction and nonfiction about philosophy, baseball, and a host of other things. You can find my stuff at https://linktr.ee/gglotzer

Attiya Batool

A passionate Teacher!

Lucie Frost, 56

San Antonio, Texas

I retired from a lifetime of practicing law and now spend my days writing humor, satire, and women's fiction. You can find me online at luciefrost.com or on all the socials (especially Instagram) at @lucieHfrost

Melissa Dean, 43

Niverville, Manitoba, Canada

I'm a classroom educator, with experience as a consultant and coach spanning grades K to 12. I began my teaching career in Toronto, ON, and am now continuing that journey in South Eastern Manitoba, Canada. Melissa is passionate about mathematics education, assessment and evaluation, and questioning the status quo in the education system. When I'm not talking to people about math, I'm working part-time at a local bakery, baking my own sourdough bread, drinking coffee, or out for a run. I'm known for continually learning and growing and trying things out, constantly buying books, and my distinctive laughter, usually as a result of telling my terrible jokes.

Allison Dunajski, 39

Chicago, Illinois

I'm a licensed clinical professional counselor, art therapist, and school counselor. I discovered my passion for working with children and adolescents while in graduate school, and can not see myself in any environment other than a school setting. While it is often very difficult work, the reward outweighs the challenges. When not working, I enjoy spending time with friends and family, especially my nephew and nieces. I also love to travel whenever possible. I'm thrilled to have been a part of this project and look forward to sharing the book with others.

Bret Williams, 63

Conroe, Texas

I'm a life-long student of spirituality and am currently writing a book based on my revelations. I live and work alongside my wife of 42 years as a strategic solutions specialist in e-commerce. I'm a third-generation Texan, I enjoy meditation, writing, photography, and giving.

Jennifer Haston-Maciejewski

Greenfield, Indiana

I'm the lead teacher of an alternative placement program and a behavior specialist/coach. After receiving training in Yoga and mindfulness, I opened my own yoga studio and started a program called Stop.Breathe.Be. My consultation program focuses on restorative practices, replacing detentions and suspensions with a mindfulness program, skills to implement mindfulness into your classroom, and developing a personal mindfulness practice.
I'm a contributing author in several books and I also sit on the board of directors for the Coalition of Schools Educating Mindfully. I'm a nature therapy practitioner and I have recently converted an old school bus into a tiny home on wheels for herself and her family of 6 to travel in during the summer! I genuinely believe that behavior and classroom management are less about managing student behavior and more about managing yours as a teacher. I continue to push educators outside of their comfort zone and ask teachers reflection questions to bring out the best in them, empower them, and make them realize just how much power they truly hold!

Akshaya Kishor, 29

Prayagraj, India

I'm an Asst. Professor of Law in India working with a reputed institution. Have a keen interest in writing and travelling. Love to experience new places, people, and cultures.
In the future, I want more collaboration with beautiful minds in writing Books and articles.

Dr. Jane R. Shore, 52

Philadelphia, Pennsylvania

I'm part of the founding team at a progressive high school that opened in 2019 in Philadelphia, PA called Revolution School. Though not my official title, I see my work as an Opportunity Wrangler and a Visual Translator. I have had the opportunity to co-found a growing professional community called School of Thought, which exists through a blog, a podcast, gatherings, and community, as a platform for amplifying the work of others, building knowledge with purpose, and co-creating in public around educational change. My latest obsession is creating hand-drawn visualizations of complex findings from research to connect them to users of research. I wholeheartedly desire, as @monachalabi puts it, "to take the numb out of numbers." I love hiking, ocean swimming, and picnic foods. I live in Philadelphia, PA (and occasionally Massachusetts) with my husband, Walker, and our two boys, Avery and Beckett. I'm on Twitter @shorejaneshore.

Natalee Tangen, 37

Shoreview, Minnesota

I'm a mother to two wonderful girls, wife to the kindest man alive, and dog mom to a sweet golden retriever. I love my family and friends and enjoy spending time with them. I'm a school social worker and am passionate about helping children and families. I'm from Colorado and love the outdoors, especially during summer!

Teresa Lien, 60

Baraboo, Wisconsin

I'm a retired public school teacher that served rural schools for 36 years. In my retirement, I'm a teacher activist to bring awareness to the complexity of teaching. As an unapologetic advocate, I'm vocal about how the role of the teacher must be renovated. The teacher shortage will negatively impact future generations.

Dr. Erik Youngman, 47
Gurnee, Illinois

I'm an education leader who is passionate about topics such as homework, growth mindset, grading, and leadership. The published books I have written include, "The Magic of Growth Mindset," and "12 Characteristics of Deliberate Homework," as well as a chapter for, "100 No-Nonsense Things That All Teachers Should Stop Doing." I have also written numerous blogs about growth mindset and grading. This is my twenty-first year in educational leadership. I'm the Director of Curriculum, Instruction, and Assessment for Libertyville District 70 in Libertyville, Illinois. Previous education experiences include being a principal in Libertyville as well as an assistant principal and teacher in Gurnee, Illinois. I earned a Doctorate in Educational Leadership, an Education Specialist Degree, and a Master of Science in Education from Northern Illinois University and a Bachelor of Arts from Augustana College. Please follow and contact via Twitter: @Erik_Youngman.

Jeff Dase, 47

Decatur, Illinois by way of Chicago, Illinois

I'm an Assistant Superintendent of Teaching and Learning that has risen through the ranks in the educational field as an Operations Manager, Chief of Schools, Principal, Assistant Principal, and Teacher in Chicago Public Schools before coming to Decatur Public Schools. Chicago made me. Of all my titles, the most important are black man, father, and student advocate. I'm also the author of my own book titled "*Rise Above: A Chicago Success Story*"

Kathy Andrew, 69

Petaluma, California

If I'm not working on my latest novel, you'll find me painting. Creativity keeps me sane. I'm a lesbian and live with my partner of forty years in Northern California, and last summer, I took up Stand Up Paddling. You can find me on Instagram or Twitter: @artyyah.

Dr. Robin Y. Green, 50 and fabulous
Charlotte, North Carolina

I'm descended from two very different women who birthed and raised 10 and 7 children respectively. One was wed to a country preacher who[worked hard to raise their children in rural Arkansas during the Jim Crow era. The other was wed to a man who passed away when her children were young, leaving her to work domestic jobs in urban Washington, DC during the same period. I was blessed to have one of these women in my life into my adulthood while the other passed away before I was born. The one thing these women had in common was they carried the seeds that made my parents, who made me. From what I can remember and what I've been told, I not only carry the physiological traits of both of these women; but also personality and affect. I'm grateful that these two women carried the seeds that made my parents, who made me who I'm- a child of God who believes in His power, a daughter in love with my mother and father, a sister who would be lost without my "big" sister and "little" brother, an aunt who is grateful beyond measure for a beautiful intelligent niece and a friend who treasures my sisters from another mister and brothers from another mother to the ends of the earth. Because of all of the things I'm, it surprises me sometimes that I'm also a career educator leader, avid multi-genre reader, active sorority member (I love my AKA), self-critical amateur writer, and voracious lifelong learner. Needless to say, two very different women, Grandma Madgie Slater Coleman and Grandma Mary Welch Green carried the seeds that made my father, Roland Green, Sr., and my mother, Elverna Coleman Green, who in December 1966 made a vow to each other that made me the proud, intelligent, beautiful and graceful Black woman I'm today.

Jessica Delfino, 45

New York City, New York

I'm a mom, host of the weekly Mom Report on Pocono 96.7 FM, and a freelance writer for The New York Times and other publications by day, but at night, she is a delightfully twisted comedic musician who sings original "dirty folk rock" songs along with mutilated classic rock covers. She has performed at clubs and festivals worldwide, including The Soho Theatre, Edinburgh Fringe Fest, Reading and Leeds, Just For Laughs, SXSW, and more. She spends most of her time between NYC and the Poconos, and online at @JessicaDelfino. Listen in to The Mom Report at Pocono967.com.

Alexandria Hulslander, 24

Dallas, Texas

I'm a creative writer with a degree from the University of Arizona, have been writing for over 10 years, and love baking!

Antonio Romayor Jr., 41

Southern California

First and foremost, I'm a full-time family man. I'm employed by an elementary school district in Southern California, working in technology. In addition, I have a passion for various things and activities: art, woodworking, music, cooking, reading and writing, mentoring, working on automobiles (and driving them), spending time with family and friends, and my rambunctious French Bulldog named Harley.

Barbara Sapienza, 77

Sausalito, California

I'm a grandma of two young women, of twenty and nineteen. Married at twenty—still married— a mother of two. I practiced clinical psychology until I turned my attention toward writing three novels: *Anchor Out*, 2017, *The Laundress*, 2020, *Dream Being*, 2023. Now I practice painting, meditation, tai chi and most currently dancing among the oak and bay laurels. I try to remember that each moment is sacred. Thank you for this project. Truly fun!

Tu Vuong, 42
Ottawa, Canada

I'm an educator who has worked in several capacities including consultant, teacher, and advocate for newcomer families and students. I have been a lead in projects with the Ontario Ministry of Education and Apple Education, and have contributed numerous content to various magazines, blogs, and podcasts. I also recently published a book titled, *Coming Home*; it is an autobiographical collection of short poems about my journey story. I love to be creative with a purpose.

Shelia Atuona

London, United Kingdom

I'm a teacher and writer from London, United Kingdom. My fiction writing has been longlisted for the Alpine Fellowship, and the Penguin Random House Write Now competitions. I'm especially interested in autoethnographic fiction as a form of cultural preservation. I enjoy watching plays, having talk-walks with friends, and cappuccinos in my free time.

Walid Abu Haya, 50
Brussels / Belgium (originally an Israeli)

I was born, to a Druze family, on April 3rd, 1972 in a small village named Beit Jann in the Galilee mountains in northern Israel. Married to Rajaa since 2001 and has 3 children. I graduated from Tel Aviv University, first with a degree in political philosophy and linguistics, and a second degree from Haifa university in international relations, specializing in conflict management and peace studies. I have been a diplomat in the Israeli foreign service for the last 23 years. During those years I was posted in 4 different missions in Zimbabwe, the Czech Republic, Switzerland/ Geneva (UN), and currently in Belgium as deputy chief of mission to EU and NATO. During my career, I was acquainted with people from many countries in the world and was exposed to different and various cultures. One of my passions, besides global politics, is exploring new cultures and cultural socializing. I love nature, animals, photography, movies, and soccer. I speak 3 languages, Arabic, Hebrew, and English with some basic French.

Jonathan Taylor (pseudonym), 30
Darmstadt, Hesse, Germany

I was born in 1992 to white-collar parents from blue-collar backgrounds. I grew up in Eastern Europe in a time of important and at times dramatic changes in the world around me. I adjusted to this new and ever-changing world by keeping an open mind and taking in as much of my surroundings as possible. In my attempts to understand the world, I also created various short stories and other narratives throughout my early life, to make sense of what was going on around me. Outside of writing and creative endeavours, I was an exemplary child, or at least tried to be. Dutiful in my school work, I kept myself out of trouble and bad crowds, and always attempted to be on good behaviour. My results in school allowed me to attend a prestigious technical university in Germany, where I soon became confronted with the rigours and trials of what adulthood and independence required. Through sustained practice and effort, I found my way into academic circles and beyond. I'm currently employed as an application engineer and enjoy discussing philosophy, history, and politics, as well as a variety of other topics.

Annabelle Perston

Kitchener, Ontario

I'm a WRDSB Kindergarten teacher! I love baking, skating, travelling and making the occasional TikTok! My favourite countries that I have travelled to are China and Iceland. I spend a lot of time outside with my puppy Kylo and love finding new and interesting ways to be creative!

Mary Dawood Catlin
Saint Augustine, Florida

I'm a Canadian writer, pianist, historian, and doctoral candidate in Music and Musicology at the Sorbonne (Paris). I'm a contributing author at the *American Institute for Economic Research*, and I have been published in numerous other outlets including the Jerusalem Post, the Times Union, the Miami Herald, and the Herald-Tribune. I'm a voting member of the Recording Academy where my debut album of classical piano music, *Nostalgia*, was considered in the first round of the Grammy Awards. I'm a member of the *International Alliance for Women in Music* and a *Bösendorfer Artist*. I'm deeply passionate about the seven arts, the humanities, and about advocating for human rights and liberties. I have lived in Canada, France, and the United States. I currently reside in Saint Augustine, Florida.

Dr. Robert A. Martinez (ResiliencyGuy), 58

Benicia, California

I have served the broader educational community for over 35 years. I have worked to improve and expand educational opportunities and access for students by expanding our collective understanding of the impacts of trauma, resilience, and the importance of being engaged in healthy relationships. I live in Benicia, Ca. with my wife Nancy of 34 years, where we raised our four amazing children. I'm an author, speaker, and educational leader, and focused on becoming a better person every day of my life.

Melissa Pritchard, 42
Switzerland

Born and raised in the Pacific Northwest (USA) in a family of five children, I attribute my relentless energy and curiosity to my active upbringing. A veteran teacher in international schools for the past 15 years, I have lived and worked in 3 different countries and speak 4 languages. Halfway through my career, I took a sabbatical to cycle solo around the world and still dream of writing a book about my adventure. My husband and I, along with our two young daughters will soon be moving to Cambodia to embark on our first family adventure living and working overseas.

Julia Knight, 43
Based in Bahrain but originally from the United Kingdom

I'm a teacher and currently head up a small, well-being-focused school in Bahrain having lived and worked in London and Bangkok before that. I have written a children's book and written for many globally recognized magazines on education. I love escaping into a good book and am currently reading Norwegian Wood by Haruki Murakami. There's nothing more peaceful in my world than writing and reading. I'm married with two gorgeous, compassionate boys aged 11 and 7.

Aubrey Lynn, 35
Santa Clara, California

I wear many hats in life including wife, mother, special education teacher, behavior analyst, and social worker. When I'm asked, I usually say I'm "just Aubrey." I have spent a lot of time working to eradicate the stigma surrounding mental health. Through advocacy and understanding, I'm working to promote classroom communities of success with structure and support. When I'm "off", I love to create comics and escape to the beach. Fueled by caffeine I hope to push kids (and adults) beyond their comfort zone to try and experience new and exciting things. I truly believe that anything is achievable if the bar is set high enough. I'm very excited to be opening my own non-profit in the foreseeable future.
Twitter handle: @spedteacheriam

Veronica Jarboe, 29

Sacramento, California

I'm a California resident and the author of "sweethearts and sorrows," and "I tell the finches" with Rinky Dink Press. I'm also a professionally trained dancer starting at age 3 and currently love teaching it as often as I can. Theatre is another passion of mine and I was fortunate enough to train professionally at the London Academy of Music and Dramatic Art. I love stories in general, in all art forms, and there is nothing I love more than getting immersed in a good book!

Mike Breza, 61
Michigan

I was born, raised, and still live in the Midwest of the United States. If you had asked me while I was in school if I would go on to write a science fiction novel, you would have gotten a 'no.' But things change and here I'm, self-publishing his first book. I have spent most of my working career in museums. Giving tours, creating exhibits, and running fun events became part of my everyday life. Back in 2010 the idea for a novel that involved 18th-century electricity, ships, and steam power first came to mind. Picking it up and putting it down over the years eventually got the story roughed out. The pandemic lockdown and an old garage as a "studio" made writing out five drafts of Aether War possible. Many rounds of proofing and refining followed, and I'm now looking forward to selling an ebook Aether War on Amazon soon.

Anna Lindwasser, 34
Brooklyn, New York

I'm a freelance writer who specializes in anime, but who writes short fiction in my spare time. My fiction tends to combine surrealism and magic with the specific, painful, and mundane details of everyday life. I also teach ELA, Writing, and Test Prep to 6th and 7th graders. I have a BA in literature and a Master's in Adolescent English Education. You can find out what I'm up to at my website, annalindwasser.com, or on Twitter @annalindwasser. In my spare time, I love writing short fiction, reading books, swimming, volunteering at a cat shelter, trying new types of tea, and listening to music and podcasts while wandering around Brooklyn.

Kimiko Shibata, 43

Ontario, Canada

I'm a wife, parent, teacher, and learner. I have been an educator in both childcare and elementary school classroom settings, and am currently an MLL Resource Teacher in Waterloo Region in Ontario, Canada. I enjoy finding wonder and adventure with my spouse and our 8-year-old daughter, creating music and videos, reading, and writing. I live by the motto "sharing is caring." I can be found on Twitter as @ESL_fairy. My resource website can be found at: sites.google.com/view/eslfairy

Lynn Sawyer, 73

Henderson, Nevada

My name is Lynn Sawyer. I'm 73 years young and live in Henderson, Nevada, right next to Las Vegas. My grandkids live 2 blocks away, which is why I moved here 3.5 years ago to be near them. Grandparenting is a big passion for me, and I feel fortunate to be involved in their lives. Reading is a bit of an obsession for me (at least one book per week). And even though I retired as a full-time coordinator of professional development in a large school district, I'm still teaching seminars and workshops for districts in the US, Asia, the Middle East, and Europe. This Next Page project has ignited an old interest in writing short stories. Thank you so much for including me!

Neha Vashist, 23

Edmonton, Alberta Canada

I'm a student, dreamer, and writer. I recently completed a Bachelor of Science in Psychology and will be starting my Master of Public Policy degree. During my early elementary years, my teachers always commented on my report card that I was too quiet and too shy. But of course, just because I was quiet didn't mean I didn't have a lot to say. Once I found my voice through writing, I never looked back. To me, writing is many things. It's a weapon for peace. It's an ointment for invisible wounds that may run generations deep. It's 3-Dimensional, and it's alive. To read more of my work and follow my journey check out my Instagram page: @nvwrites_

John Lawson, 66

Bognor Regis, United Kingdom / Pompano Beach, Florida

I recently retired after teaching 'sexy theology' for 27 years. I now work as an academic coach, a school governor, and I write a regular column for 'Teach Secondary' a UK education magazine. My latest book, 'The Successful (Less Stressful) Student', is available on Amazon.

Ezikiel Holm, 24

Tucson, Arizona

Although I was born and am still currently living in Tucson, AZ, I have moved around various places and have experienced a wide array of distinct cultures and peoples during my short 24 years of life on this earth. I graduated from the University of Arizona in 2020 with a B.A. in English and Creative Writing. I consider myself to be firstly and foremostly a writer, but also take pride in my academic pursuits, youth mentor work, volunteering, drawing, crafting, hiking, camping, and above all else spending time with my loved ones.

Olivia Lauritzen, 25
Ohio

I'm an avid reader, fiber artist, and musician with a degree in writing. Narrowing my interests down is hard because there are so many, but those three have stayed consistent.

Marie Sinadjan, 35
United Kingdom

I'm an author, singer-songwriter, and musical theatre actress from the Philippines. I recently moved to the UK with my husband, and I hope to someday make the shift to writing full-time and making music for books. I've published a fantasy novel and several short stories, and I enjoy reading the same genre, especially when mythology, folklore ,and fairytales are involved. I enjoy working with other creatives, and I believe that together, we can bring out the best in each other, so please feel free to reach out to me for collaborations and projects! I also love coffee, cheese, bunny plushies, traveling, and watching the stars.

Breanna Struss
Illinois

I'm a teacher. While living abroad in Madrid I co-ran a writer's group to meet weekly to write short stories on the spot! I enjoy writing, reading, and of course, binging the next great show! I was born, raised, and currently live outside of Chicago. I received my undergrad from Valparaiso University and my masters from the Universidad de Alcala in Spain. Writing has become one of my deepest passions, and I'm currently writing my first novel.

S. Kensington

West Coast, USA

I'm a retired educator who has spent the past 30 years living and working in various countries overseas. I've been able to indulge my love of travel through work, and hope to continue my journeys throughout retirement. I'm also the happily published author of a WWII historical novel "Just Another Girl on the Road."
I currently reside on the West Coast, writing my memoirs.

Molly Miller, 20

Sydney, Australia

I'm a University student currently studying a double degree in Arts/Education at UNSW. I have a strong passion for reading and creative writing (particularly romance) and am currently working on my debut novel! When I'm not writing or reading I'm probably binge-watching Bridgerton with my pug :)

Kim Elder, 41

St. Louis, Missouri

Hi! I'm Kim- a Reading Specialist that loves to write. I have great grammatical gratitude for alliteration and the oxford comma. I'm also thankful for family, friends, and french fries, and find felicity in foliage and waterfalls.

Angela Thompson, 40

Iowa native in St. Louis, Missouri

I've taken every experience in my life and I strive to learn and reflect to evolve. My identity continues to grow: daughter to Matt and Jeri, small-town farm girl, Hall of Fame student-athlete, coach, wife to Tavares, mother to Julius and Myles, friend to many, educator, leader, and (now) co-author. Proud and passionate about all the parts that make up my story!

Brad Darnall, 43
Paducah, Kentucky

I'm a dad to my 15-year-old son and one 4-year-old Cavapoo. I'm an elementary assistant principal. Before that, I taught math and social studies for 18 years. Before becoming a teacher, I worked as a reporter, producer, and photographer at WPSD-TV, the NBC affiliate in Paducah, KY. I have a B.S. from Murray State University in journalism and middle school education with a minor in political science. I have 2 M.A.s from Murray State in middle school education and school administration. In my spare time, I enjoy hanging out with my son, binge-watching streaming shows, traveling, and trying new food experiences. While I have no formal cooking training, I want to compete on Food Network's "Chopped" one day.

Phoebe Miles, 29

Ningbo, China

I'm from the UK where I grew up in Southampton, England. Since childhood, I was passionate about all things science, and this soon became my career centered around health and well-being. I studied nursing at university and entered the world of clinical research in NHS hospitals. At university, I also met my husband, and we were fortunate to explore China together, where his family is living. In 2019, we moved to China together and I started my Ph.D. research on smoking cessation in Chinese healthcare settings; we've lived here ever since. My passion for health extends outside of academia; anyone that knows me personally will know how much I value CrossFit and running. As an autistic person, I'm prone to talking about it – a lot! I'm thankful to have found welcoming fitness communities in China, they have also had great patience to help me develop my Chinese language ability. Moving away and taking on a Ph.D. has not been without some hurdles. I've faced a myriad of challenges throughout this journey and will be forever grateful for discovering mindfulness, my health, and having a loving husband and family.

Soma Kar

Sydney, Australia

I'm a BIPOC author of Indian origin. I hold a master's degree from the University of Wollongong, and a diploma each in Creative Writing, Music, and Fine Arts. I lived in Kolkata, India, and Berkeley, USA before moving to Sydney, Australia, where I live with my family. I self-published an illustrated book for children in 2021 on Amazon under the pseudonym, Soma Kar, winning two indie book awards. I have a growing online platform on Twitter and my website.

Ana Sofía Castellanos, 22

Sonora, México

¡Hola! My name is Ana Sofía Castellanos and I'm an Education student (next year I'll graduate) and a Kindergarten teacher assistant. I have always loved reading books, but now being able to contribute by writing a page for one is incredibly amazing. Also, I love coffee and dogs (mom of two Chihuahuas with the names Mickey and Minnie).

Breanna Tsingine

Arizona

I graduated with a bachelor's degree in Creative Writing from the University of Arizona and live in the Navajo Nation.

Benji Reese Carter, 24
Ireland

I'm a film producer, photographer, and writer who is always looking for new projects to work on. From freelance photographic work to working alongside other creatives, I have produced several short films, which have been highly praised at a number of film festivals around the world. I'm committed to every project I work on and finding unique ways to create new, brilliant, and exciting worlds

Dominique Margolis, 58
Los Angeles County, California

I was born and raised in the rural Auvergne region of France. At the age of sixteen, I had a near-death experience that changed the course of my life. I moved to the USA, became the first non-native speaker to graduate with a Ph.D. in English from the University of Denver, and even worked as an English professor for a while. I'm happiest in nature and amongst people who love and respect the earth and all the beings who cannot speak for themselves.

Sydney Barcus, 55

Dallas, Texas

I'm a behavioral scientist, living in a suburb of Dallas, TX. I help leaders facilitate large-scale change initiatives, and provide executive coaching to unleash potential. Personally, I'm an avid reader. I raise chickens, and enjoy knitting and writing. My greatest passions in life are connectedness, positivity, and allyship.

Jessica D. Frazier, 33

Las Cruces, New Mexico

I enjoy reading, writing, watching a good sitcom, and spending time with family. I'm a Pre-Kindergarten teacher who loves ALL things education! I'm not only passionate about teaching, but mental health and Jesus Christ. You can often find me basking in solitude with a great cup of coffee or some delicious ice cream.

Kimi Hardesty, 67

Lexington, Kentucky

My favorite types of writing are essays and non-fiction, but I love to read great novels. I like to break writing rules and am also a sucker for lyrical prose. Recently retired from 37 years of pediatric nursing, I spend my time between gardening, cooking, and travel – and of course reading and writing.

Anne Maguire, 62

London, England

I'm a retired engineer and construction professional who worked for many years in the public sector. I now write to feed my soul and study the craft of writing poetry, short stories, and scripts. I'm currently working on a novel. I dream of my work reaching a wider audience so people realise we are all connected. And that working-class lesbians have stories to tell.

Nidhi Srivastava, 33
Greater Noida, India

I'm a dog trainer and behaviourist, closet yogi, incorrigible book hoarder, bona fide book club person, and a flag-waving feminist. I live in Greater Noida, India, with two cats who try their very best to support my passion for writing by waking me at 4 AM every morning.

Dr. Deepika Kohli, 39
Amritsar Punjab, India

I'm an Assistant Professor at Khalsa College of Education GT Road Amritsar Punjab. I was awarded a Ph.D. from Panjab University Chandigarh. I have teaching and research experience of 12 years in a Teacher Education Institution. I'm a guidance worker and permanent member of the People's Court (Lok Adalat). Another distinguished role I perform is being in charge of the Educational Clinic in the college, in charge of Competitive Examination Centre, in charge of timetable and discipline committee, and college Nodal officer of UGC projects. I have also served as Programme in charge of B.Ed (Distance Mode) Jamia Millia Islamia and D.El.Ed. and Bridge Course NIOS. I'm an acclaimed author, researcher, and dissertation supervisor of Master's Students. My research interests are in the area of educational technology and pedagogical techniques and approaches. I'm also a mentor of eLearning Internship and SPOC, eLip (Koneru Bhaskara Rao & Hemalata Human Development Foundation). I'm also a single contact person for OERU, New Zealand. - Outreach partner. I deliver skill-based sessions across the nation and globe on innovative teaching-learning online tools and research. I'm also an active member of CCGN-Chapter India and CTE Punjab and Chandigarh Chapter. Recently, I launched a 4 week MOOC on "Innovative pedagogical strategies for gifted and slow learners under OE4Bw-UNESCO Chair. The second MOOc which was launched in May 2022 was Creativity in School Education. Total enrollment across the globe was 1400. I'm a co-moderator of various courses on MOODLE for Teachers. I'm a member of the Editorial Board of the International Journal "Joinetr." Also, a reviewer of research papers for international conferences and volunteer at CC Global Summit 2021. I'm also a lesson writer for various state and national organisations.

Jill Devine, 65
Cambridge, United Kingdom

I've been involved in teaching throughout my working life - either as a teacher of art & design, a teacher of English as a foreign language, or currently as a teaching assistant in a primary school. I like to create visual artworks, either in 2D or 3D form, using a variety of mediums from charcoal in portrait drawing to hot glass pieces (in my younger days). Creative writing has always been a passion and I'm interested in the short form or flash fiction, which has led me to be published in several anthologies compiled from tweets, and the novel, one completed and a second on its way.

Troy Knowlton, 29

San Bernardino, California

I'm a writer, a healthcare worker (x-ray technologist), and a giant nerd. I'm fairly new to the field of writing but have just released my debut novel, Seekers: The Winds of Change, a YA Fantasy. Besides writing, my hobbies include card games like Magic: The Gathering, video games, anime, swimming, and hiking (I've even dabbled in archery.)

Melody Serra

NYC, New York

My passion is teaching and empowering others by sharing what I have learned. I helped launch an arts and crafts program at a children's hospital and also taught at San Quentin State Prison. I hope to inspire others to explore and expand their creativity through web development, writing, and art.

Julisa Basak, 31

Pennsylvania, US

I'm a full-time marketing communications specialist for a global SaaS firm, and a part-time speculative fiction writer and digital artist. A few themes I like to explore in my works are generational trauma, friendship, and familiar dynamics, redemption, and coming of age. I have a few published flash-fictions, an lgbtq+ short story romance on Amazon ebooks, and am currently drafting my first full-length Spy Supernatural drama. When I'm not crafting words, I like to take commissions for character design and cover art. I also love dancing, crisp cool sunny mornings, brunch, vibey aesthetics (like purple skies), and my baby nephew, and furry niece.

Bonnie Lynn Nguyen, 67
Nassau, Bahamas

My father was a talented Vietnamese painter/artist/craftsman who married a Turks Island/Bahamian woman, twenty years his junior, and was blessed with four daughters of which I'm the youngest. I'm a former government employee, HR and Training Manager/Vice-President and Consultant in banks and insurance companies. Fortunately, I'm enjoying my retirement after 45 years in the workforce. I'm an active Catholic and churchgoer and not-so-active Toastmaster and HR professional. I love nature, gardening, photography, swimming, writing, walking and jogging the beach, & collecting shells. I have the awesome responsibility of helping to take care of my aging and invalid mother. I'm the proud mother of two daughters, Kya and Khristy, and have a grandson Judah.

Joshua Gray
Venice Beach, California

Filmmaker, storyteller, and wannabe influencer. Sharing stories that inspire, give hope, and cause action. Past projects include stories from Haiti, Guatemala, and Iraq. Currently doing a TikTok project taking video portraits of strangers. Tiktok & Instagram @joshuathomasgray

Dubravka Rebic, 32
Novi Sad, Serbia

I'm a copywriter, a published author, and a mom. My goal is to make others feel accepted and less alone. I do that through fiction and life.

Keira Lane, 38
Dallas/Fort Worth, Texas

Hailing from West Texas, I grew up the oldest of five siblings. I was introduced to the works of Jane Austen by my grandmother at a very young age. This sparked my love affair with books and writing. As a budding author, I've shown that sheer determination and resilience are keys to growing in the literary arts.

I currently reside in the Dallas/Fort Worth Metroplex in Texas with my husband and five children, two dogs, and three cats. I'm active within my community as my neighborhood city liaison, my local school district ambassador, work as a Guest Educator, and held many board positions with my local PTA.

In my free time, I enjoy reading books of all different genres, writing, photography, painting, crafts, hanging with my family, playing video games, and Moscato.

Jo Smith, 52

Croft-on-Tees, England

Hi, I'm a happily married mum of two gorgeous older teenagers. At work, I'm an Assistant Professor where I help trainee teachers with their science and look after their wellbeing. I'm passionate about increasing female representation in science, particularly in physics. I grew up on a cobbled street in Yorkshire, and was the first in my family to go to University - so if I can do it, anyone can! I wanted to be an astronaut but I couldn't join NASA in the 1980s as I was British, and possibly not clever enough. I thought I might like to be a pilot in the RAF but no females were allowed then, so I became an engineer. I wouldn't change anything unless I invented a time machine, then there is no telling what I might get up to!

Chris Keilman, 37

San Francisco, California

I'm a senior copywriter and fiction writer based in San Francisco's foggy Richmond District. Published in McSweeney's Internet Tendency and Slackjaw, I'm also writing a YA fantasy novel called the Light Catcher. As a writer, I love finding the strange, fantastical, or absurd in everyday life, channeling feelings and sensory emotions into words. When I'm not writing, I'm dabbling in musical instruments or going for long walks in the park.

Rachel K Jones, 57

Katherine, Northern Territory, Australia

I'm Rachel but, for some strange reason, many people call me Rebecca. I've been writing since I was old enough to rhyme. Poetry made me fall in love with words. It was how I learned to play with sounds and rhythms. Now that I'm older, I write prose. I'm a cosy absurdist, a proponent of talking cats, demons called Steve, and furious gnomes. I read books that carry me away to distant understandings and far-flung imaginations. Most days, I very much like avocados; mainly for their taste, but also for their attitude. My dream is to go to space; just so that I can look back toward the earth and sigh wistfully. Until then, I will continue to work in my palliative nursing role. The mask I wear is one of clinical necessity and consideration for those in my care. It has taught me how to convey everything I feel through my eyes.

Kathy Whynot, 42

Fredericton, New Brunswick, Canada

I'm a Type B personality with a passionate curiosity about life. My head is often in the clouds, but with an intense work ethic and desire to learn, I'm constantly taking on new projects and pushing myself to try new things. My main work hours are devoted to my work as an educator; I have over 20 years of experience working with all ages of learners, mostly in the areas of Language Arts, Literacy, and English as an Additional Language. I'm also a recently graduated Registered Yoga Teacher, a newly minted graduate course instructor, and a non-profit volunteer. Supporting and celebrating GROWTH, whether it's personal or professional, and whether it's within adults or youth, is my passion. I'm also a daughter, sister, friend, partner ,and mother, roles that nourish and sustain me. My most precious gift in life is that of being a mom.

Gina Marie Elia, 32
Coconut Creek, Florida

I'm a freelance writer who also teaches Mandarin Chinese at an independent high school in South Florida. My work has been published in Taiwan's CommonWealth Magazine, SupChina, and Genealogies of Modernity. I have earned numerous fellowships, including a Fulbright Award to Taiwan. I was born and raised in Boston, Massachusetts, and I earned a Ph.D. in Chinese Literature from the University of Pennsylvania as well as a Bachelor's Degree in Comparative Literature from Cornell University. In her free time, she enjoys reading, writing, listening to music, and continuing to study Chinese and other languages.

Christine Alice Coc, 30

Belize

I have an MSc. in Educational Leadership and Management from the University of East Anglia.
In 2019 I was the recipient of the prestigious Chevening scholarship, which allowed me to meet numerous leaders worldwide, specifically those passionate about education. I'm currently one of five founding members of the first-of-its-kind STEAM laboratory school in my country where I will use my cutting-edge knowledge to mentor teachers and students. Through this initiative, I aim to promote inclusive, equitable, and quality learning opportunities for my Belizeans.
My resilient attitude and tireless energy encourage others to work smart and follow their passions. I'm inspired daily by my students and family and in my free time, I enjoy exercising, travelling, and reading.

Megan Gabellieri, 38
Massachusetts

I live with my husband, Matt, our daughter, McKinley (10), our son MJ (7), and our dog, Kona (2). I have taught fourth-grade English to multilingual learners for 12 years. Writing is my favorite subject! When I'm not teaching, I'm dreaming of ways to fulfill my wanderlust!

Vira Bunoan, 27

Manila, Philippines

I'm a public school teacher based in Manila, Philippines. I teach English to high school students. As a literacy advocate, I love books and reading, so I made it my mission to share my genuine love for reading with my students.

Jody Matey, 50

Frankfurt, Germany

Originally from Pennsylvania, I'm an international educator who has lived abroad for over 22 years in China, Germany, and the U.K. I'm passionate about creating positive, meaningful, and inclusive movement experiences for all children. I love Crossfit, coffee, and hiking in the forest with my cockapoo, Puffin, and 12 year old son.

Victoria Noe, 70
Chicago, Illinois

I've worked in theatre as a director and stage manager, mostly musicals; raised millions of dollars for the arts, social services, and AIDS service organizations; sold books to Chicago Public School librarians. My fourth career is writing, which started when I promised a dying friend that I would write a book about people grieving their friends. Contemplating a fifth career if this one ever gets boring.

Steven Kolber, 34

Melbourne, Victoria, Australia

I'm a proud Public-school teacher who has been teaching English, History, English Language and English as an additional language for 12 years. I was recently named a top 50 finalist in the Varkey Foundation's Global Teacher Prize. I'm passionate about teacher collaboration which I support through organising Teach Meets and running #edureading (an online academic reading group). I research and publish around empowering teachers, professional learning via social media, and teachers engaging in research. My forthcoming publication is: 'Empowering Teachers and Democratising Schooling: Australian Perspectives' available from Springer.

Christine Salek, 32

Madison, Wisconsin

I live in Wisconsin, where I'm a grad student in library science and play in an orchestra. My prose and poetry have appeared in a bunch of places, most recently The Gravity of the Thing, Something Involving A Mailbox!, and Quartz Literary. I'm a big fan of traveling great distances to watch women's sports, making information more accessible, and having days off.

Kyle Ross, 23

Maine

My husband refers to me as "heart full, head empty" and I take that with pride! I'm a copywriter for a specialty food company by day, and one of the editors-in-chief of The Icarus Writing Collective by night. Quintessential Gemini, sweater-hoarder, cat dad – I'm all this and more. Find me at thekyleross.com

Miriam Walsh, 35

Cork, Ireland

I'm a digital media and coding educator, teaching creativity and coding across schools in my local community, and excited about the possibilities of using technology to reach all learners. Outside of work time, I enjoy travelling especially when it means capturing street art or sunrises and exploring new lands.

Tega A. Onobrakpeya
Lagos, Nigeria

I'm a Zillennial writer and lawyer from Nigeria. I live in the metropolitan city of Lagos and while I work an 8-5, I try to explore my city at night. I love to read, write, see movies, and plan hangouts where I show up with drained energy. Hehe. Being a part of this project has been a unique and engaging experience, making me look forward to more collaborations.

Maria Kornacki, 26
Michigan

I graduated in 2018 from Eastern Michigan University with a BA in Creative Writing. I've been writing for https://detroitisit.com/ for a year now. I have a passion for poetry and will have my first chapbook published with Ethel Zine & Micro Press in December '23. I plan to have another full-length collection in the world sometime around then as well or at least accepted! I also recently started honing in on my old hobby/passion for art, specifically portraiture. I'm still working on a site for that. I made an Etsy, but not sure if that's the best option for me at the moment. You can follow my portrait art page on IG: @mariamakes_faces

David Betancur, 21
Medellín. Colombia

I was always the quiet kid, sitting in the corner, daydreaming about escaping this world into an epic adventure, at one point, those stories were becoming too much for my brain to handle, so I turned to writing, as a way to give some use to them, I'm still learning a lot about the craft, but hopefully one day, I'll get one of my fantasy stories out there, and I'll inspire another quiet kid, to make his own

Lindsay Avery, 30
Derbyshire, UK

I started writing as a teenager which inspired me to study for a degree in English Literature at the University of Exeter. I took advantage of numerous creative writing workshops on offer during this time and have since taken part in various masterclasses and writing programmes. I would define myself as a writer of YA fantasy/adventure. For my day job, I work in student recruitment and marketing at the University of Birmingham, alongside studying for an MBA. I currently live on a farm with my dog, Groot.

Sarah Wallace, 34
Orlando, Florida

I'm a queer indie writer who likes to write sweet historical fantasies full of queer joy. When I'm not writing, I'm either reading or watching old movies.

Jonathan Squirrell, 45

Kingston-upon-Hull, United Kingdom

I'm an Academic Writing Support Tutor at the University of Hull. I work with a really broad range of people, from all backgrounds and studying all subjects, helping them to clearly communicate their ideas. In my creative writing, I like to shake off the shackles of convention and let the words loose. I have published a pamphlet and some short stories and am perennially working on a novel. Most importantly to me, I'm a husband and father. My family inspires and entertains me every day, and any linguistic legacy I leave will be dedicated to them.

Emily Francis, 44

Concord, North Carolina

I'm a nationally recognized English as a Second Language teacher at Concord High School in Concord, North Carolina. I serve students in 9th-12th grade with various English proficiency levels. I am a native Spanish-speaker who is originally from Guatemala and came to the U.S. at the age of 15. My experience as an English Language Learner inspired me to become an ESL teacher and affords me a deep understanding of the challenges my students must overcome to find success. I earned a BA in Spanish and a MAT in ESL from UNC-Charlotte. I'm the author for *If You Only Knew: Letters from an Immigrant Teacher*.

Made in the USA
Monee, IL
06 March 2023

29260104R00236